# IN THE WORKS

BLUE FEATHER BOOKS, LTD.

# IN THE WORKS

A BLUE FEATHER BOOK

by

Val Brown

This is a work of fiction. All characters, locales and events are either products of the author's imagination or are used fictitiously.

IN THE WORKS

Cover design by Ann Phillips

A Blue Feather Book
Published by Blue Feather Books, Ltd.

www.bluefeatherbooks.com

ISBN: 978-0-9822858-4-8

First edition: April, 2009

Printed in the United States of America and in the United Kingdom.

# Dedication and Acknowledgements

This book is dedicated to my great friend Kathrin Kotte, who complained to me that "you never see a story about a sexy or interesting engineer." Thanks for the inspiration, background, and translations.

I'm indebted also to the fall of the Berlin Wall and the Internet, because without them, I never would have met Kathrin and several other wonderful young women from the former East Germany. My life is infinitely richer by having made their acquaintance.

My deep gratitude also needs to be expressed to Reagan and Karen for the reading and opinions, and to Blue Feather's own Jane Vollbrecht for her patience and forbearance on the editing and fixing of the results of my admittedly feeble typing skills.

Finally, profound thanks to Emily Reed at Blue Feather. You're a great publisher and an even better friend. Your encouragement has been priceless.

.

# Chapter 1

Mariah Carey leaned over and sang "Hero" into Anne's ear.

The vision of the lovely singer brought a smile to Anne's face until she realized it was only the ringtone on her cell phone waking her up.

"Damn Patrick," she mumbled. Her business partner had suggested the ringtone as a joke, but now Anne regretted her decision to go along with it. Picking up the cell phone, but not raising her cheek from where it rested on the computer desk, she grumpily answered, "What?"

"How did I know you'd still be awake and working on that new project? 'It's only one a.m.,' I told myself. 'Anne hasn't gone to bed yet.' I bet you've got the design up on the old computer screen right now, haven't you?"

Anne glanced up at the video display. The screen saver was on, and tropical fish glided lazily by on the monitor.

"Yep, I'm looking at water works right now," she said, not elaborating beyond that. "What do you want at this hour anyway?"

"I wanted you to be the... let me see, one, two... ninth to know. I'm going to be a father."

Anne lifted her cheek from the desk. "You dog! It's about time. So when's my godchild due?" In her excitement, Anne's normally careful, measured tone lost its bland American sound and took on the German one of her birth.

"In November, and you must really be happy about it. It's been a while since you slipped into your German accent so heavily."

Anne laughed. "You know me. Give the customer just enough German to remind them of the superior engineering and workmanship of the Mercedes."

"And then we slip them a Ford," Patrick continued, using an old joke of theirs. "Not flashy, but damn reliable."

Anne had met Patrick Ford when they were both newly-hired engineers in the large firm of Crabtree Engineering Partners. They

1

had been the latest two engineers given jobs immediately after their Spaulding University education. Anne and Patrick were assigned to Water Projects and had done well enough to get positive attention from their division head. They blossomed under that attention until it turned to the idea-stealing, credit-grabbing kind. Anne and Patrick talked it over and decided to start their own business. They had used up the whole year of their no-competition clause and all their savings to attend to every last detail of running a business. They learned everything from bookkeeping and taxes to advertising and supply control. When Clearly Perfect Water Systems was finally born, they were ready for success.

They were still ready. Two years later, Clearly Perfect was making a reasonable profit, but it was taking all the time and hard work Anne and Patrick could put into it.

"Okay, I realize I'm a bit foggy right now, but why did you call me in the middle of the night? I like good news, but I like it better in the daylight hours."

"Um…" Patrick's hesitation had Anne immediately suspicious. "It's about the new project."

Anne reached up and tapped the computer mouse. The screen saver vanished, and a three-dimensional depiction of the early stages of the design for a wastewater treatment system appeared.

"What about it?"

"I need you to take it."

"I'm working on the design you requested, so I'm already on it. Did you forget that?"

"Of course I didn't, and I'm very grateful you took that on in addition to all the other projects on your agenda. But I need you to take it over… completely," Patrick said.

"What does completely mean, exactly?"

"A new honcho's being sent out from Bohannon Corporation's corporate offices in Detroit. It appears the situation is a lot worse than we were originally told."

"A lot worse? I thought you said they only needed the standard upgrade to the system they already have," Anne said.

"That's what I thought. That's what I was told. The truth is that Bohannon Corporation is about to get massively fined by the State of California for dumping inadequately-treated wastewater into the Prussian River from their Big Tree Paper Plant near Wood Mill. There was even some talk of closing the operation down. The interim plant manager told me Bohannon got a court order to halt both the fine and the closing, based on local economic impact.

They've been given just six months to get the plant into compliance."

"Sucks to be them," Anne said. "That's not a lot of time."

"No, it's not, and to do what needs to be done, Bohannon Corporation's serious about getting to work right away on the process. They want us out there immediately to get this problem fixed."

"And by us, you mean me," Anne said.

"I would have gone, but now with Robyn being pregnant, I don't want to be away from her. You know the problems we've had getting to this point."

Anne did know, having been Patrick's business partner long enough to feel the pain of month after month of their disappointment in trying to conceive.

"You're playing the guilt card on me," Anne said. "And it's working. I ought to report you to Human Resources. Which one of us is Human Resources again?"

"That's me," Patrick replied. "I'm Human Resources, Marketing, and Corporate Relations. You're Payroll, Supply, and Accounting. And we're both labor."

"Oh, yeah. When we get a real Human Resources department, consider yourself reported. Meanwhile, when do I leave?"

"Thursday. I'll get my ticket changed into your name."

"Thursday! When were you going to tell me that you were leaving Thursday?" Anne jerked up straight in her comfortable wood and leather chair.

"Tomorrow, at the usual Wednesday corporate luncheon. I just got the word this afternoon that we'd be needed as soon as possible. I believe the executive they're sending out is a real stickler for getting things done and getting them done right away. I'm glad you're the one going. I know you can be a real charmer when you want to be."

The sarcasm in his voice was lighthearted, but accurate. Anne bristled under any interference in her work, and it was decided early on that Patrick would be the face of the company to customers. He had the easygoing style suited for the job. Anne had been content to be in the background and concentrate on her projects. So far, the only company activity she'd had to be a part of was to sit for a photo with Patrick for the company Christmas card.

"We've got to completely redo the whole project?" Anne looked at the nearly finished plans she had hoped to give Patrick at their meeting the next afternoon.

"Looks that way. I know you put hours into it. Sorry."

"It's not your fault. It sounds like the right hand didn't know what the left hand was doing out there." Anne deleted the project from her computer with a few clicks of her mouse. "They do know what they are doing now, right? I don't want to fly from Albuquerque to…"

"Las Vegas, going through San Francisco, and then to Merced," Patrick said. "At that point you've got a rental car. This place is up in the sticks."

"Ah, getting back to mother nature. How I love it." It was Anne's turn to be sarcastic.

"Don't worry. You've got a hotel room booked in a small town about thirty minutes from the plant. Wood Mill's finest establishment, the Pine Palace, awaits you with luxurious accommodations."

"I just bet. Okay, I leave Thursday and I go to Wood Mill, California. When do I meet up with this new honcho, and what's his name? I doubt if he'll have a 'Hi, I'm the new honcho' nametag on." Anne could hear papers rustling in the background.

"Wait a sec, I wrote it down. The interim manager mentioned the name when I talked to him. Here it is. Adam Trent." Anne jotted the information down, along with a time for the proposed meeting. The conference with the client would be in the Pine Palace's lobby. Apparently Wood Mill only had one hotel.

"You're sure we want to do this? I'm going to be spending a lot of time in California. What about the other projects we've got going?"

"I can deal with them, and you can ship whatever you need to keep in touch with me. If I have questions about something, I'll e-mail you."

"Wood Mill has Internet? I figured by the name we'd need carrier pigeons."

"You're so amusing. I sure don't know why we haven't had you out there glad-handing the customers before this. Public Relations is definitely your forte," Patrick said. "Seriously, I was hoping this job would put us on the civil engineering map. When the interim guy told me about the new problems, I nearly bowed out, but I figured if we can pull this off, it's our ticket to better and higher-paying jobs."

"And maybe a third employee? Okay, you got me with that. I'll go, and I'll go cheerfully. I'll let them see the sweet and professional Anne Schneider. Even if it kills me." Anne hesitated. "I'll have to let my parents know."

"I don't envy you that. Your dad will have a conniption."

"It can't be helped. I don't have enough time for the kind of attention I need to give them as it is. Maybe getting more income will free me up a bit, and I can change that. It'll be worth it in the long term to put up with the short term inconvenience. That's going to be my explanation, anyway."

"Anne? There's something else you'd better know. The interim manager is the interim manager because the top five people at the plant were all fired by this Adam Trent. He just called them up and gave them the ax. This is a no-nonsense kind of person, so please be on your best behavior, okay? We really could use this job."

"Got it. No marching across the Prussian River and taking Wood Mill in a blitzkrieg. Geez, you've got to give up those German stereotypes."

Patrick laughed. "You are a nut. Eine Nuss," he said, using one of the translations Anne had given him. "Shut your computer down and get to bed. I'm beat. I'll see you tomorrow for lunch."

"I'm going, big brother," she replied as she clicked the power button. "And congratulations to you and Robyn. I'm totally thrilled."

"Thanks, we're a little thrilled, too. Good night." Patrick hung up.

Anne shut her cell phone, breaking the connection. Looking around her empty apartment, she felt the usual bout of sleeplessness coming over her.

"Thought I had it beat tonight." She sighed and reached to turn the computer back on.

\* \* \*

"Vati, it isn't going to be that long," Anne said to her father. They sat in the tastefully decorated living room of the Schneiders' small house in Albuquerque. A pot of coffee and two cups sat between them on a table.

"Ich brauche dich hier."

"I know you need me here. And we agreed to try to keep to English, remember? To get you both used to using it?" Anne included her mother, who was napping in the bedroom, in that statement.

"Some things I can better express in my own language," Marcel said, reverting to English anyway. "You promised if your mother and I came to the United States, you would help me take care of her. That you would be there when I needed you. Now you are running away."

"I'm not running anywhere. I didn't ask for this project, but I have it, and I intend to do a great job on it. This could be exactly the kind of exposure that will get us noticed and bring us a lot more work. I could spend more time with you if we could get the business as profitable as we'd like. We'd be able to arrange more caregivers, and maybe I could afford to hire some domestic help for you as well. That would be good, wouldn't it?"

Marcel made a sound of disapproval, something between a cough and a grumble. He reached for a nearby pipe and pouch of tobacco. He busied himself loading the pipe and tamping it down.

"What about the days I need to go to my meetings? Who will stay with Karina then? I have relied on you for that time. It's important that I keep in contact with the academics in Bonn. You know our project is almost ready to be presented to the Rektor and the committee. It would be a great honor to have them accept our idea for the research project."

"I know you need time to spend on your work, Vati. I've thought of that, and this morning I called the home care agency we used when you were ill with the pneumonia. Mutti didn't mind them, and they did a good job with her. They will come every other day, and you can call them the day before for those evenings you need to be out."

"They were adequate, but not the same as a daughter. Nothing can replace that."

"And they won't have to. We'll only need them while I'm gone. I'll get back here as often as I can, and you can always reach me on my cell phone. If there's an emergency, you know I'll be on the first plane back here. I promise."

Marcel said nothing.

Anne knew his silence spoke more than his words ever could. His lack of words didn't impair him from getting his point across one bit. Anne had felt the disapproval of it many times, but this time he wouldn't get his way. He couldn't. Anne needed to look beyond today to what would be best for all of them in the long run.

"Andrea." Anne's mother appeared at the door of the bedroom. Her eyes held the look of someone who had just woken up.

"No, Mutti, it's Anne." The pain Anne felt every time her mother had a slipping of her memory hit her like a punch to the stomach. The sensation was brief, though, and Anne put on her brightest smile. It wasn't the first time she had called Anne by the name of her own sister, Anne's aunt.

"Natürlich bist du's. Ich bin noch ein bisschen vernebelt vom Schlaf."

*Sleepiness in the mind; that's as good a way to describe it as any.* Anne rose to hug her mother.

"My little Annegret," Karina said, using Anne's given name and switching to English. More and more her speech was peppered with smatterings of both German and English. "I have missed you. Why have you been away so long?" Anne had been with her parents only two days before, but reminding her mother of that fact, the second mistake within a minute, might cause distress. Anne wouldn't allow that to happen.

"Just very busy with the business, Mutti. I'll be better about calling and visiting from now on."

Karina stepped back, but reached up to softly pat her daughter's cheek. "Always such a good daughter." Karina glanced quickly over to her husband, and then back to Anne again. "Annegret, I am afraid I've…"

No further words were needed. Anne had watched her mother's mental acuity slowly diminish since her diagnosis with Alzheimer's disease almost three years prior. It had begun innocuously enough with just little things. Car keys set down and unremembered, missing an appointment here or there. Anyone might have done those. It was taking Anne's mother longer and longer to do the marketing, until one day Marcel received a phone call from the store. Karina couldn't remember where she lived.

Subsequent trips to the doctor hadn't yielded any good news. It was especially difficult for her mother, who had been a practicing pediatrician for many years. Finally, an MRI scan revealed the truth. There was diffuse gray matter loss, definitive for the diagnosis of Alzheimer's. Now physical symptoms accompanied the intellectual.

"Vati, I'm taking Mutti in to brush her hair."

Marcel knew the euphemism for what it was.

Anne saw a profound sadness cross his features as he nodded for Anne to go.

*Sometimes the mask slips a little, and you let that caring human show.* She took her mother through the bedroom and into the connecting bathroom. As she helped change the protective adult diaper, Anne kept up a flow of chatter designed to distract her mother and limit her embarrassment. When her mother was clean and dry, Anne washed her hands, experiencing the same multi-faceted feelings as always. There was anger, but no one to be angry at. There was a sense of injustice, but no one to protest the judgment to. There was grief, but never a closure to it. There was even a tiny bit of resentment, though Anne would willingly do everything in her power for her mother. Overshadowing everything was a feeling of loss, even though her mother was still present in the flesh.

Anne brushed her mother's hair and told her about the forthcoming business trip to California. Whether Karina would retain any of the information for long was unlikely, but Anne had always confided in her mother.

"That sounds very exciting," her mother said. "A very good opportunity for you. We will miss you, of course, but I am very proud of you for everything you have accomplished. You must not worry about us. We will be just fine until you return." Clarity shone in Karina's eyes for the first time that morning, and Anne was thrilled to see it. Those times happened less and less frequently.

"Ich liebe dich, Mutti," Anne said.

"And I love you, too," Karina replied. "Now, what should we have for lunch? I'm sure I must have bought some of your favorites at the market." The mists descended again. Anne's mother hadn't been able to be trusted with the shopping for over two years.

"That's okay, Mutti. I'm having a business lunch with Patrick. I'll need to be going." Anne could see her mother had no idea who Patrick was.

"Very well, Annegret," her mother said pleasantly. "Have a nice time. And thank you for brushing my hair. It looks lovely." Karina exited the bathroom and bedroom and joined her husband in the living room.

Anne gazed at herself in the bathroom mirror for several long moments before snapping off the lights and following her mother.

* * *

"Five, right?" Adehm Trent asked as she stared out the large glass window of her office.

"Yes, five fired. Are you sure you want to give them all three months' salary as severance pay?" Rodney, her assistant, asked. "They've cost Bohannon a lot of money already, haven't they?" He jotted his boss's instructions down on a pad.

"I had to fire them for not knowing what in hell was going on right under their noses, but being unemployed in Wood Mill with no money seems like overkill. There's twelve percent unemployment there already. That's twice the national average. The paper plant is the only real industry. Those guys will need the money to get them through until they can find some other work or move to a new location."

"Bohannon Corporation's fixer is really a softie. If the rest of the company knew what I know about Adehm Trent, they'd have the hell shocked out of them."

"And if Rodney Burnett ever opens his trap about me to anyone, he'll wish he was a manager in Wood Mill."

Rodney merely smiled. "I could use three months' pay, but I like you too much to make you break in a new assistant. Besides, that would let three people in on the secret that you're an iron marshmallow."

Adehm winced at that. "Okay, okay... new subject. This outfit we hired to fix the mess at Big Tree. What's the status on that?"

"The proposal by Clearly Perfect was accepted by the corporate office, as you know. Since the project has changed, I've had the interim manager in Hartley talk to them about the big revisions needed. We've been assured they can handle it, and they've agreed to your demand that they send someone to personally supervise the planning and implementation. The engineer on the project will meet you Friday morning at the Pine Palace in Wood Mill. We got an e-mail about that. It was forwarded by the plant just a little bit ago." Rodney pulled a piece of paper from his pad, where it had been safely tucked. "Patrick Ford is unable to be out of state at this time, so the other partner, Anne Schneider, will be the supervisor on the job."

Adehm's eyes narrowed. "I don't like changes, especially on a project this important. If I can't get the plant up and compliant in six months, it's closed and we're up the creek we were inadvertently polluting. Seeing as I argued we should try to salvage the place instead of just walking away from it, maybe my job will be on the line, too."

"You haven't been wrong yet. You have great instincts as well as an amazing track record."

"And I didn't get that record by not paying attention to every little detail of a job. Rodney, my faithful assistant, you have work to do. I want a check on Clearly Perfect, Patrick Ford, and Anne Schneider."

Rodney added to the notes already on his pad. "Right away." He stood and walked to the office door. "How deep a check do you want to do?" he asked, turning back briefly.

Adehm had returned to the dark brown leather chair behind her desk. She glanced up at him. "The deepest."

# Chapter 2

"So, how did it go?" Patrick asked after the waitress had taken their orders. For two years, he and Anne ate a weekly lunch at The Piece of Resistance. This time, they opted for the Navajo tacos: a combination of ground beef, cheese, tomatoes, lettuce, and pinto beans on Navajo fry bread.

"About as well as could be expected. Mom won't really know the difference when I'm gone, and Dad thinks I'm disloyal for going in the first place. I can see the longer-term benefit, so this time I'm going to do what I think is right instead of what he thinks I should do."

Patrick took a sip of his Dos Equis beer. "I'm glad to hear it. We need to hang on to this job. It can open the door for bigger and better ones. I knew that Internet service notifying us of jobs we could qualify for would pay off."

"I'll admit, I was skeptical, but you were right on that one." Anne lifted her glass of Riesling in a toast to her partner. "Here's to money well spent." She took a sip of the wine. "Go ahead and give me the whole story on the Big Tree Paper Plant in Wood Mill, California."

Patrick sat back in his chair. "The name of the area used to be Hartley, but there's no real town there anymore except for the factory and a few houses scattered around. It's remote, but this job seemed right up our alley, routine kind of upgrade to an existing facility. You can do that with your eyes closed."

"I think I was trying to do that last night," she said wryly.

"Hmm, sorry about that. Anyway, the State of California found that the levels of toxins released into the Prussian River far exceeded allowable limits. They inspected Big Tree's equipment and found it outdated and inadequate. To make matters worse, Big Tree wasn't doing routine checking of the effluent. The State was not amused."

"With things like ammonia and phosphorus entering the river, I wouldn't think so." Anne frowned. "You know I'm not terrifically environmental, but we're not dealing with corporate crooks, are we?"

"You mean polluting and not giving a damn?" Patrick asked.

Anne nodded.

"Not that I can tell. It seems more like a case of neglect rather than abuse. The executives got complacent, didn't keep up on new codes and regulations, and managed like they always had. The trouble is, times have changed."

"Enter us and a much bigger project."

"Correct," Patrick said. "This really isn't that much bigger than what we did at Crabtree, but it's our first big one for our own company. The demand for one of us to be on the spot is an inconvenience, but in the long run, it should be worth it." He removed a paper from his jacket pocket. "Worth it in the short run, too. This is the contract." He pushed the paper over to her, along with a pen.

Opening it, she gasped. "Wow! They're serious about this. Almost triple our fee and a very generous per diem allowance. I won't have to eat peanuts from the vending machine for lunch." She finished scanning the form and then signed at the bottom next to Patrick's signature. "Okay, it's a done deal."

She set the pen down on the paper. "One of the reasons I respect you is because you've never been anything less than open with me. Remember when we were working on the Master's project at the university? You thought I was wrong on my sludge calculations. I wasn't, but you told me you thought I was. That was much appreciated, and not only because I needed the laugh."

They both smiled, and Patrick raised his glass to her.

"So," she continued, "here we are at the beginning of an almost unbelievably great job. Too unbelievable. Give me the bad news."

"There's enough of it to give," Patrick said. "The work hours will be long, you'll be gone from here almost all the time, you'll have to have all the supplies trucked in, and there's no room for mistakes. The deadline is absolute, no matter what. We mess it up, miss the deadline, or don't pass inspection, and we can kiss six months of work good-bye."

"We won't get paid at all?" Anne asked, incredulous at the thought.

"You can keep the per diem, that's it."

Anne's face must have shown how she felt, because Patrick laughed. "Missed that in the fine print, did you?" He became serious. "Look, you're the best engineer I've ever known. I've never said it, but even as far back as school, I knew it. You can do this. You can pull it off. I never would have agreed to these tough terms if I didn't think so."

"You've got more confidence in me than I have, but you know I'll work as hard as I can to get it done right, and get it done on time."

The waitress interrupted the conversation by delivering their meals. When she was gone, they resumed.

"I know you'll do everything in your power to make the job a success. I was told you're going to be working directly with Adam Trent. I have no idea if that's going to make your job tougher or easier."

Anne took a bite of her Navajo taco. "That's something I really need. A corporate micromanager watching my every move and asking a million stupid questions."

"Please answer them, okay? Adam Trent controls everything, according to the interim manager. That includes the purse strings."

That made Anne smile sweetly. "Anne will be a good engineer and play nice, I promise, no matter how big ein Arschloch Adam Trent turns out to be."

Patrick laughed. "Asshole? I just love how you can be a potty mouth in two languages."

\* \* \*

"Copy of the California environmental regulations, list of the remaining department managers at Big Tree, and your airline tickets. Your company gas and credit cards are open and clear," Rodney said. As the lengthy list of preparations was checked off, Adehm put the objects into her briefcase.

"Oh, and here's the preliminary report on Clearly Perfect Water Systems. The bios on the partners are brief, but our contacts promise the rest of the information in two days."

"That will be fine. E-mail me the rest of the material when it arrives." Adehm took a blue folder from him. "This will give me something to read on the plane. I can't stand watching those movies that have been chopped to death to make them acceptable for all ages. Might as well just have a puppet show and a pony."

"Now that's a flight I'd take," Rodney said. "Not sure if the pony could fit past the drink cart in the aisle, though."

Adehm laughed. "You should be going on this assignment. You're such a people person, and that makes you the yin to my yang."

"Hardly. You're definitely a people person, but maybe you should show it a little more. Anyway, are you sure this job needs a people person? Sounds to me like you might need to jump right into your no-nonsense-get-the-job-done-or-else Wonder Woman role."

"I can't tell yet. There are still several unknowns. The interim manager seems willing enough to work." She ticked the items off on her fingers. "Suppliers are on alert, the service companies are hired, and the construction crew is on retainer. I've done what I can long distance. I can only hope it will all come together when I'm there in person. The biggest unknown right now is the civil engineer and her plan."

"Thanks for reminding me. We got the signed contracts back from them. There's a copy on your desk."

Adehm picked up the documents Rodney indicated. "They accepted the play or no pay clause? That's good, but I'm surprised a little."

"Why's that?"

"It's a risk for them. Don't complete the work or don't pass the State's inspection, and no check will be issued. Frankly, if I were in their spot, I'm not sure I'd have the guts to do that." She shrugged as she filed the contract in her briefcase. "Believe me, if we don't make that deadline, there's a whole bunch of people who'll be out of a paycheck."

Rodney frowned. "Does that mean I should look around for a prospective new boss while you're gone?"

Adehm walked around the desk and clapped him on the shoulder. "My friend, if I don't make this work, you might just end up being the new boss."

"I'd miss you, but if I get to wear snappy clothes like you, then this rat might leave your sinking ship."

Adehm put her hand over her heart. "You'd toss me aside for a few glad rags? I'm hurt."

Rodney surveyed Adehm's "glad rags." They consisted of an immaculately tailored blue silk business suit, the skirt rising a very professional one inch above the knee. Matching Italian leather pumps accentuated her shapely legs. The whole outfit had to cost at least eight hundred dollars, but Adehm wore the clothes as casually as if she'd been born in them. Rodney knew her background and knew she hadn't.

Adehm walked back around the desk. "Want to try out my chair, too?"

"Already have. It's comfortable enough, but I think I'd want it in a lighter color."

Adehm settled into the chair. She looked almost regal, and more than once Rodney had wondered if she had chosen the dark color as a counterpoint to her blonde good looks. At five-foot-nine inches, her height might have been imposing, but the shoulder length naturally honey-colored hair and Nordic blue eyes led some people to underestimate her seemingly inborn killer instinct. Many times she had used that to her advantage, but just as many times she let whoever had crossed her path discover the truth: that Adehm was smart, she was tough, and when it came to business, she was all business.

"I'll tell you what, boss. I'll hold down the fort here while you deal with things in California. If worse comes to worst and you need a new job, I figure you'll need an assistant there, too. As long as you're willing to provide management training, I'm willing to follow you wherever you go. I'm living in Detroit, but I'm not married to it."

"Done deal. Thanks for the loyalty. Let's hope we don't need to relocate just yet."

"My fingers are crossed," Rodney said.

"Get them uncrossed. I need to dictate about six or seven letters before I leave."

Rodney picked up his pad and pen. It was back to business.

\* \* \*

"And don't forget to come by every other day and feed Angela and Helmut. You remember where your key to my apartment is, right?" Anne spoke to Patrick on the phone as she placed items in her suitcase and carry-on. "One nice outfit for meeting Adam Trent and then casual stuff for work," she said aloud.

"Don't forget to pack your manhole-dweller clothes," Patrick reminded her.

"Waterproof overalls, hard hat, and sludge boots all packed, and in the usual double plastic bags, of course." Anne looked at the clothes through the plastic barriers. "Just when did we decide that our engineering emphasis would be on work where one of the end products is sludge?"

"Way back when you were a curly-haired moppet. Oh, wait, that was yesterday. We decided on wastewater treatment plants in college when we went to work on that project for our Master's thesis. Remember how I always said, 'There's gold in that there sludge'?"

"Yeah, yeah, you said it. Curly-haired moppet? I get no respect around here."

"Maybe you would if you didn't have a baby face that makes you look like you're still in college. Sometimes I wish I had that kind of youthful looks."

"You wouldn't if you got carded every time you went to buy a bottle of wine," Anne said.

"Maybe not, now that you mention it. Okay, I'm meeting Robyn for dinner after she gets off work. Have a good flight, and call me when you get there."

"I will. And Angela and Helmut?"

"Your friends are safe with me. Don't worry."

Anne glanced over to the large cage that resembled a small city. Her two dwarf hamsters were enjoying a meal of shredded cabbage and carrots. She needed to leave Patrick a note to give the hamsters fresh vegetables in addition to the seeds, wheat germ, and rolled oats that were their main food.

"Don't be concerned, guys. Patrick will feed you. Nothing to worry about, nothing at all." She watched as Angela darted over to the exercise wheel and began running in it. "I wish I could say the same for me."

\* \* \*

Anne buckled in and settled back in the cloth-covered seat to let US Airways deal with getting her to Merced. She rued the fact there were no direct flights from Albuquerque to Merced. She would have a ninety-minute layover in Las Vegas and another in San Francisco. She didn't have anything against Las Vegas, San Francisco, or time spent in an airport, but she was disturbed that instead of one flight, she would have three. Three flights meant three takeoffs.

*Stupid, stupid engineer's brain.* Ever since Anne had taken the basics of engineering in college and had come to understand the relationship of the jet engine's thrust to staying aloft in air that normally couldn't support the weight of a feather, she had an almost irrational fear of dropping from the sky. Intellectually, she knew it was ridiculous. Still, after every takeoff, when the engines seemed to scale back from the massive effort that propelled tons of weight down the runway and thousands of feet into the sky, Anne feared the airplane might fall back to earth. After that moment of fear, she would be fine. Until it passed, she would have white knuckles.

Closing her eyes, Anne used an old trick to deal with her anxiety. She visualized the project she was currently working on and attempted to formulate solutions in her mind. A few times, problems were solved in her head that only later would be solved on the computer. She started thinking about Big Tree.

*So many problems with this one. We have to start from scratch and change everything, but at the same time, work fast. Six months isn't a long time. There isn't time to waste with unnecessary actions. Okay, first thing to do is streamline everything. Carry out things together that can be done that way.*

Anne felt the bump of the little ground vehicle making contact with the airplane in order to push it back. *I need to work it like a chess game. Stay two or three moves ahead of my current one.* The plane moved backward and out of the gate. It turned sideways to line up for taxiing. *Why don't planes have a reverse, like cars?*

Anne opened her eyes at her own unspoken question. If she physically started, the man sitting next to her, absorbed in the *Albuquerque Journal,* didn't seem to notice. *Why would I want a reverse on a plane? With my luck the pilot would accidentally bump into it as he got up to go to the bathroom and we'd all...* Anne pushed the unwelcome thoughts from her mind. The plane began to taxi toward the tarmac. Desperate for diversion, she began reading the back of the man's newspaper.

"You can have the sports page. I'm finished with that," he said.

Anne blushed furiously at having been caught. "Sorry, I was just interested in last night's city council meeting," she fibbed. She didn't feel like explaining why a rational and scientific mind would have an irrational and decidedly unscientific fear of taking off.

The plane made the final turn onto the runway, and after a brief hesitation, the engines roared and Anne was pressed back into her seat as the machine hurtled along. She closed her eyes and held onto the armrests for dear life.

\* \* \*

Adehm relaxed in the first-class cabin, with a plain orange juice on the tray table in front of her. Next to her drink, her laptop was open to the Big Tree Paper Plant file. Though she had committed all the pertinent facts to memory, she was of the opinion you could never know enough about what you were working on or with whom you were working.

The company's contacts in Albuquerque had sent the preliminary reports on the civil engineering firm that Bohannon had contracted to deal with the problems at Big Tree. Adehm skimmed the initial report on Clearly Perfect contained in the blue folder Rodney had given her earlier. The file included tax documents, business license forms, and a plethora of other information routinely available on businesses that dealt with the public.

*Nothing remarkable here, except that they seem to be just a two-mule team. There's only Patrick Ford and Annegret Schneider listed as employees. Annegret. Unusual name, but I'm a fine one to talk.*

The flight attendant came by with a selection of snacks. Adehm chose a granola bar and a gourmet chocolate chip cookie. *Now that's a balanced diet,* she thought as she returned to the files. Most interested in the person with whom she would be working, she turned her full attention to Anne's file. She scanned the photocopy of her driver's license. *Nice enough looking. Hair—brown, Eyes— blue, Height—five foot six, Weight—130 pounds, Place of Birth— Dresden, Germany.* The black and white photocopy didn't show anything special in the face, but Adehm knew all about bad driver's license photos, cringing at the thought of the one in her briefcase.

She skipped to the educational history. Annegret had attended the German equivalent of grade school, junior high school, and high school and made excellent marks. There were university studies in Belgium and graduate studies in the United States at Spaulding University. *Decent schools.*

A copy of her European Union passport was included in the file, as well as her application for United States citizenship. *How do we get all this stuff? Never mind, I don't want to know.* As Adehm looked over the paperwork, something poked at her from the recesses in her mind. *What am I seeing that's unusual?* She read the records again until it hit her. *Dresden. That was the city the Allies nearly bombed to smithereens during World War Two. Then it fell under Soviet influence afterward.* Annegret Schneider had been an East German.

* * *

"No, I'm not there yet, Vati. I'm on my layover in Las Vegas." Anne shielded her free ear from the noise emanating from the nearby slot machines in the airport. "I only wanted to know how things are going."

"And how should they be going?" her father said. "You haven't been gone but a half day. I am not so feeble as to have problems in that amount of time." Anne heard a voice in the background. "Your glasses are on the dresser in the bedroom, Karina." Marcel's voice had softened considerably as he gave his wife directions to the missing eyeglasses.

"I know you are going to be fine," Anne said. "I also wanted to remind you that I'll be on my cell phone while I'm away. You can call me anytime, day or night. And no matter how busy I am, if there's an emergency, I'll be on the first plane home."

"Yes, yes. You've said all that repeatedly. We will be fine. I ask you to remember that your mother was diagnosed while you were in America going to graduate school and we yet lived in Dresden. Her case has advanced, but I think I can manage with my resources."

Anne did remember. She could never forget the days of worry and fear when her mother's symptoms were being diagnosed and the awful day she received the phone call from her brother telling her the results. She shook the thoughts away.

"I know. I wanted to tell you..." She trailed off, once again knowing she and her father hadn't ever had the kind of relationship where she could say what was in her heart, or many times, what was on her mind. "I wanted to tell you I'll be in touch on a regular basis." She heard the initial boarding call for her flight to San Francisco. "I need to go now, Vati. I'll talk to you soon." She ended the call and turned the cell phone off for the flight.

Consulting the boarding card given to her in Albuquerque, she realized she would be in the last section to be called. She used the time to organize the paperwork in her bag to make it easy to retrieve on the flight. She was determined to increase her knowledge of the Big Tree project without wasting any time. She didn't have the luxury of slacking off.

Finally boarded, she buckled into her seat and gave the flight attendant's safety speech only half her attention, though her gaze seemed to be focused on the woman demonstrating the operation of the oxygen masks and warning of tampering with the bathroom smoke detectors. Anne had heard it many times before, and her engineer's brain was already reviewing new numbers faxed to her apartment that morning.

*Say what you like about Adam Trent's handling of the firings, his office seems to be pretty damn efficient.* The Rodney Burnett who faxed the paperwork was organized and experienced at what he was doing. He had included her hotel reservation, the door-to-door driving directions from Merced to Wood Mill, and the number to contact him if she required any assistance.

*I wish he had given me Trent's number. I could have used the time from Merced to Wood Mill to get the initial meeting out of the way over the phone. Then we could have gotten right down to business without the little pleasantries entailed by meeting a client for the first time. The handshake, the questions about the flight, and, if he's like a few of our clients, the obligatory look at my chest when he thinks I'm not aware of it.* The last one couldn't be gotten out of the way with a telephone meeting, but if she was businesslike enough, maybe the peeking wouldn't last long.

She closed her eyes as the plane left the gate. *Here we go again,* she thought. *Just keep thinking about work. Pipe dimensions, water outflow, sludge...* All thoughts were scattered to the wind as the jet engines roared, and yet again, she was propelled skyward.

\* \* \*

Adehm walked from where she had collected her baggage to the car rental counter. Her corporate card got her speedy service, and she was soon cruising out of the airport and northbound on Highway 101. She had told Rodney to book her rental car from San Francisco because she didn't like the tiny jets used for commuter service in and out of San Francisco. That had been a lie. She knew if she flew into San Francisco, she would be forced to make the side trip she was making now.

*No sense fighting it. I have to go see her. I don't think anything could keep me away if I was this close. I'm still in love with her.* Adehm felt the weight of the truth of the statement. She had never been one to struggle with self delusions. Accepting the situation as fact, she cruised effortlessly through the mid-afternoon traffic. The flow slowed a little as she approached the Golden Gate Bridge and city exit, but with the toll plaza being on the side entering the city, it did little to hinder her speed. She didn't use the built-in global positioning system for directions. She knew the route by heart.

Putting the wireless headset earpiece in place, she flipped open her cell phone.

"Call office," she stated. A momentary silence ensued, followed by a ringing.

"Adehm Trent's office."

"You staying late trying out the executive chair?" she asked Rodney.

"Why else would I be here? Not because I knew you would think of something for me to do once you landed, or anything like that."

Adehm laughed; Rodney knew her so well. "Call the hotel and ask them to leave a message for Annegret Schneider. Just say I've been delayed a bit, but I'll meet her for breakfast instead of for dinner tonight as originally planned."

"Anything wrong?" Rodney asked.

"No, not a thing. I'm going to stop in and see an old friend." She didn't elaborate beyond that.

"Very good, then. I'll call the Pine Palace and have them leave her a message. Drive carefully, boss."

"Will do." She tapped the earpiece to disconnect. She waited a moment and then tapped the earpiece again. "Call," she said and repeated the phone number she had known by memory for years.

"Hello?"

"Donna?" she asked when she heard the familiar voice. "It's Adehm. I'm in the neighborhood. Well, about forty miles from the neighborhood, anyway. I thought I'd drop by, if that's okay."

"You know it is," Donna Roth replied. "I told you that you'd always be welcome. I'll never change my mind about that. I assume you've flown into the city for some reason?"

"I'm passing through on business." Adehm didn't say that her business was in the opposite direction of the way she was driving. "I need to come up there."

There was a momentary silence.

"I understand that. It's the same for me. I'll meet you by the ranch road."

"Thanks, Donna. Traffic isn't too bad yet, so give me a little over half an hour or so." Tapping the headset, Adehm ended the call. She turned her attention fully to driving, trying not to think about the woman in Cotati.

# Chapter 3

Anne stood at the car rental counter and attempted again to get her ears to pop. The quick ascent and descent from San Francisco on the small plane had worked on her nerves more than usual, and it didn't help that the nineteen-seat plane was the smallest she had ever flown on. Worry about the safety of the small prop plane had taken Anne's mind off the need to swallow forcefully to equalize the pressure on her eardrums. Opening her mouth widely, she mimicked a large yawn and managed to get the right ear to pop. The left one stubbornly remained closed.

"Here are the keys, Ms. Schneider. It's the blue one at the end." The rental car agent handed her the keys and rental agreement after pointing out the Ford Taurus. It had taken less than ten minutes to complete their transaction.

"You're a lot more efficient than I would have expected for a small airport." Anne pulled up the handle on her rolling suitcase.

"We only have thirty-one flights a week into Merced. We have a lot of time to get efficient," the agent said. He came around the small counter and helped Anne get her bags to the vehicle.

"Whatever your secret is, I hope you spread the word."

"Can't do that, ma'am, because then I'd be inundated with efficiency experts watching my every move and getting in my way. Then I might not have time for my second job."

"Which is?" Anne asked.

"Who do you think took the bags off your flight? When you work at a small airport, you need to multitask." The agent placed Anne's large bag in the trunk and closed the lid. "Yep, your bag hasn't lost any weight, that's for sure."

Anne laughed. "I'll bet it hasn't. Thank you, Brian," she said, reading the name on his airport badge. "I'll see you in a few months."

"I'll look forward to it," he replied. "Oh, you might need this on your way, Ms. Schneider." He pulled out a pack of gum and offered her a piece. "This is California, and nobody would look at you sideways for driving down the road making faces and yawning, but I figure there might be an easier way to get your ears to pop than that."

Anne pushed on the small plastic bubble holding the gum in the pack and caught it in her palm. "Thanks again."

"Just another part of our multitasking efficiency." He held the door open for her and closed it after she slid behind the wheel. "Drive carefully, now."

*I'm definitely going to have to rethink my preconceived notions about weird Californians.* Anne started the car. She placed the gum in her mouth, turned on the air conditioner, and headed out of the parking lot toward Wood Mill.

*   *   *

Adehm drove up Highway 101, enjoying the early summer weather. The fields were still partially green and were at least a month away from their true summer color of golden brown, brought on by the intense valley heat and nearly bone-dry conditions.

The window was down, and Adehm's thick blonde hair blew freely in the breeze. The fresh and welcome smell of the business of agriculture came in through the window, stirring memories in her that were at times pleasant and at other times, less so.

She had found an old favorite station on the radio and was grateful it hadn't changed the format it had been playing for as long as she could remember. The tunes were familiar, and she tapped her fingers on the steering wheel and sang out loud as she drove, changing to singing under her breath as she passed other vehicles.

The comfortable aura pushed back the butterflies she was beginning to feel in her stomach. It had been six years since she'd driven up this road, and the circumstances of the last trip had made her vow she wouldn't pass this way again.

*Never say never,* she thought. *Wow, I must be getting old if adages like that are popping into my head.* In truth, Adehm looked younger than her thirty-eight years, but she had cultivated an image of maturity and responsibility that made many people overestimate her age by ten years. If they saw her in the clothes she had changed into at the airport, they might change that estimate drastically. She had opted for a faded pair of Levi's and a cool, red cotton shirt. Except for the lack of a tan, she might have been any local California woman out for a drive on a warm afternoon.

The sign for the exit to Cotati came up, and Adehm merged over into the slower lane. She thought Cotati itself was an apt allegory for a merge into a slower lane of life. The town of sixty-four-hundred residents was less than an hour from San Francisco, but it might as well have been a thousand miles away. The rural flavor of Sonoma County came through loud and clear.

Adehm exited the highway and drove through the town, past the historic plaza, and out the other end. Nearly a mile from the town limits, a dirt and gravel road branched off from the paved one. A wrought iron gate stood wide open under an arching sign proclaiming the Donna Stop Ranch. Next to the gate and sign stood Donna herself. Adehm slowed the car as she eased onto the ranch road, trying to kick up as little dust as possible. It didn't matter; Donna kicked up enough of her own jogging around the front of the car to meet Adehm with a huge hug.

"My gosh, it's been too long," she said, depositing an enthusiastic kiss on Adehm's cheek. "I'd about given up ever seeing you around here again. You promised you'd come back someday, but I thought you were just blowing smoke up my ass to make me feel better about you leaving in the first place."

"I had to go. It was too painful to stay in California." She returned the affection given by the older woman. Donna had been like a second mother to Adehm. "At least I kept up with you by e-mail."

"After you bought me the computer and paid for lessons for me to learn to use it. I don't think I'll ever be able to thank you enough for that," Donna said. "It opened up a whole new world for me. I connected to people outside my little life here, and I learned a lot about Shannon and people like her. It helped."

Adehm looked down, unable to meet Donna's eyes. As best as Adehm could tell, the gray-haired woman had never felt sorry for herself, and she most assuredly had helped Adehm through some dark days. Adehm felt like her life hadn't moved along much, despite her rapid rise with Bohannon Corporation.

"It's okay," Donna said, lifting Adehm's chin so she could look directly at her. "Everybody heals at a different rate. I had longer with Shannon, but you had it deeper. We both hurt, and we'll both heal. I promise you."

Adehm nodded and swallowed thickly. Memories from eight years before came flooding back. And the memories brought back the pain. Adehm knew her face was clouded with emotion.

Donna took her hand. "Do you want to go see her?"

"Yeah, I do," Adehm replied. "We can take my car."

Donna got into the passenger seat, and Adehm returned to her place behind the wheel. "It's up this way, right?" She indicated the paved county road that continued on beyond the turnoff for the ranch.

"Yep, it's just about four miles from here. You can't miss it. The tree has gotten a lot bigger, but other than that, it's about the same."

Adehm nodded, checked her rearview mirror, and drove back onto the paved road. She glanced over at Donna. "How are things with you?"

Donna gave a tired smile. "Not too bad, but I really am slowing down. I can barely get up with the chickens these days, and believe me, those chickens need a lot of seeing to. I decided not to sell them anymore, but my little brood still takes up my time."

Donna had lived on the ranch for almost thirty years, surviving her foray into young widowhood by raising Plymouth Rock chickens on the small ranch she purchased with her insurance money. In Donna's estimation, ten acres of rolling pasture dotted with scrub oaks and a few pines qualified as a ranch.

The business of egg and chicken selling was good to Donna. It let her have a measure of independence and let her raise her daughter, Shannon, in the place she chose. That it was a success was due to Donna's hard work, but it hadn't come easy. In the early days, she was learning the retail side of what had only been a hobby during her marriage. Even directions occasionally were a challenge for Donna, especially before the county put down blacktop on the road leading toward the ranch. Many times, she had missed the turn to the ranch as one gravel road blended into another.

"Donna, stop!" she would correct herself as she slammed on the brakes and backed up to turn in at the ranch, which was marked only by small surveying stakes. After a few times of admonishing herself out loud when Shannon was in the car, the child had taken to calling out, "Donna stop!" whenever they traveled on the dusty road from Cotati. The moniker stuck, and when Donna finally earned the money for the front gate, the name of the Donna Stop Ranch was made official.

Adehm drove the four miles carefully, aware of the area's penchant for stray poultry, livestock, and wild animals. She had no intention of adding to the roadkill population. Finally, around a sweeping curve, the Foothill Oaks Cemetery came into view. The small memorial park contained a mix of graves, some recent, but some dating back to the 1870s. The headstones in the older sections were upright, but often tilted and battered by the California weather and earthquake-prone land. The newer section had grave markers that were flat to the ground, allowing for easier upkeep of the area. Despite a hundred and forty years of interring residents, the cemetery was still small by modern standards.

Adehm turned onto the dirt road drive and took an immediate left to the newer area. A few graves had freshly-turned earthen mounds. She followed the road around the cemetery to the very back and parked next to an olive tree.

"It's changed some since you planted it. It won't get much bigger, but it's bearing a lot of fruit. I've put up quite a few quarts since it started producing," Donna said. She pointed to the misshapen trunk. "I've always thought of olive trees as tortured souls, so twisted and almost painful looking when they grow wild like this."

"But it's such a hardy tree," Adehm observed. "That one will be around long after you and I are only memories on this planet. Even after memories of us are gone. I wanted a tree with longevity. That's something Shannon didn't have." She turned from the tree and started across the grassy field. She hadn't been there in almost eight years, but she found her way unerringly to the marker.

"Hello, Shannon," she said. "It's been awhile. I've missed you. I miss you every day, it seems."

Donna caught up to Adehm and overheard the last few words.

"I miss her, too," Donna said quietly. "Sometimes I think you and Shannon will come driving up on a Saturday like you did when you lived down in the city. Those were great weekends. You two made me laugh, even when I was putting you both to work on the ranch."

"She's still in here, you know." Adehm tapped her chest. "She stays with me. Not like she was at the end, but like she was before the damned colon cancer and chemo made her so sick. We shared some tough times, but I'll always remember her out here by the ranch, well and happy in the place she loved so much."

"Thanks for agreeing she needed to rest here. She's keeping her dad company now." Donna pointed to a slightly older part of the cemetery. "And I'll join them here when it's my time."

"Got room for one more?" Adehm asked, her eyes never leaving the granite marker.

"No, we don't."

Donna's answer caused Adehm to look up at her quickly.

"You're too young to be planning your gravesite. Shannon would kick your ass if she knew you said anything even remotely like that. She loved her life, and if she thought you were wasting yours by not moving on, she'd be pissed."

"I know you're right, but how do you move on from somebody who was your life?" Adehm felt genuinely perplexed. "How do you just forget somebody who was part of your ability to breathe in and out for four years? When Shannon died, I felt like I was suffocating because she wasn't there to remind me to take in air. How do you forget all that?" Adehm's voice was steeped with emotion, and she crossed her arms, as if holding herself physically could help hold herself together emotionally.

"You don't forget all that, but you let it go. You let it go to allow Shannon to do whatever it is she has to do now, and you let it go to let yourself do whatever the many years ahead of you have in store. That's the way it is in this world."

"Tell it to my heart," Adehm said.

Donna didn't reply.

They stood quietly and listened to the songbirds singing from the boughs of nearby trees.

At last Donna spoke again. "I don't have to tell your heart, Adehm. One day it's going to tell you."

* * *

Anne drove south on Highway 99 as she had been directed. The breeze coming in through the car window kept the bright sun from making the drive too uncomfortable. Since she'd never been to California before, her eyes wandered frequently to the scenery. She had never realized how agricultural California was, but the guidebook she bought before she left Albuquerque said it had been the number one state in agricultural production for more than fifty years. Somehow, that hadn't squared with Anne's vision of California, which consisted of big cities, bad traffic, movies, and tourists. She was already getting an education.

The breeze blew in a savory aroma. Somewhere out of Anne's vision, onions and garlic were cooking. The entire area smelled like a pot of spaghetti sauce, and Anne's stomach rumbled in response. It had been many hours since she'd had breakfast at home.

Pulling off at the nearest exit, she drove to a familiar fast-food restaurant and ordered a chicken sandwich and fries at the drive-through window. She pulled into a shady spot in the parking lot to eat. She sipped her diet cola and reviewed the directions to Wood Mill again. The turn-off from Highway 99 was about 10 miles ahead, and from there, she'd follow local roads out from the valley into the foothills.

*So much riding on this. I know I can do it, but can I do it as fast and as well as I need to?* Self-doubt she would never speak of to Patrick entered her mind. *I have to do this for the business and to get us to the place we've been working so damn hard to be.* She'd taken on huge responsibilities before, and this would have to be just another in a string of chances she would take. She nibbled on the sandwich and fries until the burgeoning fear in the pit of her stomach made finishing them impossible.

Anne stepped out of the car and deposited all but the rest of her drink in a nearby trash can. She looked down the highway in the direction she had come. She'd had an odd sensation since starting her drive. She'd checked her rearview mirror several times, almost as if she were expecting to see someone she knew following her. As far as she remembered, none of her acquaintances lived in the state. She thought about people she went to the university with and had worked with, but no one came to mind.

Must be her mind playing tricks on her. She paid a brief visit to the restroom before getting back into the car. Hoping some music would shake the odd feeling, she toyed with the radio until she found a station with music she liked. She tapped her fingers on the steering wheel as she pulled out of the parking lot and drove to the highway entrance. She checked her mirrors and pulled onto Highway 99. The feeling was there again, but it wasn't creepy or upsetting. It was just strange, and strange she had been dealing with for a long time. She could handle strange. Smiling to herself, she joined the southbound flow of traffic.

\* \* \*

Adehm drove across the Golden Gate Bridge, taking Highway 101 opposite to the way she had driven hours before. There were more direct ways to Highway 99 and eventually to Wood Mill, but she couldn't resist taking the slower route through a city she still loved.

Adehm was a native of the City by the Bay, and she never felt more at home than when she felt the cool breeze off the Pacific flow across her face. San Francisco was where she had grown up and gone to school from kindergarten through college. When Adehm had graduated from the University of San Francisco with an MBA in Management and Policy, she had joined the West Coast branch of the rapidly expanding Bohannon Corporation. Her academic program had prepared her for a life in the world of business, but she hadn't been prepared for a personal life at all. Then Shannon changed her perspective and priorities.

Shannon Roth was a young lawyer in the small Mergers and Acquisitions section of the San Francisco office of Bohannon. When she brought a prospective buyout opportunity to Adehm, it was as though Adehm's whole world had shifted on its axis. She still outperformed most of her colleagues, but the view had changed.

The quick pick-ups from The Lexington Club and late nights of drinking and dancing at The Cafe came to an end. Adehm found she missed neither of them.

Within a few months, Shannon and Adehm moved in together and looked forward to a long and happy life. That long and happy life lasted exactly four years. Diagnosis to death took up half their time together.

Adehm pushed the still-painful thoughts from her mind and turned her full attention to her driving. The sun was setting on California, and the cool of the evening was just beginning. She joined the flow of traffic south on Highway 99, leaving behind the long day and lingering ghosts.

*   *   *

Anne drove into Wood Mill and was surprised at the size of the town. She had pictured a sleepy community with wooden sidewalks and none of the conveniences of modern life. She was wrong. Although dependent on a single industry for most employment, Wood Mill had managed to attract a variety of businesses to support those who lived there. An independent grocer, a gas station, a hardware store, a video store, an antique shop, and a small bakery lined the road. At the end of the aptly named Main Street stood the two-story Pine Palace.

Anne parallel parked in front of the small hotel. Townspeople in the nearby shops and on the streets didn't pay as much attention to a stranger in town as she'd expected they might.

They must be used to people they didn't know coming here because of the plant. She thought again of the five terminated managers. *I wonder if the townspeople will treat Adam Trent as casually. I guess I'll see when he gets here.*

She exited the car and removed her bags from the trunk. She stepped up onto the curb and into the lobby of the Pine Palace. As its name denoted, the lobby was paneled in pine planks, and the check-in desk was made of the same material. An elderly man sat reading a thick book. As she crossed to the desk, she could see it was *Moby Dick*.

"Hi," she greeted the man. He was short and clean-shaven, with a white ring of hair around the back of his head and a dozen unruly hairs springing up from the top. He had a nametag that read, "Len."

"My name is Anne Schneider, and I have a reservation. It was made for me by the Bohannon Corporation."

"Yes, ma'am, we've been expecting you." He tapped keys on a laptop computer that seemed at odds with the rest of the décor. "Would you like a room in the historic part of the hotel or the modern section?"

"What's the difference?"

"Same price. The historic part is upstairs from the lobby here. It dates back to the Gold Rush days, and it's as authentic as we could keep it. The only changes are private bathrooms, a phone, and a computer port. Heaven forbid that today's traveler be without those."

His teasing tone made Anne like him almost immediately.

"The modern part is just that. It was built in the early sixties and looks like every motor lodge you'll find on the back roads. The rooms have their own entrance in the back where the lodge attaches to the hotel. It's strictly your preference. I've got rooms in both parts."

"I've always been a fan of history. I'll take upstairs."

"You got it, ma'am. Good choice. You've got a lovely four-poster bed along with all original furnishings." He pushed a registration card across the desk toward her. "Name, address, make and model of your vehicle, and the usual what-have-you's." While Anne filled out the card, Len turned and pulled a key from a pigeon-holed repository on the wall.

"No card key?" Anne asked in a surprised tone.

"We seem to find keys still work pretty well up here, at least in the historic part, so we decided to keep them around in case they become valuable antiques one day." Len winked at her. "Now then, as I'm hotel clerk and porter, can I help you with your bags?" Anne shook her head.

"No need. Never pack more than you're willing to haul around is my motto. A couple of boxes will come for me in a day or so. I'd appreciate your help then."

"Not a problem. I'll bring them up as soon as they get here." He handed her the room key. "Your room is number 12, top of the landing, turn right, and go down three doors. It has a nice view of Main Street."

"Thanks. I'll let you get back to your book now."

"*Moby Dick*," Len said, visibly brightening. "It's pretty good. You ever read it?"

Anne nodded, not adding that she had originally read the German translation.

"I went to work logging around here when I was fourteen. I worked steady until I retired, and then I took this part-time job. I figured it was a chance for me to make up for lost time, just for the pure pleasure of it."

Anne had a scholar's love of books and could understand the sentiment. "One of these days I'm going to do something just for the pure pleasure of it. Right now, I'm going to settle for a shower." Anne picked up her bags and turned from the desk.

"Ms. Schneider?" Len called. "I almost forgot. There's a message for you."

Anne stopped as Len read from a slip of paper he had been using as a bookmark. "An Adehm Trent's office called and there's been a delay in travel plans." He squinted at his own handwriting. "No dinner meeting. Make it breakfast at eight in the morning instead, and you'll meet here in the lobby." Len looked up. "And that's it." He looked at the note again. "Adehm Trent. Interesting spelling."

Anne walked to the staircase wondering exactly how many ways there were to spell Trent.

\* \* \*

Several hours later, Adehm walked into the lobby of the Pine Palace. Finding it empty, she tapped a bell she found on the check-in desk. When no one responded, she tapped it twice more. An elderly man entered from a back room, pulling suspenders up over his shirt as he did.

"Okay, ma'am, give me a chance," he said good naturedly. "I'm seventy-six years old, and it takes me a bit to get out of the recliner."

"Sorry," Adehm said. "I didn't mean to seem impatient."

"And I didn't mean to fall asleep in that recliner," the man said, laughing. "What can I do for you?"

"I have a room booked. The name is Adehm Trent." She was a bit surprised she didn't get the usual questions about her unusual name.

"Got the reservation right here, ma'am. One room, modern section in the back. Is that correct?" He pushed the registration card toward her as he asked.

"It sure is. High speed Internet, right?"

"Wireless and secure. The instructions are printed on a card on the desk in your room. You have an oversized Jacuzzi tub and a mini-bar for your convenience. Your parking space is numbered and right outside your door. Just drive around to the back of the hotel. I can come out and help you with your bags," he offered.

Adehm filled out the card quickly and accepted her key card. "No need, I can find my way to my room, but I will need a seven a.m. wake up call."

"Seven a.m. it is. Have a good rest."

"I will, thank you. It's been a long day. Oh, has an Anne Schneider checked in?"

"She has. She's in room 12 upstairs and will meet you in the lobby at eight in the morning. You can dial her directly by pushing nine-one-two if you need to reach her this evening."

"No, tomorrow morning is soon enough. Good night."

"Good night, ma'am. If you need anything, just call me by pushing zero on the phone. Just don't need anything too quickly."

Adehm laughed with him and waved as she left the lobby.

*It starts at eight o'clock,* she thought as she got back into her car. *Anne Schneider, I hope you don't freak out when you find out what you're in for.*

# Chapter 4

At seven-fifty-five the next morning, Anne came down the stairs searching for the executive from Bohannon Corporation. She found only Len sifting through paperwork behind the desk.

"Did Adam Trent get here yet?" she asked.

"Sure did. Checked in after ten o'clock last night. Should be along any minute now."

"I've never actually met him," Anne admitted. "So, anything you can tell me about Mr. Trent would be helpful."

"Mr. Trent is sixty-one-years old, works as a branch manager for a mortgage company, and lives near Santa Barbara with Mrs. Trent," Adehm said as she walked into the lobby. "However, if you're looking for his daughter, representing Bohannon Corporation on this project, then you've found her."

Anne could only stare.

"I'll give you the standard explanation so we can get right to our meeting, if that's okay by you. I'm Adehm Trent, that's A-D-E-H-M." Adehm extended her hand to Anne, who shook it. "I was a late-in-life child, and my dad thought I would be his only chance for a namesake. Adam didn't quite fit the gender expectations of the day, and that's the reason for the odd spelling. Little did my dad know if he had only waited fourteen more months, he could have given my younger brother that name."

"What is his name?"

"Mary."

Anne's mouth dropped open, and Adehm laughed. "I never get tired of that joke. My brother does, but I don't. The truth is he got dad's middle name, which is Harper. Now that we've dispensed with my family designations, I propose we take ourselves to the café up the street, get some breakfast, and start work on this little difficulty that Big Tree seems to find itself in."

Anne went along with the suggestion. Adehm Trent had a commanding personality that Anne felt as soon as Adehm had entered the room. For now, she would be content to let Adehm lead things.

They walked down Main Street to Ruth's Café. Several patrons were already enjoying their breakfast. Adehm and Anne followed a sign's direction indicating they should seat themselves. A large redhead walked to the table with a pair of menus and a glass coffeepot.

"Good morning. Coffee?" she asked as she gave them each a menu.

Both Anne and Adehm turned up their mugs for a generous cup of the aromatic liquid.

"You've saved a life with this," Adehm said as she reached for the cream. "What do you recommend?"

"The Logger's Breakfast is good. That's two eggs any style, two pieces of toast, two pieces each of bacon or your choice of sausage. Home fries on the side."

"Sounds good to me," Adehm said. She handed the menu back to the waitress. "I'll have them scrambled with link sausage and wheat toast."

"You got it," the waitress said. She pulled a pad and pen from her pocket and jotted down the information. She addressed Anne. "Do you know what you'd like, honey, or do you need a minute?"

"Just oatmeal and a half of grapefruit," Anne said, closing the menu.

The waitress took it after noting Anne's order. "I'll get this up right away. Meanwhile, if you need anything, just give me a shout. The name's Brenda." She tore the order off the pad as she returned to the kitchen.

"You dieting?" Adehm asked.

"No, not really. I mean I like to eat as healthy as I can at breakfast. I'm not a fanatic about it or anything, but you never know what's the next thing they'll find out is bad for you."

"Sensible, I suppose." Adehm took a sip of her coffee after adding more cream from the small metal pitcher. "Maybe your good eating habits will rub off on me. I'm going to give you a chance to do that, because I'd like to hold a daily meeting with you. This project is under my personal supervision, and it's vital I be kept up on the progress as we go along. I don't know what every day will hold for us as far as workload and priorities, so I'd like to schedule our meetings here at eight each morning. Any problems with that?"

"None whatsoever, as far as I can tell," Anne said. "If there's ever a scheduling conflict, I'll give you as much notice as I can.

Unless there's an early delivery or work-related issue, I can't see any difficulty." She added sugar substitute from a small blue packet to her coffee. "Keeping you up to date shouldn't be a problem," she added, as she used a spoon to stir the mixture.

"It's not simply not a problem, it's essential. I'm the point person here. I've got the ability to cut through red tape and make things happen that others don't. But I can only help if I know what's going on."

Brenda delivered their breakfast.

Adehm closed her eyes and inhaled deeply. "God, I love the smell of sausages in the morning."

"I'm sorry, I couldn't hear what you said over the noise of your arteries clogging." Anne stopped sectioning her grapefruit mid slice when she realized what she had said to the representative of the company for which she was consulting.

"Good one." Adehm dug into her eggs. "I would have hated to work with someone afraid to talk to me."

Anne's only reply was a weak laugh and a mental kick to her own backside for the remark. *She isn't Patrick, and if I don't want to go back to Patrick explaining how I lost this job, I'm going to have to watch what comes out of my mouth.* She looked up to find Adehm adding a generous dollop of grape jelly to a slice of her wheat toast. *No matter what.*

\* \* \*

After breakfast, Adehm and Anne agreed to meet in the parking lot of the hotel to drive to Big Tree. Anne wasn't sure what items she might need at the mill, so she packed for any contingency. She had several necessary measurements and inspections to make, and some would call for her to don her manhole-dweller clothes.

Adehm negotiated the road skillfully. It was wide and well-paved. Anne surmised it was built to deal with the traffic of logging trucks and the tractor trailers that hauled product out from the mill.

"Why didn't they build the town closer to the mill, Ms. Trent?" Anne asked, realizing they would have a fifteen- or twenty-minute commute each way every day.

"My name is Adehm, and originally I think the town did exist closer to the plant. Hartley was small, but lively, back in the day. Then the railroad built a spur line through the spot where Wood Mill is now, and the town sort of relocated. The spur hasn't been in use for years, but the town stayed put. Too much trouble to repack, I suppose." Adehm slowed for a tighter curve and then accelerated again. "We just ship straight down to the valley and put the containers on the train there. Not far from the gate, you can still see a few buildings in what's left of the old town."

"Like a ghost town?" Anne asked.

"You've been reading too much Western lore, but I suppose you could call it that. I'd call it abandoned, run-down, and a haven for rattlesnakes."

Anne winced. She had always been concerned about finding slimy or furry creatures on her forays into the world of wastewater treatment. Now she had to add venomous to that list.

"Anything wrong?" Adehm asked.

"No, not a thing. I just realized I forgot to tell you to call me Anne."

"Great. Anne it is then," Adehm said as she drove through the gates of Big Tree Paper Plant.

\* \* \*

Adehm walked Anne into the manager's office at Big Tree and motioned for her to take a seat opposite the modest desk situated there. Anne dropped her bag and settled in to wait for Adehm to reveal why she had asked Anne to the office. Anne wanted to start in on the necessary testing right away. Not knowing laboratory facilities in California, she had no idea how long it would take to get results back.

"I think I have something that may interest you," Adehm said as she opened the top drawer on a file cabinet.

"The main thing that interests me right now is to shrug into my working clothes and get down to the current treatment plant and find out what I'm up against," Anne replied.

"Like I said…" Adehm pulled a thick file from the drawer and took it to Anne. "I think you'll find this helpful. I may have missed something, but I used the recommendations from the State inspectors to have some preliminary testing done. I hope this will be of use to you."

Anne took the folder and leafed through it. It contained page after page of lab results. She looked at the data, allowing the information to flow through her agile mind and become sorted into the good, the bad, and the impossible.

"This is incredible. These tests are exactly what I would have done." She looked up at Adehm. "You ran these on the outlet pipe, right? These are the outflow numbers?"

Adehm nodded. "Frankly, I didn't know an outlet pipe from a hole in the ground, so I can't take any of the credit on that. I still don't, but I know who to go to for the information."

"You got great information." Anne flipped through the pages. "Magnetic inductive flow measurement, nitrogen, phosphorus, chemical oxygen demand, biological oxygen demand, and a measurement by a photometric probe. Everything's here."

"I looked at some of the tests. It's all Greek to me. A photometric probe sounds like something an alien who abducted you would do."

Anne looked up at Adehm and smiled.

"It suits you," Adehm said. "The smile, I mean."

"I always smile when someone saves us a hell of a lot of time." Anne tapped the folder. "Our timeline is tight, but this definitely helps. Very good work."

Adehm gave a short bow from the waist that acknowledged the compliment. "This is why I want a daily meeting. This is what I do best and why I'm here. You let me know what we need to push this project through to completion, and I'll get it done. Company policy, red tape, purchasing, working with the State people, or whatever you need."

Adehm walked around the desk and sat in the chair. "Look, I'm going to level with you. This project means my ass. I made the decision to rehab this place, and I backed it up with my professional judgment and reputation. Like it or not, you're the king in this little chess game. Ultimately, you're the piece that will determine whether Bohannon wins or loses. I'm the queen. I have the power to make our game plan work. We'll have to work together to get things to happen. That's why I insisted on the all-or-nothing contract. I need you to be as invested in this as I am." She sat back as though waiting for Anne's reaction.

"The contract doesn't make any difference to me," Anne said quietly. "I take great pride in everything I do. This is my professional judgment and reputation as well. You would never need to resort to extortion for me to put every ounce of effort into the project."

"I couldn't take that chance," Adehm said. "The corporation awarded you the contract, but I didn't know you at all. My comments weren't meant as any personal disrespect to you."

Anne thought a moment and then nodded. "None taken then. Now, what do you say I look at the system and start doing what you're paying me for?"

"Great. Anything you need me to be doing while you're having that look?" Adehm asked.

"Yeah, you made me smile once," Anne replied, holding up the folder of lab results. "I'd like to see if you could do that again."

"Just say the word."

"The word is—I mean the words are—work space."

\* \* \*

Two hours later, Anne returned to the manager's office. She carried a clipboard tucked under one arm and an industrial grade flashlight in the opposite hand. She dropped the flashlight on Adehm's desk, and Adehm looked up from the file she had open on her computer.

"I saw everything I needed to," Anne said. "And a few things I didn't want to see."

"What's that mean?"

"It wasn't as bad as I thought. It's worse." Anne looked around for someplace to set her clipboard and stopped mid-look. "Hey, what's all this?"

"As per your request, you now have a place to work. You told me you needed space for two computers, a small file cabinet, and a few other minor requests. I made it happen. It was easy to put together. We've got a lot of workers with nothing but time on their hands."

"This will do perfectly. My computers should be here later today or tomorrow. I'll need both of them to set up the design for the wastewater treatment plant. I've already started on it in my mind. The numbers you gave me, plus my visual inspection, have given me an idea of the scope of your problem."

"And is Bohannon going to like the scope of the problem?"

"I very much doubt it." Anne took her clipboard, flashlight, and gloves to her new work area. "I can't give an accurate estimate until I get the computers." She unzipped the coveralls and pushed off the work boots.

"I put your shoes under your desk." Adehm watched Anne emerge from the bulky outerwear. "Like a butterfly," Adehm said.

Anne glanced over to Adehm as she stepped out of the coveralls and folded them. "Pardon?"

"I said you're like a butterfly. You've been in that green cocoon and hard hat, and now you emerge to be the engineering professional."

"Hmm." Anne put the coveralls and boots into their plastic bag and sealed it up. "Sometimes my cocoon can get a little stinky," she said.

"How long before you might have an initial estimate on the new system? The home office is two hours ahead, and I thought I might be able to send them your figures."

"I can give you a broad estimate for the total job, but you can't hold me to it until, as I said, I run it on my computers. Then I can tackle the details and match up our needs with contractor prices around here. The subcontractors' costs for labor have to be considered, as well."

"Okay, I get your point." Adehm held a pen above a yellow legal pad. "This is only a ballpark figure. I'm just hoping to get an idea of what this project is going to add up to."

"Let's say approximately seven-hundred-thousand dollars. That's the closest I can come right now."

"Wow. Big ballpark." Adehm pushed her hair back off her forehead. "I'll e-mail your first number with the caution that it's just a beginning figure."

"Will you need me to submit another bid proposal when I get the completed figures?"

"I think that would be a good idea. We already hired you based on your previous proposal, but a new one for the revised project files would be valuable back at Corporate. Any chance you can get me a timeline for the wastewater treatment plant? We have a deadline, and that would help me keep track of our progress and let me work with you to keep us on schedule."

"I can rough one up for you," Anne said, "but that will take longer because of contractor and subcontractor availability. I'll need a week for that."

"You got it."

Anne sat in the comfortable chair at her workstation. She slipped on and tied her shoes.

"Adehm?"

Adehm looked up from the e-mail she was composing to send to Detroit. "Yes?"

"I haven't worked with you or Bohannon Corporation before, and this is a big project with the possibility of cost overruns. I need to know for myself that they, and you, aren't going to just up and pull the plug on the whole thing rather than spend the money."

"Hang on a second. Let me send this off to Detroit." Adehm quickly typed another line before hitting the send button. Then she turned to face Anne.

"This is how I see it. Bohannon has a huge investment here. We own the factory and grounds, but we also own large tracts of land we get our lumber from. Plus, we have contracts for logging on other tracts. We do millions of dollars of business and are heavily into a reforestation program to keep us supplied for our lifetime and maybe a few more. In addition, we're the biggest employer in this area. If Big Tree goes under, so do a hell of a lot of employees and their families."

"And Bohannon Corporation cares about all that?" Anne asked.

"Truth?"

"That's why I asked."

"Bohannon probably cares more about the bottom line and dividend per share, but I care about all the rest of it. I have to, because I believe everything we do right here goes into profit and dividends. The reason I've gotten where I am is because, so far, my beliefs have been right. I'm not naïve. I know if I get something severely wrong, I can be replaced. That's why I like to be involved and be right." Adehm watched as Anne organized the papers on her clipboard and made a few additional notes in the margin.

"Was that your subtle way of telling me your job is on the line with this project?" Anne asked, without looking up from her papers. When there was no reply from Adehm, she glanced up. Adehm was looking directly at her with an unreadable expression. "Sorry, that's none of my business."

"That's just it. It is your business," Adehm said. "Maybe if this thing gets screwed up in some way, and we don't pass the State's test in six months, I'm out the door. Let's just say we're all in this together and leave it at that."

"I can do that," Anne assured her. "So what do you want to do together first?"

"Have dinner with me?"

"Are you sure you don't want to have some time to yourself? You've been forced into proximity with me all day. I wouldn't want you to suffer from an overdose of Anne."

"That's not likely, but if it makes you feel better, let's make this a work-related meal. I was supposed to bring a list of subcontractors with me to give to you, but I left it in my hotel room. Show up, eat a meal, and be edified."

Anne hesitated.

"My mistake, my treat," Adehm added.

"Sold."

# Chapter 5

The dining room at The Rose was decorated after the style of the 1850s. Hardwood paneling adorned the walls, which were speckled with interesting shadows cast by refurbished mine lanterns. A pickax, shovel, and gold pan were among the decorations on the walls. A young girl wearing a simple, floor-length, Victorian housedress seated Adehm and Anne at a corner table. After providing them with menus and ice water, she took their drink orders and left to assist other patrons.

"Nice place," Anne said. "If the customers weren't dressed in modern clothes, I could almost imagine us being here in the Gold Rush days. At least what I think the Gold Rush days might have looked like. I have only Hollywood's version to go on."

"The actual Gold Rush happened farther north, but I believe there were placer miners all over California."

"What's a placer miner?" Anne asked.

"Placer miners were prospectors looking for loose gold, usually by panning or running shovelfuls of dirt and rocks across screens and water. The gold was heavier, so the soil would wash away, leaving gold to be found among the weightier and cleaner rocks."

"I'm impressed." Anne took a sip of her water.

"Don't be. I went to public school in California. That's part of the history of the Golden State."

"It's still interesting to a stranger."

Conversation was interrupted by the waitress returning to deliver their drinks and take their orders.

"I'll have the hamburger steak with baked potato, and I'll start with the mixed field greens salad," Adehm said. "Do you have a house dressing?"

"It's crushed peppercorn ranch," the waitress informed her.

"Sounds good to me. Can I get that on the side?"

"Absolutely." She looked to Anne.

"I'll have the petite filet, medium, with steak fries. I'll have the salad with house dressing, too."

The waitress nodded as she wrote. She took the menus from them. "I'll have the salads out to you in just a minute," she said.

After she walked away, Adehm resumed their conversation. "Before the waitress came to take our orders, I was going to say that maybe California history is interesting to read about, but I think it's definitely more interesting to live through history like you have."

Anne raised her eyebrows, and Adehm added, "I hope you don't think I'm foolish enough to work with someone I haven't checked out. I also hope you don't take it personally."

"No, not at all. We aren't a big company... yet." Anne stressed the final word. "I can tell just by this first day you didn't make your way to where you are by luck. You're very thorough. I only wish I'd had time to Google you. Maybe then I wouldn't have expected some old man instead of, well... you."

Adehm laughed. "I stopped minding the name-spelling, appearance-shocking mistakes a very long time ago. I told you my dad thought I was going to be his namesake. My mom had been convinced by her family that the way she carried me during her pregnancy meant I'd be a boy. They called me 'Adam' the whole time I was in the womb. So, with a little spelling change, the name stayed.

"I'll admit, I occasionally like to use it to my advantage. It's almost embarrassing how many Neanderthals are still in the business world who don't mind taking orders and accepting takeover bids, as long as they're issued by a man."

"I agree," Anne said.

Adehm continued. "I noticed in your bio that you were raised and went to school in Germany."

"Dresden born and bred," Anne said. "I don't normally advertise that fact, but since you already know, I don't mind talking about it."

"Do you take a lot of grief for being from what was East Germany?"

"Not so much anymore," Anne said. "People have gotten away from the stereotype that an East German woman must be a testosterone-using, muscle-bound Olympic competitor. It helped that I spoke the American version of English with my studies. I worked on the pronunciation with language CDs."

"Your English is excellent," Adehm said. "Thanks for meeting me for dinner tonight to get my notes on the various contractors available in the area. Sorry I didn't remember to bring it to the office. I'll move all the rest of the files and notes in the morning."

"You said, 'my mistake, my treat.' How could I turn down a chance for a free meal?"

The waitress returned with their salads.

"A free and massive meal, if this salad is any indication," Anne added.

The Rose provided generous portions, and Adehm and Anne were silent as the server added fresh ground pepper to the salads and they ate their first satisfying mouthfuls.

"What was it like living under Soviet control and then changing when the two Germanys were reunited?" Adehm asked.

"As a child, I preferred East Germany. The schools were run efficiently, and the curriculum was more difficult and diverse. Unfortunately, you couldn't learn English there. You could take Russian from the third grade onward, but I didn't start learning English until the reunification took place. Then we did the classes, including poetry, all in English, to learn it. There's nothing like a little Faust in English to sharpen your skills.

"As an adult, I definitely prefer the West German model that's been adopted by the unified country. It provides better opportunity to become successful." Anne raised her glass. "May I propose a toast to capitalism?"

"I'll drink to that," Adehm said.

They clinked their glasses together and drank.

"As I passed through the lobby on my way to my room this afternoon, Len told me he had been notified of a delivery tomorrow morning for me."

"Len?"

"The man at the check-in desk. That must be my computers. Would it be all right if I drove myself to the mill after they're delivered? That way I won't have to hold you up."

"Sure, no problem. I can take care of e-mail and a few other things with the home office. I'll also have the plant crew install an additional outlet or two near your desk. Being so far away from the beaten path at Big Tree actually has its advantages. We have our own fully trained plumbing, electrical, and maintenance teams. They can't install a wastewater treatment plant, but they can make sure a malfunctioning switch or leaking toilet doesn't stop all work at the plant."

"I'm very appreciative of that. Not enough outlets can be a hassle. You think of everything."

"I try to," Adehm said. "Thinking ahead can smooth out the bumps on many projects."

The women finished their salads as their entrees were delivered. Their conversation continued between bites and covered a range of subjects, not always work-related.

"This filet is really very good and cooked perfectly," Anne said. She dipped a steak fry in ketchup and popped it in her mouth. "Ketchup and fries is a habit I picked up in the United States. There are way too many fries here for me. Would you like a few?"

"Maybe just one." Adehm reached over to Anne's plate for a steak fry, dredged it in ketchup, and finished it off in two bites.

"Baked potatoes are nice, but they aren't good with ketchup," she said. "Such a versatile vegetable. Hash browns, home fries, steak fries, French fries, baked, twice baked, au gratin, mashed, potato skins, and chips. It's like a little miracle."

"Not really," Anne said. "When you get down to it, it's still just a potato, but like people, it has many possibilities."

Adehm ate the rest of her steak. She dabbed her mouth with her napkin and set her fork and knife across her plate. "When I came in here tonight, I didn't think I'd be having a philosophical discussion about vegetables, but it's a nice change from an all-business dinner meeting. How about we make sure we have some non-business time in all our meetings, just to keep our sanity?"

"Agreed."

The waitress came to ask about dessert and coffee. Both women declined. Adehm took the check. "Like I said, we'll make this one on me."

"But the next one's on me, and my per diem from Bohannon, of course."

"So generous of you," Adehm said.

"It's just my way."

They picked up their bags and left the restaurant. The evening was warm and neither needed the light jackets they'd brought. They slowly walked up the planked sidewalks of Main Street.

"I didn't really discuss much business with you at dinner tonight," Adehm said, "but I wanted to find out what the first step is in the actual process of upgrading the wastewater treatment plant."

"Normally, that would be to start the digging for the project, but that depends on whether you want to keep part of the factory going while we change things. If you want to close it down completely, that's another story."

"We can keep some of the mill productive? That's great news!"

"But it won't be the whole factory, and not even the part we keep running will be able to operate at full capacity. You'd have to test the water samples nearly every day to make sure you weren't exceeding State guidelines."

"It's not worth it then," Adehm said after some thought. "The full-time people will need to be satisfied with part-time work for now."

Anne could tell she was troubled by that decision. "Isn't part-time now and full-time later better than no job at all?"

"You'd think so, but try telling that to an employee whose income has been cut in half. I only hope we don't lose too many of the mill workers between now and the time we're back in full production."

Anne reached over and took hold of Adehm's hand. "I'll do whatever I can to make sure you're back in full production as soon as possible."

"I know you will." Adehm patted the hand in hers. Each pulled back a little and released the other's hand. They continued walking up the street toward the hotel.

Anne swallowed hard to quiet the quickening of her heartbeat.

* * *

The arrival of Anne's computers sent the project into a higher gear. Adehm helped unpack the boxes. She recognized in Anne the same independent streak she had, so she moved out of Anne's way while she put her system together.

Adehm retreated to her desk where she had spent the morning organizing her work area. Anne's desk was identical to hers and supplied just as well.

The phone on Adehm's desk rang. "Adehm Trent's office," she answered.

"Hey, that's my line. If you think you can impersonate your own executive assistant just because you're in California, then you're sadly mistaken."

"I humbly admit I couldn't function without you, Rodney. You're irreplaceable."

"Now that's what I like to hear. You especially needed my gift for forging your signature this week. Personally, I'm impressed by the amount of mind-numbing reports you've read and signed lately."

"And my gratitude will be properly shown on my return to Detroit. Was there anything interesting I learned in those reports?"

"I've summarized each of them with the most salient points indicated. Why these corporate nimrods can't do the same is beyond me."

"Job security, I suppose. Some of those executives at Bohannon think if you can say something in one hundred words that might only really take ten, then they've worked ten times as hard. I think they've wasted ninety words," Adehm said.

"I received the rest of the background checks on Clearly Perfect Water Systems. Do you want me to fax them or e-mail them to you?"

Adehm glanced at the fax machine, located halfway between her desk and Anne's.

"Go ahead and e-mail me that information. I'll take a look at it today sometime. Anything else urgent on the agenda?"

"Yes, Neil Hammond called and wants you to call him back today. His assistant said he'd be in a meeting until four o'clock, but would be free after that. I put a reminder on your computer's day planner."

Neil Hammond was Bohannon's comptroller. Adehm figured the e-mail with Anne's initial cost estimate was the issue. Neil was a great comptroller, but could be notoriously tightfisted with project dollars. Adehm opened the personalized day planner on her computer.

"Great job. I see the note about the phone call to Neil right where you put it, under four o'clock."

"Yep, efficient as always. Remember that at bonus time."

"I'll tell you what. How about at bonus time, I forget you didn't change from Central to Pacific time? I would have missed him by two hours." Adehm grinned as she pictured Rodney fuming at his desk. He was a perfectionist at his job, one of the traits that made him a good assistant.

"I'm changing your calendar right now to reflect your location," Rodney said. Adehm's computer agenda page refreshed and now showed her phone call to Neil Hammond to be made at two o'clock.

"That's perfect," Adehm said. "Is there anything else?"

"Just me needing thirty lashes for that boneheaded mistake. Anyway, I'm sending the background checks as I speak."

"Thanks, I'll take a look when I have time. I'll e-mail you if I think of anything else I need you to take care of, and I appreciate everything you've done while I'm here." Adehm hung up the phone and noticed Anne had her computers booted up. "It's all working?"

"Sure is, just as I will be in a minute. I can use your list of contractors in the area to give you a more precise estimate in terms of time and dollars. A lot of money will be spent getting the facility ready for the new system. Things are pretty decrepit down there. Who deals with your sludge?"

"I beg your pardon?"

"Sludge. Wastewater treatment plants have two end products, and those are treated wastewater and sludge. A certain amount of the sludge is recyclable, but there's other sludge left and that needs to be dealt with." Anne paused for a moment. "My God," she said and laughed. "I lead a fascinating life. Sludge and wastewater. When I was a schoolgirl, I never would have predicted I'd be doing this." She began putting numbers into the computer, transferring them from her clipboard of notes from the previous day.

"Will it bother you if I occasionally talk to you while you work?" Adehm asked.

"I've done this many times, so go ahead. I'll definitely tell you if you're bugging me. Trust me, I'm not afraid to tell you what I think."

"I appreciate that. I was just wondering what you did want to be when you were a little girl. I really can't imagine little Annegret saying, 'I think I'd like to be a civil engineer.' Even if you have turned out to be a good one."

Anne's head popped up. "You said 'Annegret.'"

"Was that wrong? Your biography said Annegret Schneider."

"Yes, that's my name, but no one calls me Annegret except my parents. It just took me by surprise."

"I like Annegret. It's unusual and pretty," Adehm said.

"It's very German. And little Annegret wanted to be an archeologist." Anne's eyes took on a distant look. "I wanted to be in some ancient habitation, using a dental pick and toothbrush to find the fossil record of our prehistoric ancestors."

"What changed your mind?"

Anne tilted her head as she thought. "Two things, I think. First, I am definitely not a camping-out-at-the-dig-site kind of person. Second, I eventually learned what archeologists make. It didn't seem like much for such tedious work."

"And being a civil engineer is good money?"

"It is these days," Anne said with a smile. "It seems some desperate executive decided she needed to throw money at me. Thank you, oh desperate one."

"Don't thank me just yet. You're definitely going to earn the money. That is, *if* you earn the money."

An Instant Message box popped up on Anne's computer screen. Patrick Ford was sending her a message.

"How's it going?" he wrote.

"I'd better get working if I plan to make the beginning of my fortune," Anne said.

"No problem, Annegret." Adehm turned her attention to her own computer.

Anne typed into the chat box. "This is a big project, and time is tight, but I think it can be done."

"That's good," Patrick wrote. "You probably already know Adehm Trent is a female. Probably some kind of dried-up prune of an executive who is a corporate mouthpiece?" Anne glanced over to where Adehm was absorbed in something on her computer screen.

"Not really. She seems quite nice, and she's very attractive." Anne thought about her reply and deleted the second half of the sentence, placing the period after the word "nice." She hit the send button.

"Then you might not need any information on her, but I called in a favor from an old friend who did a little digging on Ms. Trent. I'm going to send you the file now." A file transfer box opened on the computer, and the information downloaded. She was very tempted to read the information the file contained, but work was waiting.

"Anything else?" she typed.

"One more file for you, and it requires your immediate attention." The file transfer box appeared again and the content was sent through. Anne opened the file, but wasn't sure what she was seeing.

"I'm either looking at a Rorschach blot or a gray peanut on a black blanket," she wrote.

"Is that any way to describe my child's first picture? By ultrasound of course, but it's still a picture. That peanut is the baby."

"The peanut is gorgeous. It looks just like you, my friend. Now, I have work to do, proud papa, and money to make."

"Let me know if you need anything from me. Bye." Patrick signed off. Anne was very tempted to open the file on Adehm Trent right then.

*It wouldn't be ethical,* she sighed to herself. *I have numbers to come up with, and personal things should be done on personal time.* She stood up from her desk and walked to the coffeepot that had been newly installed in a corner of the large office.

"Coffee, Adehm?" Adehm was obviously deeply involved in her work, because she jumped a little at the question.

"Yes, please, with a teaspoon of that fake creamer stuff, if you would."

Anne poured the two cups of coffee, adding a packet of sugar substitute to hers. She took the cups to Adehm's desk.

"Anything interesting?" she asked, nodding at Adehm's computer.

"No, just the usual corporate stuff."

"I'll let you get back to it, then." Anne returned to her desk. Now that she was on her coffee break, she quickly used her mouse to open the file Patrick had sent her. She scanned the information. It seemed to be mostly compiled from Internet and Who's Who type sources. She breezed past the usual résumé-filling things, although they seemed impressive, and finally found what she was looking for. Adehm's early life was nothing out of the ordinary. Middle class family, two kids, raised in various California locations. Registered domestic partner in San Francisco, Shannon Roth. Anne could barely resist smiling. *Adehm is a lesbian.* Then all thoughts of smiling left. Shannon Roth was noted as deceased three years after she and Adehm had registered as domestic partners. *Adehm is a widow.* Anne glanced at Adehm and, noting her dedication to work, felt guilty for slacking off. She closed the file and resumed entering numbers into her computer.

Adehm heard the tapping of fingers on a keyboard and immediately felt guilty for reading the in-depth check on Anne while she was working so diligently. Some of the information was a repeat of what she had learned previously, and she skimmed through it. Scrolling down, she found the details on what had piqued her curiosity. Anne Schneider had dated only two people seriously in college, Dana Saunders and Maureen Harrison.

*So, Ms. Annegret is gay. I'd call that kind of valuable fact well worth whatever we paid our investigators.*

Adehm couldn't resist a quick peek at Anne. She had paused a moment in her work to take a sip of her coffee. Their eyes met briefly, and they both gave a half smile.

Adehm and Anne returned their attention to their own computers, and the workday continued. Adehm's eyes may have been on her work, but a bit of her mind was elsewhere.

# Chapter 6

Several days passed as both Anne and Adehm worked hard to get the wastewater treatment plant project off the ground.

Anne completed her measurements and began calling contractors and arranging for estimates. She had a number in mind for each step of the process, but different companies could quote vastly different prices depending on grade of materials, cost per hour of labor, and even what kind of price break they might be willing to give in anticipation of future business.

Once Anne received an estimate from a contractor that she approved of, she transferred the information to Adehm to check out the company thoroughly, as quality and speed of work were going to be equally as important as price on the Big Tree project.

The process was going as rapidly as it could, considering everything had to be right the first time. There wouldn't be time for a second round of bidding if the original winners failed to deliver.

While obtaining estimates, Anne was also firming up the entire project's cost and bid proposal. It seemed strange to be working on the bid proposal for the project and the actual project at the same time, but Anne understood the need for a clean and organized paperwork file. The State inspectors would be looking at the project from every conceivable angle before certifying the plant to run at full capacity again.

The third and most immediate part of Anne's job was the removal of Big Tree's old wastewater treatment plant and upgrading everything needed for the new one. After her preliminary inspection, she decided the old system was wholly inadequate and antiquated. Initially, it would be costlier to start from scratch, but the savings in the long run from doing the project with one hundred percent quality would be substantial. This was where Anne would earn her money, and it was also the area in which she excelled.

True to her word, Adehm helped Anne in every way she could. Secretarial help was kept to a minimum, with Adehm preferring to print out contracts, sign, and file them herself. She really trusted Rodney with those details, but as he was needed in Detroit, she decided to rely on the only other person she trusted… Adehm Trent.

The most exasperating assignment on Adehm's plate was dealing with Neil Hammond. His almost-daily phone calls and e-mails asking for more paperwork, updates on signed contracts, and progress reports on the project wasted more of her time than any other single person.

Adehm hadn't told Anne the full truth about Neil Hammond. She didn't want to add to Anne's pressures. It was true that Neil was one of the few people Adehm reported to, and therefore all his requests were probably legitimate. It was also true that she'd turned down several of his date requests when she had first been promoted to the executive level. Then there was an unfounded rumor two years previously that Adehm was next in line for Neil's job whenever he left, voluntarily or not. The rumor was completely untrue, and their working relationship continued to be amiable on the surface, but Adehm had the feeling that no matter how big a hit the company might take, Neil wouldn't exactly grieve if she failed at Big Tree and was terminated. She was determined not to give him the satisfaction.

* * *

By the end of their first full week on the job, Anne and Adehm were ready to take a day off. The plant was completely shut down, all the part-time workers had the weekend off, and the contractors Anne and Adehm needed to talk to were unavailable. That forced them to take Sunday off.

Anne woke shortly after ten, her sleepy eyes struggling to read the clock. Calculating the current time in Albuquerque, she detached her cell phone from the charger plugged into the wall socket. She used the number two position on the speed dial.

"Hello?" Patrick's groggy voice came over the line. Anne rapidly recalculated the time in her head. She was right; it was noon in Albuquerque.

"What are you doing sleeping in so late?" Anne asked. "You're usually up mowing your lawn by now."

Patrick groaned in reply. "That would be on a normal Sunday. Nothing has been normal since this pregnancy began."

"Complications?" Anne asked in a concerned tone.

"Cravings," Patrick replied. "Guess how many stores I had to go to last night to find Ben and Jerry's Cherry Garcia? Go on, guess."

"Three?"

"Six. Six, can you believe it?" He groaned again, but in the background Anne thought she heard giggling. "And she thinks it's cute." More laughter in the background. "Frankly, I think she's just making this stuff up to get me out of the house at midnight. I'd like to know what goes on while I'm gone." A thump that sounded suspiciously like a pillow meeting a head came over the line.

"And it seems she can't take a joke anymore either," Patrick said, amusement evident in his tone. Anne loved the affectionate and fun relationship between Patrick and Robyn. It seemed to her they were best friends as well as husband and wife. Anne thought they were role models for the kind of relationship she'd like to have someday.

"I hate to interrupt your good time by bringing up work, but how is everything going without me there?" she asked.

"Things are going smoothly so far. We got the final payment on the Levin project, and it looks like we're getting the Humphries job now. The new job isn't big, but it will tide us over until we get paid for the work you're doing out there. We will get paid, right?"

"Barring any sudden catastrophe, we should. This project needed me here. It's turned out to be a lot worse than we were initially led to believe."

"And how is Adehm Trent to work with? I've been calling her 'Machine Gun Trent' in my mind."

"She's really good and has certainly been very helpful. For a corporate executive, she's surprisingly intelligent and extremely nice." As she spoke, Anne realized that assessment, especially the last part, was very accurate. "But why do you call her 'Machine Gun'?"

"Because she just kept firing, of course. Just make sure she doesn't fire us, okay?"

"I'll have you know I haven't had to say anything to her that wasn't perfectly pleasant," Anne said. "I told you, she's been helpful. You know I can't stand corporate types messing around while I work. Not only does she not interfere with my work, we even share an office, and it isn't intolerable."

"Egad, stop the presses. Anne Schneider has found someone who doesn't annoy her. That's good. I was getting so lonely in that club."

"And whatever gave you the idea you were a member?"

"For that reason. If you didn't like me, you wouldn't speak to me. If Adehm Trent gets to know you like I do, then she'll be a lucky woman. I kind of miss your pain-in-the-ass presence. Our company lunch on Wednesday just wasn't the same."

"I miss you, too," Anne said. "Look, this is my first day off since I got here, and I want to do something besides work, so I'm going to let you go. I'll be in touch regularly. Oh, how are Helmut and Angela?"

"Fine. They still don't like anybody but you messing around in their cage, so I let them run around in their exercise balls while I clean their houses. They're well-fed and appear happy, in a dwarf hamster kind of way. I'll check on them again Tuesday when I go by to pick up your mail. I'll send on anything that looks important and leave the junk on the table in the kitchen."

"Sounds good. I'll call you later this week, okay?"

"Do that. Take care and continue to be a good engineer. I knew you were the woman for the job."

After Anne sent along her love to Robyn, they hung up. Then she pressed the number one position on her speed dial.

"Hello?"

"Hello, Vati, it's me," Anne said. "How is everything?"

"Some good days and some not as good," Marcel said.

Anne figured that meant that there had been no significant changes for the worse, and she was satisfied with that. The days of expecting anything to be better with her mother were long over.

"How is the work in California?" Marcel asked.

"It's very busy and will continue to be so, but I think we can get the work done in the six months we were given."

"Good then. I think your mother misses you. Sometimes she asks for you, but I tell her you were here yesterday. She does not remember it, but takes my word and is happy. Until she forgets again."

Anne had nothing to say about that.

"Your brother called us two days ago."

"What was the occasion?" Anne asked. Her brother's lack of helpfulness with their mother's illness irritated her.

"Annegret, that tone isn't necessary," Marcel said.

Anne suspected her father was as disappointed as she was annoyed, but Marcel was much better than she at concealing his feelings.

"Dieter told us his business would be bringing him to Phoenix next month, and he will fly from there to Albuquerque for a visit."

Anne was suspicious of the visit. Dieter was probably checking to see that his inheritance wasn't being squandered. She made a mental note to e-mail him and casually mention the visit to see what she could learn. Anne decided she wouldn't question her father about it.

"That will be nice for you and Mutti. How is your work coming?"

"We will publish some initial work in two months. We've contacted the main journal in Germany, and they have agreed to assist us in having it professionally edited and translated. We will send the Rektor and the Council a copy of the translated version and hope for full funding of the project." It was the first time in the conversation that Anne detected animation in Marcel's tone.

"I did ask the caregiver to stay with Karina two days last week. You were correct. It did give me time to work, but it was not the same as trusting you with Karina."

Anne was being given a free ticket for a guilt trip, and she knew she might as well climb on the bus. "If there's anything I can do from here, just let me know."

"We will be fine. If we need anything, maybe your brother will help."

More guilt and consternation. "I need to go, Vati. I have work on the computer to do."

"Fine. Annegret, don't work too hard. Take care of yourself."

Anne knew her father's words for what they were. "I love you, too, Vati. Bye."

Anne disconnected from the call and thought about the day sprawling before her. Usually, filling free time was easy, but without her games and gadgets, she was somewhat lost. Her room phone rang.

"Hello?"

"It's Adehm, and it's our day off. I've only been up two hours, and I'm bored already. I was never good at doing nothing, so I thought maybe if you didn't have other plans, you'd like to go on an adventure with me."

"I didn't have anything planned, but what kind of adventure are you talking about?"

"If you have to ask, you aren't the adventurous sort," Adehm challenged.

"You don't really know me yet, do you?" Anne's words brought to mind exactly what she had learned about Adehm from Patrick's information.

"Okay," Anne said. "Just tell me when, where, and what to wear."

"Great. One hour, in the lobby, and wear something that won't shrink. Oh, and bring a towel, too." With those cryptic words, Adehm hung up.

Anne looked at the handset before hanging it up. She had no idea what was going to happen, but she was ready to find out. She threw back the covers and hopped out of the bed.

\* \* \*

"That was incredible," Anne said, dropping into the passenger seat of Adehm's car. Her flushed skin and still-damp clothing were leftovers from the three-hour white-water rafting trip Adehm had arranged. "Adventure" had been exactly the right word.

"I suppose it was more fun from your seat," Adehm said as she leaned in the driver's door. Her honey-colored hair was still dripping, and Anne could see where the helmet had been on her head. Her clothing was soaking wet.

"I'm just glad I decided to sit in back of you instead of beside you. I got a great view of you hanging on for dear life at a couple of those rapids." Though she didn't mention it, Anne actually had an excellent view of Adehm's nicely-sculpted body, as well. The damp clothing had left little to the imagination.

"I know I swallowed half of the Prussian River. Just let them try to organize a rafting trip with the water level at half normal. Paybacks are a bitch!" The towel Adehm was using to dry herself was completely inadequate for the job.

"I threw a few extra clothes in the trunk before we left the hotel," she said. "I've got to change into something drier than these."

The rafting group they'd gone with had sat on the bus returning them to their vehicles for half an hour, but even the warm California air wasn't enough to dry Adehm out.

Anne remained in place as Adehm pulled clothes from the trunk. They were the last to leave the secluded parking lot, and

Adehm removed her clothing and put on a dry pair of shorts and a loose-fitting top. She took her soaked shoes and socks off, swapping them for a pair of flip-flops. Then she tossed her wet clothes into the trunk, along with the towel.

As she closed the trunk lid, her eyes met Anne's in the passenger side mirror. She realized her change of clothes had been in view of that mirror, and Anne would have seen her stripped to her skin if she'd been looking. Anne appeared perfectly at ease, though, and Adehm believed Anne probably hadn't seen anything.

*I would hope my naked body could muster some kind of a reaction anyway,* Adehm thought. *Especially now that I know Anne's preference from our in-depth check of her.* She joined Anne in the car for the drive back to Wood Mill.

"All set?" Adehm asked, as she started the engine.

"Sure," Anne replied, busying herself using the towel she'd brought along to dry her hair.

Adehm gave her a surreptitious peek. *Was that a blush, after all?*

# Chapter 7

By the end of the first month of the project, Anne and Adehm had settled into a comfortable routine. They would meet at breakfast, go over the agenda for the day, and discuss what they hoped to accomplish, what they needed to plan for, and what they respectively needed to do to make those things happen. They were getting to know each other personally, as well.

When Brenda, the waitress at Ruth's Café, came for their breakfast order, Adehm stopped Anne.

"Wait. Let me try." To the waitress, she said, "She'll have an egg white omelet, two strips of soy bacon, fresh fruit, wheat toast, and coffee with sugar substitute."

Anne was impressed and indicated the choices were to her liking by nodding. Brenda jotted the order down.

"I want a chance at that," Anne said. "She'll have a Denver omelet, two strips of crispy bacon, home fries, sourdough toast, coffee with cream, and ice water with a lemon."

Adehm smiled as Anne got the kind of breakfast she liked, exactly right.

"If you two had an order pad, I'd be out of a job," Brenda said. "Do either one of you want to guess what I had for breakfast?" she added with a smile

"Waffles," Anne said immediately.

"Wow, how did you know? You're absolutely right."

Anne shrugged. "Just one of those psychic kind of feelings."

"Damn, you're scary. I think I'll back away slowly from the table and go put your orders in pronto." She hurried off.

"Okay, I give. How did you know?" Adehm asked.

"She had a little syrup on her blouse. That meant either pancakes or waffles. I took a guess."

Adehm laughed. "Brilliant deduction, Sherlock. I don't think I'd like to try to hide anything from you."

Their conversation was interrupted momentarily by Brenda bringing their drinks.

"Speaking of that," Anne said, "I've been trying to work up the nerve to apologize for something my business partner did that I took advantage of. He has a friend who does skip traces and things like that for insurance companies. Patrick asked him to find out more about you, so I would know who I was working with. I'm sorry, I didn't know you'd be so approachable and easy to talk to. I feel like I could ask you any question I might have."

"It's okay," Adehm assured her. "I told you I'd had you checked out, as well as Patrick Ford and Clearly Perfect. Turnabout is fair play." Adehm squeezed the lemon wedge into her water. "Learn anything interesting?"

"Maybe a thing or two."

"I'll bet. If you need any clarification on the information, you be sure to let me know."

"You'll be the first," Anne said.

Brenda returned shortly with their orders. "I had them put your orders to the front of the line. Made the toast myself." She put their plates down in front of them. "Say," she said, addressing Anne. "You ever get one of those psychic feelings about lottery numbers?"

"Not yet," Anne replied, buttering her toast. "So far it's only co-workers' breakfast food, but if I ever do, I'll give you a heads-up."

"Suits me," Brenda said as she left them.

"So, what were we talking about?" Adehm asked.

"Work," Anne said with a faint blush. "I'm definitely sure it was work."

\* \* \*

The first problems on the project appeared over the next few weeks. Adehm was working on final contracts in the manager's office at Big Tree when Anne and a man Adehm didn't know came in. Both were wearing coveralls, work boots, and hard hats.

"Adehm, this is Lucas Barr. He's the plant grounds supervisor." She waited as Adehm shook the man's hand. "Lucas, tell Ms. Trent what you told me, please."

Lucas nodded. "Yesterday, as I was making a routine inspection of the plant grounds, checking on seismic compliance, condition of infrastructure, and various other things, I noticed a problem along PR Four."

Anne had gone to her desk and retrieved a large roll of paper. As she unfurled the roll, Adehm saw a map of the plant facilities.

"PR Four is Plant Road Four, which is here." Anne indicated the spot on the map.

"On my inspection, I noticed an area approximately here," Lucas said, placing his finger next to Anne's. "The road surface has cracked. I thought at first it might have been a little temblor, because we're not that far from the San Andreas Fault. I still think that was the root cause."

"Of what?" Adehm asked.

"This area of PR Four is where your outflow pipe to the river is," Anne said. "I think that outflow is probably cracked and leaking. I can't say how long it's been like that. When the plant was shut down by the State, the pressure on the outflow pipe was decreased dramatically. We might never have noticed this problem until after we put in the new treatment equipment and started pumping again. You might say this is a blessing and a curse."

"How so?" Adehm asked.

"It's going to let us fix the problem now instead of at the last minute, which might cause us to fail inspection. Of course, the curse is the extra time and money this will take."

"Any idea how much of each?" Adehm asked.

"The current outflow pipe is made of concrete. That has to go. Concrete was considered acceptable years ago, but these days, the preferred material is either cast iron or HDPE, high density polyethylene. I think I would recommend the HDPE in this area."

"Cost?" Adehm asked, taking up a pen and making notes on her ever-present yellow legal pad.

"I'd say two-hundred-and-forty dollars per foot under your asphalt and one-hundred-and-eighty dollars where it runs under the grass. That's a rough estimate."

Adehm winced at Anne's projection. "Time? We don't have much to spare, you know."

"If you can expedite the contract process, that will help. You might have to abbreviate your bid time. A good company can place about sixty feet a day."

"I can check with some of the companies we're already doing business with to see if they have the equipment and expertise to do the outflow pipe. I'll ask them to give us the bids as quickly as possible," Adehm said. "I'll approve the contracts immediately and even type them up myself, if need be. Just put down what's required, and I'll get right on it."

"Will do. As long as we have to replace the outflow pipe, we might as well add a measuring pit. That will allow us to take samples of the effluent before it gets to the river. It will save time and make it easier to make sure the plant stays in compliance in the future." Anne began jotting down her numbers along with cost projections.

Adehm realized Lucas Barr was still in the office. He had removed his hard hat to reveal a much younger man than Adehm had expected. He was blond and fair and very handsome.

"Good thing you noticed that cracking, Mr. Barr," Adehm said. "How long have you been at Big Tree?"

"Sixteen years. I started part-time as a general laborer right out of high school. There's not many chances for steady employment if you want to stay in this area. Anyway, I moved up to line work and then floor supervisor later. Now I'm the plant's grounds supervisor."

"Big Tree is lucky to have you," Adehm said. "Do you know Fred Kendall?"

"Sure, he was my first supervisor here. He's the day shift supervisor, and I guess he'd be called the interim plant manager since you…" He hesitated. "Since some of the others left the plant."

"You were right the first time, Mr. Barr. I did dismiss Mr. Kendall's predecessor and a few others. We're rehabilitating a business here. Bohannon is spending over three-quarters of a million dollars. We aren't going to do that and not have our best people running Big Tree. I trust you can understand that."

"I suppose I can. We're local, but we still have to answer to the corporation."

"Exactly right. We need sharp minds and observant eyes to make sure this kind of thing never happens again. Do you want to be a part of that?"

"Yes, Ms. Trent, I do."

"Then report to Fred Kendall. As of tomorrow, you're the new assistant to the interim plant manager. This is on a trial basis, of course, as Mr. Kendall has indicated he prefers to keep his original supervisor's position."

The stunned and pleased look on Lucas's face told Adehm he agreed to those terms.

"I'll see Mr. Kendall right away. Thank you."

"You're welcome. You deserve it, and besides, we need to start training up new management here. You've got a good start on an excellent track record."

Before Lucas opened the door, he stopped with his hand on the doorknob. "Ms. Trent?"

"Yes?" Adehm expected the question of money to come next, but she was wrong.

"Is Ms. Schneider an employee of Bohannon Corporation also?"

Adehm glanced toward Anne, who shrugged her shoulders. "No, she's an independent contractor here. Why?"

"Just didn't want to possibly break any of Bohannon's non-fraternization rules in the future." He gave both women a wide smile and left.

Neither woman spoke for a moment.

"It seems you have an admirer," Adehm said finally. She couldn't for the life of her figure out why that fact bothered her.

"Do you hear that?" Anne asked, as she cupped her hand to her ear.

"Hear what?" Adehm asked, listening intently. "I don't hear anything."

"Then you missed the sound of Lucas Barr barking up the wrong tree." Anne sat down at her computer.

Adehm grinned, not needing further explanation, and both women got back to work.

\* \* \*

"It's late here, Neil, and I'm beat. We've worked all day to nail down the contractor and cost for the new outflow pipe. I've faxed you the price." Adehm listened as Neil Hammond made his usual request for more paperwork and even more details on the expenditures. "Ms. Schneider and I can put the rest of the numbers you want together and on the fax machine in the morning. We just need time to get the information collated."

Anne was packing papers into her bag in preparation for leaving Big Tree for the day. Her attempt at trying to look as though she wasn't eavesdropping was failing miserably.

"I know it's even later there, Neil. My home's in that time zone, too, remember? Look, I'm too tired to argue with you. You'll have what you need by the time you get into the office in the morning. Will that work? Fine, then."

Adehm hung up the phone and addressed Anne. "I don't know why Neil Hammond works such long hours. It must make him late for his meeting of the Annoying Jerks Club. Of course, they wouldn't start without their president." She began stacking folders on one side of her desk. "He says there's a meeting of the accounting staff at nine o'clock in the morning, and they need all the appropriate requests, documents, and contracts to process the funds before close of business because it will be Friday. I need that money to start the extra work. We need to get the road torn up and that faulty pipe removed. The polyethylene tube should be here by next weekend, and I want to have the area prepped and ready to go." She ran her hand through her hair, and only then discovered she'd been stomping around the office as she spoke.

"Now he has me pacing. I swear, when I get back to Detroit, I'll figure out a way to deal with his micro-managing the financials. Until then, I can tell he's going to enjoy making me fill out a form in triplicate to request more triplicate forms."

Anne calmly sat at her desk, watching Adehm let out her frustrations. It had been a busy week, made even more so by the unforeseen pipeline complication.

"Look," Adehm said. "He hates me, and you shouldn't have to be punished for that. It's my little cross to bear. Give me the data you have on the things we've been working on, and you can head back to the hotel for the evening. I'll catch a ride with one of the late shift crew when I'm done." Adehm returned to her desk, looking utterly unhappy.

"No."

"What? What did you say?" Adehm asked, looking up from the stack of work in front of her.

"I said no. I'm not going. Well, I am going, but I'm not going in the manner you suggested."

"Really?" Adehm asked in a tone that made it clear she wasn't used to having her orders or suggestions ignored. "You have a better idea? Maybe you know a good bulldozer operator to push all this paperwork around for me?"

"Nothing that good. We're leaving here together. We'll have some dinner like normal people, and then you and I will work on Mr. Hammond's requests together. We'll get it done a lot faster that way, and we won't have to look at the inside of this office any more today."

"That's very nice of you to offer, but I can't let you do that. I'm the executive on this project, and you're a contractor. Bohannon and Neil Hammond don't have the right to ask you to burn the midnight oil. So please, just go on back to town."

Anne listened politely to all this, adding a few extra supplies to her bag as she did. "So," she said, "now that you've protested enough, can we please get out of here? When we get back to the hotel, you'll have one hour. Do anything you wish with that, but after that one hour, be sure to bring some food because I'll be starving. I need to take care of a few things, which should be finished by the time you get to my room. After that, we'll work. We'll work until we have whatever it takes for your Mr. Hammond to be satisfied. We can fax the papers from the hotel office when we're through."

Adehm stared slack-jawed at Anne during her instructions.

"You can stand there for as long as you want, but it's going to change nothing. I've made up my mind, and I can be a little stubborn."

Adehm snapped out of her fog and began tossing files and papers into her own bag. "My God, you're as pushy as I am. I didn't think it was possible." As they left, Adehm turned off the lights in the office. "I have a question," she said as she closed the door. "What's the German translation for 'bossy engineer'?"

"Annegret Schneider," Anne said, leading the way to the car.

\* \* \*

Fifty minutes after arriving at the hotel, Adehm stood at Anne's hotel room door. In one hand, she carried a large plastic bag bulging with Styrofoam cartons, and in the other hand, she carried a brown paper bag holding recently-purchased drinks. She used her foot to knock on the door to room 12.

"Annegret, it's me," she called.

"You're early, but come on in anyway," Anne said from inside the room.

Adehm used both hands as she struggled to open the door, puzzled by the lack of assistance from inside. She wasn't puzzled long. Anne was stretched out on the carpet on her stomach. Her arms were along her sides as she lifted her chest and legs off the floor simultaneously.

"What are you doing?" Adehm asked, taking the food and drinks to the table in the room.

"My sports." Anne relaxed to the carpet and then arched up again. "Or exercise, whatever you want to call it. By any name, it's good for me. After a long day, it takes away some stress and keeps me flexible."

"You were pretty inflexible with me an hour ago." Adehm removed containers from the plastic bag. "I got Chinese. I hope you like it."

"Sounds good. I'm almost done here."

Adehm opened the food containers and removed the paper plates and plastic utensils from the bag. Out of the corner of her eye, she watched Anne exercise. Even on the rafting trip, she hadn't noticed Anne's firm body and smooth muscles the way she was noting them now.

"Twenty-nine… thirty." Anne dropped out of her last arch and rolled to her side. "All done." She stood then and picked up a nearby hand towel, dabbing a faint sheen of perspiration from her brow.

"You do that every night?" Adehm gestured to where Anne had been exercising.

"I try to, but at least three times a week for sure. Engineering is more of a mental than physical job, obviously, so I need the exercise if I expect to indulge in whatever smells so good in those containers." She sat down in one of the two chairs at the table.

"I didn't know what you'd like, so I got small portions of several different things. Let's see…" Adehm opened the first container. "We've got chicken with green beans, snow peas with water chestnuts, sweet and sour pork, house fried rice, and shrimp with honeyed walnuts." As each container was opened, a new enticing aroma permeated the room.

"Maybe eighty sit-ups and thirty push-ups won't be enough," Anne said, spooning food onto her plate. "I wouldn't have had time for more, though. I was barely getting through my thirty back scrunches when you knocked."

"Have you been exercising the whole hour?"

"Just the last half hour. I brought our work bags up here, did a quick errand, and then changed into my workout clothes." Anne indicated her black shorts and matching tank top.

Adehm had already noticed the snug outfit that accentuated Anne's fit body.

"I approve of your choices for our meal, by the way. I'm surprised you can get such good Chinese food in Wood Mill. Doesn't seem like the place for it."

"The Chinese have probably been here as long as anybody else. They worked here from the days of the Old West. Many of them came over as laborers to work in the new camps and towns, and eventually, on the roads and railroads."

"Foreigners coming to America to make their fortune. Never heard of such a thing."

"I know you went to college here, but I'm curious as to why you stayed in the States after you were finished. You didn't want to go home? Don't get me wrong, I'm glad you're here, but I am a little curious."

"My home is wonderful, but it was changing. It was bound to happen with the reunification. Some changes were good, and some I thought, not as good. When I got here, I had a whole new culture to get used to. Once I did, I loved my adopted country as much as my birth one. I had a job, I was still seeing someone I met in college, everything just seemed right for me to stay. Then my friend Patrick and I decided to start our own business. We relocated to where his girlfriend, now his wife, came from. I really enjoy Albuquerque. Then I helped my parents move there, which works well for my father. He's working on a joint project with local professors he contacted on the Internet. He's a very intelligent man."

"The apple doesn't fall far from the tree," Adehm said. "And how does your mother like the States?"

"My mother was diagnosed with Alzheimer's three years ago. She's as content as she would be anywhere." Anne dropped her gaze from Adehm's.

"I'm so sorry." Adehm could see her innocent question had brought up a painful subject. She reached over and put her hand on Anne's arm. "Annegret, really, I'm terribly sorry to hear that."

"It's okay. You didn't know. I've had three years to get used to the idea of it. Time doesn't make it much easier, though. I see my mother, and I see the changes. It's as if the disease is robbing me of the woman I've known my whole life. She's there, but then again, she's not. It's difficult."

Adehm didn't think; she only reacted. She left her chair and went to Anne. Taking her in a hug, she tried to convey her sympathy and support. She wasn't sure how Anne would take the gesture, but she couldn't think of anything else to show what she felt. After a moment, Anne moved back.

"Thanks for that. Let's change the subject for now, okay? We need to finish this great meal you brought, and then we need to get to work."

Adehm sensed Anne's need to lighten the mood. She returned to her chair. "Yes, Annegret Schneider," she said in a deliberately meek voice.

"Were you using my name or calling me 'bossy engineer'?" Anne asked with a smile.

"I don't know. I don't speak German."

# Chapter 8

"Is there anything more exciting than seeing a backhoe finally breaking ground on a new project?" Anne asked, walking into the manager's office. She was wearing a long-sleeved red shirt, Levi's, and her hard hat.

"Let me think. That's a tough act to follow," Adehm replied. "Okay, how about watching paint dry, having Neil Hammond on vacation for the next two weeks, and observing an engineer in a hard hat being excited by the backhoe thing." Adehm placed the folder she had in her hand into the file cabinet. "Of course, that's just off the top of my head. I can do better if I'm not under such pressure."

Anne took her hard hat off and hung it on a hook she had installed on the wall for just that purpose. "When I'm not in the office, I forget all about that sparkling wit of yours."

She went to her desk to update the plans on the computer. "Is Neil Hammond really on vacation for two weeks, or was that just wishful thinking on your part?" She used her mouse to bring up the work in progress.

"Not only is he on vacation, as the e-mail I received this morning informed me, in my mind he is gone from the face of the Earth altogether. I wonder if there's any chance he won't come back? Nah, that's just me wearing Neil Hammond-sized rose-colored glasses. I'm not that lucky."

"Maybe if he's left the face of the Earth, the aliens will keep him," Anne said. "I'll help you think positive."

"You're going to do more than that, Annegret Schneider. You're going to help me celebrate. As executive on this project, I am giving us the rest of the day off."

Anne appeared wary at the announcement. "This doesn't involve any more rafts, does it? Summer's coming to an end, and I don't think I could handle the chilly water today."

"You're not even close, my engineer friend. I've picked out something fun, interesting, and dry."

"Then I'm ready."

"Good. Grab a jacket. We might get back a little late."

Anne and Adehm shut down their computers and secured their files. They were preparing to leave when a knock sounded on the office door.

"Come in," Adehm called out. Nate Perdue, one of the two security people who manned the front gate, opened the door.

"Delivery for you, Ms. Schneider. This is the first time I've ever seen anything like this here." He carried a large vase of flowers, with daisies and miniature roses being the most prominent blooms.

Anne hurried to take the vase from Nate.

"There's a card in there somewhere," Nate said. "I need to get back. Twenty-two years I've been here, first flowers ever arrived. Something new every day, I guess." He left and closed the door behind him.

Anne set the flowers on her desk and found the small card inside a white envelope. She read the writing on the card aloud. "Thanks for bringing me to the notice of the executive level. I hope you'll let me thank you in person sometime soon. Your friendly new interim assistant plant manager, Lucas Barr." Anne blushed a little. "I may need to do some gentle discouraging with that one. Nice flowers, though."

"Very," Adehm agreed. In truth, she didn't care for the blooms much at all. "Do we need to stand around here admiring your gift, or can we head out on a much-needed break?"

Anne raised her hand. "Call on me, teacher. I know the answer to that one." She pulled her jacket from the back of her chair. "Let's go."

\* \* \*

The town of Webster, California, was nearly thirty-five miles from Wood Mill. Adehm elected to take the gently winding back roads instead of the nearest freeway. It was their afternoon off, and she was in no hurry.

First Fall Festival had been celebrated in Webster for over 110 years. The mayor of the small town at the time of the first one had been a veteran of the War Between the States. To be precise, he was a veteran of the Army of the Confederate States of America. After the South's loss, he drifted westward to California. Even after marrying and settling down in Webster, he was never able to forget that huge defeat. He was determined that Webster would be victorious in something. As mayor, he decided that although many towns held festivals in the fall, Webster's would be the first one each year. Some argued the date was actually in late summer, but in the State of California's regard, Webster had the first fall festival.

Adehm drove into Webster, and a helpful volunteer directed her to a parking spot. She had read online that Webster's population nearly quadrupled during the weekend of the First Fall Festival.

"I read about some of the activities they have going on here, and we can pinpoint what we want to see and do, or we can just wander around. It's your choice," Adehm said.

"Let's just wander. Sometimes you get lucky, right?"

Adehm thought about Anne's statement, and then thought about Anne herself. "Yeah, sometimes you do."

They locked the car and walked to Cafferty Street, which seemed to be the main thoroughfare. They took their time exploring the various art sellers, craft booths, and historical displays.

"What do you think of this?" Adehm asked. A local artist had skillfully used leaves, grasses, and tree bark to create a picture in a shallow shadow box. The scene was of a homey room with a fire blazing in the hearth.

Anne studied the piece of art. "I like it. I especially like how she uses local materials to produce a scene that might be from anywhere."

They perused the artist's other works, but Adehm kept returning to the first picture they'd looked at.

"There's something about this one I like. It's as though I can see myself living in that scene." Adehm asked for the artist's card, which noted she had a website for her work. Satisfied with that, they continued wandering through the festival.

At the end of the street, they discovered a section devoted to games and prizes, with the usual variety of carnival competitions. Adehm and Anne decided to try their luck at one game each, determined not to lose more than a dollar apiece. In one game, contestants used a water pistol to squirt water into a clown's mouth, thereby blowing up a balloon affixed to the top of the clown. The first contestant to pop their balloon would win.

Adehm chose her pistol, deposited fifty cents for the right to play, and aimed carefully. The attendant moved to one side and pushed a button, causing a bell to ring, which indicated the start of the game and activation of the water pistols.

The intensity of the flow of water through the pistols surprised Adehm, and for the first few seconds, she shot erratically. Water went every place on the clown's face except into the mouth.

By the time she had improved her aim, a balloon farther down the line popped. A groan issued from five out of the six contestants in the game, including Adehm. Three clowns down, a youngster with thick glasses and a retainer raised his arms in victory. The game attendant exchanged the small bear in front of the boy for a larger one.

"Nice shooting, kid," Adehm called to him. "He's good at this because he probably spends every spare minute of his time playing video games," she said in a low voice to Anne, who was standing behind her. "He's going down, though. I've got the hang of this game now." She plunked down her other fifty cents for the next round.

The attendant picked up the money and moved out of water spray range again. The bell rang, and a much more competitive round was underway. This time, Adehm's aim was perfect, and her balloon began expanding right away. It had nearly burst when, three clowns down, the balloon popped. Adehm's smile at the youngster was strained this time, and she fished in her pocket for more change.

"This is why we said one dollar each," Anne reminded her.

Adehm reluctantly left the game. "I could have taken him, you know. He's probably a ringer."

"Sure he is. I had to pull you away to keep you from embarrassing the poor child."

"You choose something now," Adehm said.

Anne had looked the games over and decided to try knocking over a pyramid of milk bottles with a baseball.

"You realize you only get one throw for your fifty cents, right?" Adehm asked. "You have to knock over all the bottles with one ball. Do you have much experience doing that?"

"Not really. Baseball still isn't big in Europe, and I've only seen it on television here. It looks like something I'll be able to do though. It can't be that hard."

"That's exactly what they want you to think." Adehm snickered. "It's a lot harder than it looks, but go ahead and give it a try."

Anne gave fifty cents to the man running the game. He gave her a baseball and told Anne to make her throw whenever she was ready. Anne hefted the baseball in her hand, getting a good grip. Reaching back, she made her throw. The top three milk bottles fell, leaving the entire bottom row intact.

"You won't be winning the Cy Young Award this year," Adehm said. At Anne's puzzled look, she explained, "Famous old-time pitcher. They named an annual award after him. Never mind. Go on, try it again."

Anne gave the man behind the counter her other fifty cents.

"I think I've got the feel of it now," she told Adehm.

"Of course you do."

Once again, Anne reached back and threw the baseball. This time, the throw was accurate, and all the milk bottles fell.

"You see, everybody, this is an easy game," the attendant announced in a loud voice to other potential customers. "Pick a prize, young lady." He indicated a row of small stuffed animals.

"What's that one?" Anne asked, pointing to a brown critter wearing a red bandana.

"That's an armadillo, ma'am. Also known as the Official Texas Road Kill Mascot."

"I'll take it."

He delivered the armadillo to her, and she stepped aside for the next patron.

"How did you do that?" Adehm asked. "No matter what that guy says, the milk bottle game is tough."

Anne inspected her armadillo. "I looked at it as a physics problem. The equation needed to come out to the answer of where to hit the grouping to cause all the bottles to fall. Once I worked that out in my head, I had to hit that spot. I'll admit there was a little luck involved there."

"Beating a carnival game using engineering. I never thought of that," Adehm said, scratching her head.

"What shall we name him?" Anne asked, lifting the brown armadillo. "With this bandana, I think he needs a Western name."

They began walking away from the games area, and she looked to Adehm. "Any suggestions?"

"Western names... the only really Western names I know are from movies and television shows." Adehm ran through a list of names. "Let's see, there's Bat Masterson, Matt Dillon, Chester, Pecos Pete, Yosemite Sam..."

"Chester, I think. Yes, definitely Chester."

They walked toward a large tent that held the judging for homemade food items. They looked in briefly.

"You know, it might be a good idea to hit one of the food stands before we go much farther. I'm famished. Must have been why my aim was off earlier," Adehm said with a smile. "Any preferences for a meal?"

Anne scanned the choices. "No preference, really. You choose the food. I vote that we try the wine tasting afterward. I saw a sign earlier that said two local wineries are here, and I do like a good glass of wine now and then."

"Maybe you can tell me what kind of wine goes with a corndog and garlic fries."

They purchased their meal and ate at one of the picnic tables located nearby. When they had finished, Anne directed them to where she had seen the sign for the wine tasting. They easily found the restaurant that was hosting the event.

Merry Mountain Vineyards and Laughing Jack's Wines had several varieties of their wines available for tasting. Anne persuaded Adehm to try most of them. It was obvious to Adehm that Anne had a thorough knowledge of wines. After tasting the offered vintages, she purchased a bottle each of a sweet wine made with plums, a dry Chardonnay, and a Merlot she had pronounced "very nice."

Adehm thought they had all tasted nice and was now sporting a mild buzz. They returned to the food area.

"Why don't you sit here with Chester, and I'll get us a cup of something hot to drink. You look like you could use it," Anne said.

Adehm waved Anne away. "Go, go. I'll be sitting right here at this table when you come back." She wasn't drunk, but she was feeling very warm and happy. She watched festival-goers as Anne went to get their drinks. Anne soon returned with two steaming cups of coffee.

"I'd like to see a few more craft stands before we leave, if that's okay," Anne said.

"My head is clearing up quite nicely now," Adehm replied. "If we take our time going through the craft area, I'll be fine by the time we're ready to drive back."

They sipped their coffee as they strolled to the craft area.

Anne found a string tie for Patrick and a one-of-a-kind baby's rattle made by a local Indian tribe for whenever Robyn had her baby shower. She purchased a dream catcher for herself. She added several other gifts for her parents and friends.

"You have bad dreams?" Adehm asked, nodding at the woven basket. It was made for catching nightmares and bad visions and letting the good dreams filter through.

"Hardly ever, but I'll take no chances."

It took both women to carry Anne's purchases. "You're not going to buy anything?" she asked as they reached Adehm's car and placed the bags in the back seat.

"No, I like to travel light. I'll just ignore my more materialistic side."

"I give in to mine," Anne said. "That's much more fun." Anne got into the passenger seat as Adehm slipped behind the wheel.

"Speaking of fun, from the look of your flowers today, I'll bet you could have a lot of fun with Lucas Barr."

Anne made a face at Adehm's remark. "I'm going to have to explain a few things to him when I see him next. However, the flowers were lovely."

"I wish I'd thought of sending them." Adehm glanced at Anne, whose expression gave nothing away. "I mean, you've been working very hard and doing a great job."

"I think I know what you meant," Anne said. She leaned across the front seat and gently kissed Adehm. After a moment she moved back. "That was nice. Once more?" she asked.

Adehm nodded.

Anne leaned in again, and this time Adehm met her halfway. The kiss was sweet and exploring with questions asked and interest expressed.

Adehm pulled away first, her emotions hovering somewhere between pleasure in the kiss, and guilt for enjoying it. A work romance could never work. Or could it? So many thoughts. For the moment, all those thoughts were pushed aside. "You were right, that was nice," she said. "I think we should be getting back to Wood Mill though."

"You're the driver," Anne said with a soft smile.

There was little conversation on the trip back. The winding road, now in darkness, required Adehm's full attention. When they arrived at the Pine Palace, Adehm helped Anne carry her purchases to her room.

"Would you like to have a drink?" Anne asked. "I suddenly seem to have obtained a nice supply of wine."

"I better not. I should head back to my room and take care of a few e-mails before I go to sleep."

Anne's disappointment was very real, but she decided someone who had lost a partner, as Adehm had, might have second thoughts about getting involved again.

"Okay," she said as she walked Adehm to the door. "I guess I'll meet you in the morning for breakfast as usual." She tried to keep an even, pleasant tone to her voice.

At the door, Adehm turned and took Anne into her arms. She rested her cheek against Anne's.

"I'll meet you for breakfast," Adehm agreed. "But I don't think it can ever be as usual again, Annegret." She kissed Anne's cheek, then left the room quickly, leaving a smiling Anne standing in the doorway.

*   *   *

"I have a huge goddamned headache." Adehm had her head in her hands as Anne walked into the manager's office at Big Tree.

"Are you okay?" Anne rushed to Adehm's side. She didn't recall Adehm saying anything about feeling unwell on the drive from Wood Mill. As a matter of fact, Adehm had seemed cheerful and upbeat. Even though she hadn't said anything specific, Anne had hoped the good mood was because of the new facet to their relationship.

"You don't think it was the wine we had yesterday, do you?" She put an arm gently around Adehm's shoulders. "Can I get you anything?"

"No. I'll be okay, and the only thing I need is to take a powder." She turned her head to look at Anne. She saw confusion on Anne's face. "Taking a powder is an old-fashioned way of saying I'd like to get out of here."

"That makes your phrase easier to understand, but the reason behind it still escapes me."

"Neil Hammond is the reason."

"The comptroller from your company? Is he making demands again? Wait a minute, I thought he was on vacation."

"He is," Adehm said. "He's on vacation in Wood Mill." She stood, causing Anne's arm to drop from her shoulders. Adehm paced the room. "He told the office he was going to the Pacific Northwest, but I guess he decided on a little side trip down here first, the rat bastard."

"When did this happen? How did you find out?" Anne was sure Adehm hadn't known at breakfast.

"It seems our friend Len at the Pine Palace likes the fact that we're staying there and being generous with our tips. He called me on the cell phone number I left him in case of an emergency. Neil

Hammond drove in a little after we left this morning. When he signed the check-in card and used the company credit card, Len thought he would alert me to the presence of one of my colleagues. Neil asked for directions out here. Len told him how to get here and where he could get some breakfast. After he eats, I think we can expect a visit from him." She walked over to the file cabinet containing all the paperwork on the project. "At least that will give me time to double-check everything."

"What can I do to help?"

"How's the trenching coming? Do they look like they're on schedule?"

"I talked to the supervisor for the contractor. They may even be a little ahead of schedule. They're doing very nice work. We picked a good company."

"Then you're doing everything you have to," Adehm said. She began perusing the files again.

"I know I've done what I have to, but I want to help." Anne blushed a little. "To be honest, this project has grown a little more important to me lately."

Adehm turned from the files and faced Anne. "I feel that way, too, and I'm very interested in seeing where this might go, but Annegret, not while Neil Hammond is here, okay?"

Adehm's words stung a little. "Does he have a problem with two women having a relationship or whatever it is that we do… or will… have?"

"I don't know about that, and I don't give a good goddamn about his views on same sex relationships. That's none of his business. He will, however, have a problem with an executive responsible for a three-quarters-of-a-million-dollars project having any kind of relationship, other than business, with a contractor. Even if she is the cutest engineer in all of Wood Mill."

"Just in Wood Mill?" Anne said, relieved to hear Adehm's concern.

Adehm took Anne into her arms and pulled her close. "Maybe in all of central California. I doubt any of the other engineers fill out a pair of coveralls like you do."

Anne gave a little laugh; she was glad to see Adehm hadn't lost her sense of humor.

"But," Adehm said, as she pulled back a little to look directly at Anne, "while Neil Hammond's here, it will have to be a more formal relationship, I'm afraid. After Neil's gone, though, I'd like to drop the formality right away and see you on a much more social basis. I like you, Annegret, in case you hadn't picked up on that."

"I had an idea of that last night," Anne said. "However, a brief reminder might be in order, especially as it will be the last reminder for a little while."

Adehm glanced at the door. "One reminder coming up." She brought her mouth to Anne's in a kiss much more exciting than the previous night's.

Anne felt a heat rising between them that had to be quashed before it threatened to rage out of control. She broke the kiss, her breathing rapid. "Wow, I'm not likely to forget that." She held on to Adehm, steadying herself.

"It's burned into my mind, I can tell you that." Adehm no sooner said, "How about another reminder?" when the office phone rang.

"Must be him," she said. "How about we refresh our memories again after he's gone, Annegret?"

"Why, Ms. Trent, how very unprofessional of you," Anne said, as Adehm went to the phone. "And, I'd love to."

Adehm winked at her as she answered. "Adehm Trent." She paused for a moment. "Of course. Escort him up to the manager's office, please." She replaced the phone. "Boy, do I wish I was an engineer right now," she said to Anne, who was returning to her desk.

"Why is that?"

"If there was ever a time to put on coveralls and slip down a manhole, this is it."

\* \* \*

"And that brings us back to our starting point, Neil," Adehm said, ushering him into the manager's office. He walked to Adehm's desk and seated himself in her chair.

At six-foot-three-inches tall and two-hundred-and-forty pounds, Neil Hammond created an imposing figure behind the desk. As a prop to indicate power, the desk wasn't bad. Adehm smiled inwardly, knowing she had used the same tactic herself from time to time. It didn't make the maneuver any less irritating. She didn't allow her annoyance to show on the outside as she took a seat across from him.

"Is there anything else I can answer for you?" she asked. Another question was actually the last thing she wanted after fielding them for the last six hours, but she'd be damned if she'd let him know that.

"No, I can see everything's in perfect order here. Of course, my visit here was strictly informal, really just a show of my support."

*In a pig's eye,* Adehm thought. *It became informal when you realized you couldn't find anything wrong. If you think I'm letting my guard down because you're trying to look harmless, you seriously underestimate me.*

"It's nice to know I have your full backing," she told Neil.

"I'll admit there were skeptics when you decided to take this project on," Neil said, running his hand through his thinning brown hair. "Not me. I have great faith in your work and judgment, but there were voices saying you were wrong to try to save this place. They said we should abandon this property and rebuild nearer the main transportation arteries. Even I was a bit surprised when you came up with your plan."

*I wonder who was the choirmaster for those voices, you crocodile.*

"Thinking outside the box is what keeps Bohannon competitive," Adehm said. "Less than a million to get Big Tree operable seemed worth a try, rather than the several million it would take just to buy the land for a new plant."

"I don't think we should count our chickens before they're hatched. You've still got a big project ahead of you and then the inspections to pass before there can be any real celebrating here."

"Not to worry. We're too busy around here to celebrate." Adehm thought briefly back to the kiss she and Anne had shared just prior to Neil's arrival. She rose and went to the coffeepot to hide a rising blush.

"Coffee?" she asked over her shoulder.

"Black, please."

Adehm was pouring the coffee when Anne entered the office. "Would you like some coffee, Ms. Schneider?" With her back still to Neil, Adehm gave Anne a brief smile.

"That would be nice." Anne removed her hard hat and placed it on the hook. "The HDPE pipe has arrived. The contractor's people are going to unload it and lay it out to start installation in the morning."

"That's great," Adehm said. She was proud of their handling of the complication of the fractured pipe. She handed Anne her cup of coffee.

"Ms. Schneider," Neil said, "we really didn't get a chance to chat much when I arrived. Adehm tells me you've been doing an excellent job here."

"I appreciate the assessment. Ms. Trent has been putting in long hours on this project as well. Just this morning, I was saying she should have a bit more recreation time. It's difficult to maintain the pace she's been working at."

"And is she providing all the assistance and backup you need to get the job done here?" he asked.

"She's been giving me everything I need," Anne replied with a straight face.

"I forgot your sugar substitute, Ms. Schneider," Adehm said, returning to the coffeepot quickly to hide her blush.

"You see that, Mr. Hammond? Ms. Trent is very helpful. She knows how much I enjoy a little sugar."

"I'm sure your coffee wouldn't be the same without it," Adehm said, rejoining Anne and Neil. Her cheeks still felt faintly heated.

"It's after five already," Neil said, checking his watch. "How about we meet at seven for a bite of supper? I slept on the plane last night, but the drive here and the day at the plant have tired me out. I'd like to turn in early, because I want to get an early start in the morning. A few old friends have invited me up to Washington State for the opening week of deer hunting season."

"That sounds very interesting, Mr. Hammond," Anne said. "There's a restaurant in Wood Mill called The Rose. We can meet you there, if you like. Anyone can give you directions. It's close to the hotel."

"That's fine with me. I think that concludes my business here. You're both doing a remarkable job, so far."

"I trust you'll pass that observation along to the board of directors," Adehm said.

"With my vacation, I really won't have time to give the board a report. Just keep sending those updates to me. My office will know how to reach me." With that, he rose and left.

"I'd like to reach him," Adehm said. "I'd like to reach my hands around his neck and choke him like a chicken. Damn! It felt like I was put on a spit and slow roasted for six hours." She walked around her desk and dropped into her seat. "I can tell you, if he'd found something wrong here, he would have attended the next board meeting with a bullhorn to squawk all about it."

"But he didn't find anything wrong, did he?"

Adehm shook her head in response.

"Then we look at this dinner as a victory meal. We have supper with Neil, and then he can take his black cloud away, and the sun will shine on us again."

"That would be a very nice prospect, if only Neil Hammond didn't cast such a huge shadow."

# Chapter 9

"Adehm Trent's office."

"You just get better and better at that," Rodney said. "If I hadn't become so personally secure in my position, I'd worry about your self-sufficiency. Fortunately, just today I overheard something in the executive floor employee lounge that gives new purpose to my employment."

"And what are the chickens clucking about in the secretarial coop these days?" Adehm asked. "And good morning, by the way."

"Good morning to you, too. The executive assistant coop was carrying on when I, your loyal minion, traipsed in to heat up my Ramen noodles. Pretending to be adding just the right amount from my seasoning packet, I heard that you are doing fine on the project in California."

"How gratifying to know Neil Hammond has been in touch with his staff," Adehm said. "I'm waiting for the point to all this."

"Is it true that Anne Schneider is invaluable, irreplaceable, and the only reason you're managing at all there?"

"That's ridiculous. Anne Schneider is integral to our progress, but she's not the cog in the machinery that makes everything else work. You sure you heard that right?"

"I swear on my sainted grandmother's dentures. It appears Neil Hammond is letting it be known in a subtle way that Anne Schneider seems to be carrying you on this project. Without you here to refute the garbage in your no-nonsense way, the rumor mill is working at time-and-a-half."

"Anything you can do on your end?" Adehm asked. "I know I've been gone several weeks, but I just can't fly to Detroit to make an appearance and quash gossip."

"The way I see it, there are three possible solutions to this problem. One, I can try to downplay the Anne Schneider thing. I can minimize her role, or at least bring it into perspective, using the same gossip pipeline. Two, we can counterattack with our own rumor about Neil Hammond."

"Such as?" Adehm asked.

"I don't know. I'll think of something. How about if I say that, at certain times of the month and late at night, Neil Hammond eats shit and howls at the moon?"

Adehm laughed at the picture her imagination created at that suggestion. "Not bad. What's my third option?"

"You can dismiss Anne Schneider. Without the kindling, there's no fuel for the fire and subsequent smoke screen."

Adehm felt like she had been kicked in the stomach. It wasn't just the potential loss of a great co-worker, or the loss of someone she considered a friend. Anne was the first person she had... responded to... since Shannon.

"That third option is out of the question," Adehm said, more harshly than she intended. "I mean, I won't throw an innocent bystander under the bus just to squelch rumors Neil Hammond is floating. It'll be enough when I get this plant up and running at capacity after passing the State inspection. My gamble will pay off then."

"Anything you say, boss, but at least I can still let it be known around Corporate that Neil Hammond wears women's underwear."

"As much as that visual both amuses and repulses me, I think we can try to stick to the truth. Anne Schneider's work on this project is too important to mess up because of office politics."

"Thanks for the compliment, but what politics could mess up my work here?"

Adehm hadn't heard Anne return to the office. She stood just inside the doorway, her hard hat tucked under one arm while she removed her work gloves.

"I have to go, Rodney. Thanks for the heads up. I'll speak to you in the morning." Adehm hung up and gave Anne her full attention.

"You've never mentioned any other troublemaker, so I'll presume that Neil Hammond has been causing problems again." Anne tucked her gloves away.

"Normally, I try to discourage presumptions, but in this instance, you're absolutely correct. Our little ray of sunshine is spreading rumors back in Detroit that you are my wastewater muse, and I'm just along for the ride, using your talents selfishly to further my own ends." She watched as Anne went to her computer and moved the mouse to stop her screen saver and bring up the project plans.

"That's pretty much how I see it. Neil Hammond might just be more intelligent than I thought."

That comment caused Adehm to sit straight up at her desk. "Ha! If intelligence was gas, Neil Hammond wouldn't have enough to prime a pissant's motor scooter. I can't believe you're agreeing with him." Adehm rose and went to Anne's desk.

"I'm an engineer and not an executive for a national corporation, but it seems to me that business is all about using each other. You use my trade to get your plant open. I use the prestige and experience I'm getting in working for you to increase my own value and my company's reputation. Done right, a business deal seems like the ultimate symbiotic relationship."

"Neil is making sure it seems more like a parasitic relationship than anything else. He's saying you're the only reason I'm making any progress at all."

"Okay, that's going a bit too far. I'm good, but I'm not that good," Anne said with a smile. "I'll tell you what. Keep Neil Hammond away from this office, and we will make real progress here. When he was hanging around, I felt like he was staring at my chest half the time and going over your books with a microscope the other half. I'm surprised he isn't complaining that we caused him to have eye strain."

Adehm gave a short laugh, breaking her annoyance with Neil.

"Did I mention I'm really glad you're here? Neil Hammond's perfidy has no chance against your humor." Adehm became serious. "Want to know something? I really am glad. I said it lightly, but I mean it. Being with you is fun and interesting on a lot of levels. We work well together as professionals, and I certainly have a great deal of respect for you, but we laugh at the same things, and I think our idea of entertainment is the same. We're definitely individuals, but it's really nice to work with someone I find so compatible." Adehm perched on one corner of Anne's desk.

"Thanks for the compliments, and I think it's safe to say those sentiments go both ways."

"Anne, were you seeing anybody in Albuquerque? I mean in a personal way. You don't have to tell me, of course, but I've never heard you mention anyone special."

"There's no one to mention," Anne said. She released her computer's mouse and sat back in her chair. "I've dated people off and on, but it seems like most of the time, it stalls out or we become friends instead. That could be my fault. I've put a lot of time into the business and helping my father take care of my mother." Anne spread her hands, palms up. "That's the boring story. And don't worry, you can ask me anything, as long as you don't expect a fascinating answer in return."

"How would you like to go out on a date with me?" Adehm asked the question quickly, afraid she'd lose her nerve. "I'm a bit rusty at this, but I believe that something like dinner and a movie is still traditional."

"I'd really like that… if you're sure Neil Hammond won't hear about it and use it against you in some way."

Anne's reminder about Neil's presence in their lives was disturbing, but not enough to make Adehm change her mind. "I don't care if he knows or if he says anything about it. This is my personal time, and I'll do as I please. Now, if you can't think of any other objections…"

"I'd love to go out with you," Anne said. She met Adehm's gaze straight on. "Very much."

"Excellent." Adehm slapped her thigh with the flat of her hand. "Let me put some details together, and I'll let you know when, okay?"

"Sounds good."

Adehm returned to her desk, and both women resumed their work.

"You know, you were wrong in what you said a little bit ago." Adehm broke the silence. "Some of your answers are quite fascinating."

\* \* \*

It was mid-fall in Wood Mill. The new pipeline was installed, a gleaming black length that Anne was sure could withstand all that the California terrain and tectonic plates could dish out for at least the next hundred years. Removal of the elements of the under-functioning wastewater treatment apparatus was being completed, and subcontractors came and went, preparing Big Tree for its new equipment.

Anne opened the door to the manager's office and dragged herself in.

"Don't be surprised if when I come out of that manhole one day, I've completely changed into a mole. Start worrying when I come up with dark glasses and a white cane. Then you'll know I've been underground too much." She went to her desk and dropped into the chair. She was still wearing her coveralls, hard hat, and work boots.

Adehm didn't look up from her computer. "Got it. Start worrying if the farmer's wife comes after Annegret with a carving knife. I'll make a note of that."

Anne laughed and removed her work boots. "What are you working on? Whatever it is, it's got your attention."

"It's two things." Adehm glanced up. "And both things have me more than slightly nervous. All my plans might be ruined if I can't make this work." She clicked the computer's mouse twice and began typing.

"I'm really sorry. I didn't know it was that serious. Is there anything I can do to help?" Anne removed her coveralls and stored her gear away.

"Maybe," Adehm replied. "Let me do some more work here, and I'll let you know in a minute."

"No problem at all. I'll be right here." Anne tried to concentrate on a set of plans Patrick had e-mailed to get her opinion on, but her mind strayed time and time again to Adehm across the office. Something was definitely wrong with her. Just as Anne feared she might expire from a cross between curiosity and concern, Adehm raised her eyes from the computer screen.

"Aha! I think I've made it all work out."

"That's great," Anne said. "Whatever it is, that's great."

"It is from my point of view. I've been trying to come up with an idea for our date. I had a few plans made, but then I got this a couple of hours ago. I've verified it with Detroit." Adehm pointed to a printout of an e-mail sitting next to her computer. "Let me summarize the corporate lingo for you. I've got to go to Detroit for a meeting to finish up another project I've been working on. The law team has finished litigation, and I'm expected to be at the settlement meeting."

"Oh, you'll be leaving, then. Will you be gone long?" Anne asked, missing her already. She went to Adehm's desk.

"Five days," Adehm said. "As long as I'm heading back east, I'm going to clear up a lot of work Rodney has been handling. I need to put in an appearance for my position, too. I hope that doesn't sound shallow or like I'm power hungry."

"It might sound shallow if I knew what you meant by all that."

Adehm stood and faced Anne. She gently wrapped her hands around Anne's upper arms.

"I have a position at Bohannon. No one gave it to me. I didn't inherit it. I've worked really hard to get where I am. To be honest, I have a bit of a reputation as a tough-minded executive there."

Anne's mind drifted back to the time she had first heard of "Adam Trent" and the firing of the five managers at Big Tree. She smiled.

"What?" Adehm asked.

"I'm glad you don't feel you need to keep up your reputation here with me. Don't get me wrong. You were the very model of professionalism during Neil Hammond's visit, but I sure get the feeling I have the rare privilege of seeing the real person you are."

"I'm glad you think so. We haven't known each other very long, but it's important to me that you see me as a person and not just as the executive on your project."

"It would be impossible not to notice you as a person, Adehm." She leaned forward and kissed Adehm on the cheek. "Can you please now enlighten me about how I figure into your Detroit plans?"

Adehm dropped her hands from Anne's arms. "You're in my post-Detroit plans. I'll be gone five days, but on day six, I'll be back for our date. I've made a few arrangements for that event, and I hope you'll like what I've planned. It's a little difficult, you know. I didn't know whether to arrange something I know you'd enjoy or plan something I'd enjoy so you could get to know me better, or try to find something we both would enjoy to emphasize our common ground."

"And which did you decide to do?"

"All three," Adehm said as she clasped and unclasped her hands. "This is technically our first date, and I want to make a good impression."

"No question about it, you already have. Are you going to enlighten me about the plans for our date or do you intend to keep me in the dark? Correct me if I'm wrong, but I believe I have a leading role in this two-person play."

"Curiosity only kills cats. I don't think you'll expire from yours. Give me a little bit of time to polish up all the details."

Anne gave a short bow from the waist. "Whatever you wish, you shall have. So when do you leave?" she asked.

"The day after tomorrow. You can handle everything here the rest of the week. I haven't been disappointed in your work yet."

"You make my heart flutter with such sweet talk."

Adehm laughed. "I might need to polish up on my compliment giving. Speaking of talk, will it be okay if I call you from Detroit?"

"It will be very okay and very welcome. I might just miss you around here. I can certainly understand you wanting to keep up on what's happening on the project."

"I can assure you, my calls won't have anything to do with work," Adehm said.

Her meaning caused Anne to blush. "Like I said, that will be very okay and very welcome."

# Chapter 10

Adehm was already at her desk, sorting through a massive stack of correspondence when Rodney came into the office.

"Welcome back," he said. "I didn't expect you in so early. Let me get a pot of coffee going, and we can start to tackle some of that pile."

"I already made the coffee," she said, pointing absently at the mug sitting on her desk. "There's more. Help yourself."

Rodney stood, unmoving, in the doorway. "You made coffee? Since when?"

Adehm laid the letter she was holding on her desk.

"Just because I let you do it doesn't mean I can't. In California, I routinely make the coffee."

"That's very democratic of you." Rodney removed his jacket and hung it on a coatrack in the corner of the outer office. He helped himself to a mug of the hot coffee. "Very good," he said, taking a sip. "You're definitely the new barista around here."

"Don't get used to it. I'm only back for a few days this time. The project in California is entering a crucial stage. Getting the actual wastewater treatment plant installed is the most important thing, next to passing the State's test. There are details in Wood Mill that require my personal attention," she said, cryptically.

"You'll have less to deal with now that the Marzlin business is settled. You worked a long time to get them to agree on that settlement. That's a nice prize in your pocket."

"Hard work made it happen. It was a team effort to get the results we wanted."

"Whatever you say, boss. I sure would like to be the recipient of your Christmas bonus this year. Be modest and a team player if you wish, but Bohannon knows it got a good deal when you climbed on board."

"I think that's what happens when you're a workaholic with a broken heart and no personal life."

Rodney was one of the few people who knew Adehm's personal background and history.

"And not much has changed by the looks of it. You're in earlier than ever."

"I just don't want to be burning the midnight oil around here. What do you say we shoot for being out of here at five tonight?"

"Five? As in five p.m.? The sun will still be up. Are you sure you'll be able to find your way home in sunlight? Hey, wait a minute. I take back what I said. Things have changed. I don't think I've ever heard you talk about getting off work at a reasonable hour before. Have you finally made some lucky woman in Detroit happy?"

Adehm leaned back in her chair. "I think I have, and that woman is me."

*　*　*

Three sharp raps on the manager's office door caused Anne to lift her gaze from the file on the desk before her. The knock heralded Lucas Barr's appearance a moment later. He leaned into the office

"Hey, Anne, am I disturbing you?"

"No, no. Nothing that can't wait for a minute or two. Come on in."

Lucas entered the office, leaving the door open behind him.

"Is anything wrong?"

"Not at all," he said. "I just know you and Ms. Trent usually have dinner together." At Anne's concerned look, he added, "It's a small town, and people notice things. Anyway, I figured you both were strangers here and decided to pair up for meals. I can understand that. I hate to eat alone at a restaurant."

Anne relaxed a little. "You're right. That's no fun. Adehm does provide nice company, and she understands my work here, the non-technical things, at least."

"That's why I'm here. With Ms. Trent gone this week, I'd say seeing that you have company for dinner falls to me. After all, I'm the assistant to the interim plant manager in large part due to you."

The hopeful look on Lucas's face made it plain that a strictly business dinner wasn't what he had in mind. Anne felt she should be honest with him.

"Dinner, and company for it, would be fine, Lucas, but that's all it can be." Anne stood and came around the desk. "I think you're bright and personable, and if you'd like to be one, I'd appreciate a friend here. I just don't want you to think there could be more than friendship for me."

Lucas's face showed a mixture of curiosity and disappointment. "Is it because I'm an employee here? Or maybe because in the refitting job, you're kind of a supervisor to me?"

"That doesn't make any difference to me. The fact that I'm gay does."

"You're a... lesbian?"

Anne almost laughed as she watched Lucas fish for the appropriate term to use.

"You'd never know it."

Anne did laugh then. "I'm going to take that as the compliment I think you meant it to be."

"You know what I mean," Lucas said. "You don't act all manly or whatever. You seem really normal."

"And so I think I am," Anne said, almost enjoying Lucas's distress as payback for the stereotyping. "We frequently are, you know." She punched him lightly on the arm. "I suppose I'll need to start wearing my 'I'm gay' T-shirt to work now."

"No way," Lucas said. "I'm not going to tell anybody. I don't have a problem with it, and it's your secret."

Anne took a step back and sat on the edge of the desk. "I should make this clear to you. It's not a secret. My family knows, my business partner knows, and I'm not ashamed of it in the least. If it had been the tiniest bit relevant to my working with you, then you would have known as well. It just isn't relevant to working on a wastewater treatment plant project."

"Does she know?" Lucas asked, jerking his head slightly toward Adehm's unoccupied desk.

"I believe that Ms. Trent thoroughly knows everyone who works with her, so I would have to say yes. She hasn't held it against me, though." Anne smiled at her own inside joke.

"That's good," Lucas said. "It wouldn't be right if she did."

"So, you still want to accompany a gay woman to get some food?"

"Sure, if you still want to go. You'll be the first lesbian I ever took to dinner."

"Now there's a shock." Anne closed her computer down and retrieved her jacket. She became very serious. "There is one thing you should know if you're going to eat dinner with a gay woman."

All of Lucas's attention was focused on her.

"What's that?"

"Lesbians tip better," she said, as she walked past him and out of the office.

* * *

"I can't believe you told him that," Adehm said into the phone. She could imagine Anne lying on her bed in the Pine Palace with her head propped up and the phone tucked against her neck.

"I almost had him believing me when I told him to add the usual thirty-five percent to our dinner check, but I couldn't keep a straight face."

"Speaking of straight, how did he take it when he found out you weren't?" Adehm was in her brown leather wingback chair in the living room of her apartment. Her shoeless feet were propped on a matching ottoman and directed at a crackling blaze in the fireplace. A glass of wine sat next to her on an oak end table.

"Fairly well, but I think he belongs to the lesbian-only-because-she-hasn't-met-the-right-man-yet club. Despite that, he has the respect of the crew at Big Tree, and I don't think you'll regret his promotion."

"Nice to know my instincts about people can still be trusted." Adehm stretched and glanced at a regulator clock hanging on the wall. It was getting late in Detroit, but she didn't want to hang up anytime soon. "Have you ever noticed that sometimes it's easier to talk to a person on the phone than it is to sit across from them and look them in the eye?"

"I think it all depends on what you have to say."

"I wanted to say a lot to you all day, but now that I have you on the phone, it seems like this is enough. Not talking about anything important, just connecting."

"I'm not known for being a talkative person, but I think I could get used to this." Anne hesitated a moment before adding, "The office seemed too empty today."

"I hope you won't think poorly of me if I admit I'm happy to hear it."

"I don't believe I could think poorly of you at all," Anne said. "Ich habe dir eine kleine Aufmerksamkeit geschickt."

"German is an interesting language. Remind me to learn it someday. Until then, can you translate that for me?"

"I said, 'I've sent you a little gift.'" Anne's words in English still held a strong German accent.

"You sound more like a native of your country right now. What's making the difference?"

"Maybe just a little wine with dinner and the fact someone I could be interested in is a long way off."

"That's really... Hey, did you say you sent me a gift? I almost breezed right past that," Adehm said.

"Let me spare you the effort and tell you not to bother asking me what it is. Remember, I'm a former East German, and we know how to keep secrets. When you never knew who could be trusted, you trusted no one."

"You can trust me."

"I know." Anne hesitated. "Adehm?"

"Hmm?"

"I wish I could kiss you right now."

Any reply Adehm might have made was rendered impossible by her lack of breath.

"Me, too," she managed to say, finally. "That would be incredibly nice."

Neither said a word for almost a full minute.

"You still there?" Adehm asked.

"Yes," Anne replied. "I was listening to you breathing. With my eyes closed, I could almost convince myself you were here next to me."

It had been several years since Adehm had been, or wanted to be, near someone in that way. She felt a lump come to her throat and moisture gather in her eyes. Blinking to clear her suddenly swimming vision, she sat up in the chair.

"Annegret, you make me feel something I haven't been interested in feeling in a very long time. I hurt so badly, and because of that, I convinced myself I could do without those feelings. Now it's..." Adehm trailed off, her usual self-assured conversational skills deserting her.

"There's no need to try to discuss this right now. We can talk about it when you get back."

Adehm felt a wave of relief wash over her at Anne's words.

"That's a date."

"Speaking of dates, are you ready to let me in on ours yet?" Anne asked.

"Nope, it's going to be a surprise. Don't try to get any information from me. I'm going to be as silent as the Sphinx. Don't worry. I'll give you plenty of time and information to be prepared for it."

"Thank goodness. I truly hate being over- or underdressed."

"Oh yeah, I bet you stay up nights worrying about it."

"Now that you mention it, Adehm Trent, it's getting late back there, so you'd better trundle off to bed."

"That's true. Would it be impertinent if I said I wish you were here?"

"No," Anne said in a thoughtful tone. "It would be damn sexy and very complimentary."

"In that case, I wish you were here." Adehm was silent for a moment. "You're very easy to talk to."

"Even if I'm not saying anything?"

"Seems to me you say the most when you don't use words at all. I have to tell you, I'm rarely comfortable with silences when there are lapses in a conversation. That's not true with you. The times we're both in the office and working on our separate things, I don't feel the need to fill the void with words."

"Then I sure hope you won't mind me calling you tomorrow and saying a few."

"You'd better," Adehm said. "Anytime after seven should be fine."

"It's etched in my memory. Good night, Adehm. Sweet dreams."

"They will be… now. Sleep well."

They hung up simultaneously. For a minute Adehm sat just staring into the fire, a smile playing about her lips.

"I'd tell you all about our date, Annegret, if I had a friggin' clue about it myself. No matter what I've led you to think, I haven't got the faintest idea what we're going to do." She moved her feet off the ottoman and stood up, then walked down the hall to the den, where she removed the laptop computer from her briefcase.

"Internet, don't fail me now."

* * *

Rodney walked by the door to Adehm's office and stopped dead in his tracks. Adehm had left for lunch forty-five minutes earlier, and now he was sure someone was in her office. Whoever it was, he wasn't being very discreet. The noise he was making was a dead giveaway to his presence. Leaning in the door, he saw something that deeply startled him.

"Don't move," he said. "I'm calling security. I don't know who you are, but this feeble attempt to impersonate my boss isn't going to work."

Adehm swallowed another bite of her sandwich and took a sip of water from the bottle on her desk. "Want to tell me what you're talking about, or should I just have you committed immediately and bypass the lengthy explanation?"

Rodney circled the desk, eyeing Adehm suspiciously. "Oh, it's a clever disguise, I'll grant you that, but you aren't Adehm Trent. Aha! Even more proof," he said, pointing to the computer screen she had been looking at.

"You need serious medication. You're crazy." Adehm leaned back in her chair and regarded her assistant.

"Crazy like a fox. Let me present a little evidence to you, Miss Whoever-You-Are. First, Adehm Trent does two things during her lunch hour. She either works in the office or she works out of the office. She does not surf the Net." He gestured at the screen of Adehm's computer that was displaying something not remotely work related. "Nightclubs. The real Adehm Trent has no interest in such things."

Adehm dropped the lid of her laptop computer, belatedly shielding it from Rodney's view.

"Adehm Trent also has no time for lunch," Rodney continued. "I bet you think this is a sandwich," he said, pointing to her meal. "You'd be wrong if you did. It's an obvious error in your masquerade. Nutrition in the middle of a workday is not very Adehm-esque."

"Okay, you caught me enjoying a meal at lunchtime and not working while consuming it. That's a pretty weak case, Perry Mason."

Rodney stopped his circling at the front of Adehm's desk, a triumphant smile on his face. "You were humming, madam," he said, crossing his arms.

"I was?" Adehm asked, looking genuinely perplexed. She took the last bite of her sandwich. "You know, you're right. I think I was humming. That's not usual for me. Maybe I'm not who I think I am." She patted her own shoulder and down her arm. "And yet I seem to be. What do you make of it?"

"You've been different since you came back to Detroit. There's something in California that's been good for you."

"It's not a something. It's a someone."

Rodney uncrossed his arms and took his usual seat next to Adehm's desk. "It's the engineer, isn't it?"

"Yeah. How did you guess?"

"You're at the same hotel, your expense account receipts show meals for two, you're in the same office, and when I suggested she get removed from the project, you nearly snapped my head off long distance. It didn't take a rocket scientist to put the facts together."

"I suppose not."

"Don't sound so glum about it. I doubt anyone around here but me would recognize the signs." He rose and walked toward the outer office.

"Of?" she asked to his back.

"You're falling in love, big time. If you're not there already."

"Noticing a few outward signs doesn't mean you know what's going on in my heart," she called out a bit defensively.

Rodney disappeared through the door, but returned a few moments later carrying a box.

"I got a call from the mailroom earlier. They had this delivery for you from... oh, what a surprise... California. Do you know an Anne Schneider, or should we call the bomb squad and have this defused?"

Adehm popped up from her desk and went to Rodney, relieving him of his burden.

"I nearly forgot. She told me she was sending me a gift."

"It appears she didn't lie. I'll let you have some privacy to delve into the contents of that box." As Rodney exited the office, he started to pull the door closed behind him, but hesitated.

"Adehm?"

"Yeah?" she answered, already using her letter opener to loosen the sealing tape on the box.

"That humming you were doing earlier. I recognized the song. I just wondered if you did." He did leave then, quietly closing the door.

Adehm stopped tugging at the tape and replayed the scene in her mind. She moved slowly to her desk chair and dropped into it. She remembered the song now; her choice had been strictly unconscious at the time. She winced in acute embarrassment.

She had been humming "Love Me Tender."

\*   \*   \*

Anne had been at Big Tree only an hour when Lucas Barr dropped by.

"I had a good time at dinner last night."

"Me, too," Anne said. "Thanks for the invitation. That was nice of you."

"Nope, what's nice of me is telling you that, at this very moment, your new wastewater treatment plant is making its way up here from town in the back of an eighteen-wheeler. Should be here in about forty-five minutes or so. The driver called on his cell phone to verify the directions."

"That's great news, Lucas, the best I could have heard this morning. We'll need a crew for the unloading and transport into the plant. Round up some of the staff and equipment, okay?"

Lucas nodded and touched his hand to his hard hat. "You got it. How about if I give you a call on the office phone when it gets here, and you can come down to give us the word on how you want it done?"

"Perfect. We'll get everything ready, and then we can get the installation company here tomorrow."

Lucas left, giving Anne the chance to round up her hard hat and other equipment for use at the work site.

Mozart's *Eine Kleine Nachtmusik* began playing on Anne's cell phone. The ring tone indicated a number not saved in the phone's address book. She didn't recognize the number displayed on the screen

"Hello?" she answered.

"Is it right that you take Bohannon's money and still spend time on personal phone calls?" Adehm asked.

"Damn, you've found me out," Anne replied with a laugh. "Since you left, I've locked myself in the office and done nothing but make phone calls, hour after hour."

"Potentially dozens and dozens of calls today, and yet I haven't received a single one. I'm hurt."

Anne's voice took on a slightly suggestive tone. "That's because these were personal calls. When it comes to you, I think I'd like to get right down to business."

"Hang on. I'm going to put you on hold a second," Adehm said. Her voice was replaced on the line by The Eagles performing "Take It to the Limit."

*I'm trying,* Anne thought.

"That's better," Adehm said, returning to the phone. "I just needed to close the office door. I'm already taking a ribbing for humming today. I don't need to add fuel to the fire."

"I'll bet you're good at heating things up," Anne said. Now that she knew about it, she was enjoying Adehm's discomfort.

"You're going to cause me to lose track of why I called you, not that it wouldn't be a pleasant diversion. Just let me get this out, please. Thank you, Annegret Schneider. You shouldn't have, but I'm so very glad you did."

Realization dawned on Anne. "You got your present. I'm happy you like it. I was going to save it until Christmas, but it seemed like a much better time now."

"It was a going-away present?" Adehm asked.

"More like a come-back-quickly one."

Adehm smiled as she looked down into the box Anne had sent. In it was the shadow box scene she had admired at the Webster First Fall Festival. The sight of the artwork brought back the pleasant memories of that day.

"To say I'm stunned would be an understatement," Adehm said. "When did you get it? And how? This is one of the most thoughtful gifts I've ever received."

"It was easy, really. When you were working through your wine buzz and I went to get coffee, I detoured by the woman's display again. I bought the picture and asked her to ship it to the hotel. Have credit card, will travel."

"You're marvelous," Adehm said, her tone adding significant impact to the simple words.

"Thank you. I'm pleased it's made you happy. Oh wait, I can make you even happier I think."

"You have no idea what things flashed through my head as you said that. Kind of naughty things."

"Unless wastewater treatment equipment is naughty in your mind, you're going to be disappointed. For now."

"It's there?" Adehm asked excitedly. "Don't think that 'for now' comment slipped by me, but I'm really interested in the equipment."

"Yes, it's here, or almost. It should be arriving at Big Tree any minute."

"That's fantastic news. Getting the system there before the late fall rains start puts my mind at ease about this project. This means we're a tiny bit ahead of schedule."

"That's true. I'll have to adjust my timetable on a few fronts."

"Me, too, definitely," Adehm said. "Okay, I'll let you go deal with the equipment. I'll be thanking you again for the art, in person next time."

"Now there's something I'll be sure to add to my schedule."

"Put it down for five days from now."

"I'll be looking forward to it."

Anne sat in the manager's office with a grin on her face. A phone rang again, but this time it was the manager's office line.

"Be right there, Lucas," she said, not bothering with a greeting. She disconnected and gathered her equipment. "Five more days," she mumbled as she left the office. "It's going to be the longest five days of my life."

# Chapter 11

"This isn't what I was expecting," Lucas said. "I thought the wastewater treatment plant would be one big unit. This looks like a plumber's jigsaw puzzle."

"That's one way of looking at it." Anne ticked items off on her clipboard as they were unloaded. "Once I make sure everything's here, I'll call the company we've hired to install it. They can be out here in twenty-four hours." She checked off a set of pipes on her list. "They better be, because that's the contract they signed. Adehm Trent is a tough negotiator."

"This job called for nothing less," Lucas said. He climbed up on the back of the truck and helped the Big Tree crew move another piece of equipment forward. "To be honest, a lot of people here and in town aren't so sure it can get done." He bent at the knees to help lift a long crate.

"It can and it will." Anne checked the contents of the crate off on her list. The cell phone in her pocket rang, and the caller information showed her a number with the Albuquerque area code. "Lucas, can you finish this for me? Just be sure everything on this list gets unloaded off that truck."

"Sure thing." Lucas jumped down from the truck bed and took the clipboard from her.

Anne moved a little bit away from the workers. "Hello?"

"Annegret, it's Vati." Her father's voice was as welcome as it was unexpected.

"Vati, I'm surprised to hear from you at this time of the day. Is there something that can't wait until my usual phone call to you tomorrow night?" Anne was trying to keep her tone light, but a slightly uneasy feeling fluttered in her midsection.

"It's Karina. I know how very important your project is there, and I have appreciated all that you arranged before you left and what you have done while you were there..." He trailed off.

"What's the matter? What's happened?"

100

"Your mother is much worse. The state of her mind, her memory, the physical frailty. I had not thought it would progress as rapidly as this. Could this be my fault? Should I have tried to be with her more? Is there something I could have done?" The anguish in Marcel's voice was evident.

"You know the doctor explained that no two courses of Alzheimer's go quite the same way," Anne said. "In what way is Mutti worse?"

"So many things. There are days when she doesn't even seem to know me. Yesterday, for several minutes, she actually resisted me when I tried to help her with her personal needs. She acted as if I would try to violate her. We have been married for over thirty-five years, and she acted as if I were a stranger." His voice was laden with emotion. "Eventually, things seemed to fall in place for her, and she became docile and cooperative. She called me by my name and remembered me again."

Anne knew there was more.

"She has also been falling. She has fallen three times since you left. Nothing more serious than a small bruise or two with the first ones, but this morning she was wandering in and out of the bedroom. I was working, and the caretaker was preparing her some tea and toast. Karina's gait seems to be affected now. She shuffles along. Apparently she tripped in the doorway of the bedroom and fell. We believe she tried to stop her fall and landed on her left hand and arm. There is a break in that arm now."

"Oh, my God. Is she going to be all right? Where is she now?"

"The doctor tells me the arm will heal in time. She is at this moment having a cast applied. They gave her some sedation and pain medication so they could manipulate the arm into proper alignment first. They're going to keep her in the hospital overnight to observe her and have a physical therapist work on walking with her to see if they have any suggestions for us. I will need this day to arrange an around-the-clock caregiver to stay with us."

Anne did a mental calculation of the expense, doubling what they were currently paying for a daytime person. She winced at the figure.

"I can help more, Vati. I can send some extra money. Can you ask your insurance company if it can cover any more hours? And what about Dieter?" She was almost sure she already knew what her brother's answer would be.

"I haven't yet spoken to him today. He will be here in three days for a planned visit. He is on very important business right now, so I will mention it to him when he arrives."

Anne had never heard her father sound so lost. It was as though major pieces had been chipped away from the Rock of Gibraltar, leaving it in danger of collapse.

"Vati," she said softly, "when Mutti was first diagnosed, we spoke of possibilities in the future. I know we never expected her decline to be so rapid, but we may need to consider other arrangements soon." The specter of a nursing home had loomed over their earlier conversations, but they had both pushed that possibility to the back of their minds, a subject too painful to contemplate.

"I don't know," Marcel said. "I don't know if I can do that. I will try to take her home for now with more help there. And I will ask Dieter his opinion when he gets here."

*And it will still be up to us*, Anne thought bitterly.

"You do that," she told her father, keeping her voice even. "I'll call you tonight to check on her. And you," she added. They said their good-byes and hung up.

Anne kept her back to Lucas and the other employees unloading the truck. Her eyes were misty, and her hand clutched the cell phone tightly.

*I shouldn't have come out here and left them,* she thought, awash in guilt. Then she thought of Adehm, and what not coming out to California might have meant, how they might never have met at all. That thought was equally distressing. Like her mother's Alzheimer's, there didn't seem to be any easy solutions.

* * *

The next few days flew by for Anne. Now that all parts of the wastewater treatment plant had arrived, the actual installation of the system was happening. Her job of overseeing that process—one she only observed on a routine job—took up large chunks of her day on the Wood Mill project. Her responsibility was to ensure that everything was installed correctly, that not a component was damaged or misplaced, because the schedule held no room for error. Consequently, she watched as each piece was installed by the company they had hired for that purpose, and then she stayed around in the evening to double- and triple-check the work done that day. The result was that it was one very tired engineer who trudged up the steps every night to room 12 in the Pine Palace.

"You're dead tired," Adehm said over the phone. "I need to let you sleep."

"No," Anne said quickly. "I'm fine, really."

"Then it must be my stimulating conversation that's made you yawn three times in the last minute and a half. Anne, you're working too much."

"Nope, must be all that fresh, woodsy air catching up to me each night," Anne lied. She twirled the coiled phone cord between her fingers as she spoke, wishing the hotel room had a cordless model so she could wander around the room a bit. "The truth is, I don't want to miss any of this time with you, even if it is on the phone."

"You really can say the nicest things to a person." Adehm's reply was almost humble.

"I don't think it's being nice if it's true, like it is in this case."

"I hoped you'd be in the mood to spend time with me, but in person this time. I want to talk to you about our date."

"What date?" Anne asked. "You mean the date that's going to happen in..." She glanced at the calendar on the wall. "Three days from now?"

"No, not that one," Adehm said. "The one that's going to happen in twenty-one hours."

Anne sat up straight on the bed and assumed a cross-legged position. "You're coming back early! That's great! What do I need to wear for the date?"

"A car."

Anne was completely baffled by Adehm's statement and thought she must have misheard. "A car?"

"I was wondering if you'd be willing to meet me at the airport in Merced. I have a weekend field trip planned for our first date."

Anne was intrigued by what Adehm had in mind. "Going away for a weekend as a first date? Isn't that a bit presumptuous of you?"

"Are you complaining?"

"Not at all. E-mail me your arrival time, and I'll be there."

"Always prepared for an adventure, eh?" Adehm asked. "Were you a Girl Scout when you were younger?"

"We didn't have those in the German Democratic Republic. I could have been a member of the Young Informants League."

"You really had something like that?"

"You're entirely too gullible, Ms. Trent, and woefully misinformed about the former East Germany. I was joking, of course."

"That's me, anything to provide a friend with amusement. Your point is well-taken, and I should know more about Germany. I have a lot of questions."

"Such as?"

"Language, for one. How would you say something like, 'I miss you very much,' in German?"

"Ich vermisse dich sehr."

Adehm repeated the words over the phone, trying very hard to copy the accent correctly.

"Ich vermisse dich sehr. That's nice. And how would you say 'I wish I was with you right now,' in German?"

"Ich wünschte ich wäre jetzt bei dir," Anne said,

"Okay, Ich wünschte ich wäre jetzt bei dir. Got it. And last, how would you say, 'I would love to be holding you and kissing you at this very instant, and if you don't meet me at the airport tomorrow I'm going to explode just from the pure pain of wanting you'?"

Adehm's voice had taken on a lower timbre with the last question. It left Anne having a difficult time remembering the whole thing. "Um… Ich würde dich wahnsinnig gerne jetzt sofort in den Arm nehmen und küssen und wenn du mich nicht morgen vom Flughafen abholst, sterbe ich vor Verlangen nach dir.' I think."

"Wow, thank you. I didn't realize you wanted me back in California so much."

Before Anne could point out she was just providing a translation, Adehm continued. "You keep saying beautiful things like that to me, and I'm sure I'll have a lot more translating for you to do. Maybe we'll just start with single words or short phrases. Something like, 'there' or 'don't stop' or 'more,' for instance."

Anne swallowed audibly. The conversation was making her wish that the next twenty-one hours would simply evaporate.

"Du machst dir keine Vorstellung was dich erwartet."

"What does that mean?" Adehm asked.

"You'll have to come back to California to find out."

"Never let it be said that I don't love a mystery. I'm going to go e-mail you the itinerary details now. You get some sleep. Sweet dreams, Annegret."

Anne wondered how she would be able to sleep at all.

\* \* \*

Anne was alone in her room at the Pine Palace. She picked up the plastic water glass as if it was the finest crystal stemware. It had been fifteen minutes, and she figured the red wine had breathed sufficiently. She poured the wine into the tumbler and lifted it to her nose. She inhaled deeply.

*Berries, a mixture of them, along with a hint of pepper.*

She took a small sip and allowed the flavors to spread pleasantly in her mouth.

*Mein Gott, I needed this.*

She took another drink, and then set the glass on the bedside table. She dropped onto the bed. Two pillows propped against the headboard cushioned her as she leaned back and closed her eyes.

*Twenty-one hours. Adehm wants to meet me in twenty-one hours.*

Now that the initial elation of Adehm's invitation had worn off, more practical matters were foremost in her mind. As anxious as Anne was to see Adehm, it was the time constraint that had her worried. She visualized the wastewater treatment plant, clearly seeing the progress made in the installation of the apparatus.

*We picked a good company. They've been exactly on time, and they haven't made any mistakes that I could find.*

She opened her eyes and reached for the wine again. The third drink began to relax her.

*Not too relaxed, Anne Schneider, You've got a lot of work to do.*

She maintained her hold on the glass as her thoughts turned to the entirety of the Big Tree project.

*Any good engineer knows there are several critical times on a project. Big Tree is at one now. Then again, I think I'm at a critical point with Adehm, too.*

She lifted the glass to her mouth and drained the remainder of the wine.

*Time management, that's all this problem is. I merely need twice as much time on this phase as I have. It's simple.* She grimaced. *Simply damned awful. If she were in my shoes, what would Adehm do? Good grief, when did I start thinking like a bumper sticker?*

She turned on the bed and sat up. She stomped her feet on the rug in consternation.

*If I call Adehm and tell her I'm not leaving the job, will I run the risk of messing things up with her? I really want to see where this relationship might go. At the same time, if I do leave and my absence in some way causes the project to fail, I could lose any chance with Adehm anyway. More importantly, I'd lose respect for myself. Paging Solomon.*

She stood and walked to the bathroom. She splashed cold water on her face and then dried it with the soft, white, hotel towel. She stared at the image in the mirror.

*I'm an engineer. I solve problems all the time. I can solve this. What if I take every bit of peripheral work away from the installation company and let them focus solely on getting the plant mechanism in place?*

Quick mental calculations followed until Anne was certain she was making the correct decision. Going to her bag, she pulled out her cell phone and a scrap of yellow paper. She punched in the number written on the paper and waited for an answer. Lucas Barr answered on the third ring.

"Lucas? It's Anne. Listen, I've had a glass of wine, so I don't want to drive. Can you give me a lift back to Big Tree tonight?"

She listened to his reply.

"Good. Let's say fifteen minutes in front of the Pine Palace. While you're driving here, start coming up with a list of Big Tree workers who'd be interested in a little overtime."

\* \* \*

Anne waited outside the security checkpoint in the Merced Airport. She craned her neck to see the passengers making their way off the concourse and over to baggage claim. The small number of passengers heading toward her made picking out Adehm exceedingly easy.

"Adehm!" she called, waving her hand in the air. Adehm stopped, looked around, and spotted Anne. A warm smile replaced the mask of the traveler that had been on Adehm's face.

Anne recognized the mask as being the face most people wore when they traveled alone and sat very close to people they didn't know and didn't want to know. The look said, "Let's just pretend your elbow isn't invading my personal space for three hours, and we'll be fine."

Adehm walked out from the checkpoint to where Anne waited.

"How were the flights?" Anne asked, pulling Adehm in for a hug. She was warmed merely by feeling Adehm's return embrace.

"Not bad. The weather in Detroit wasn't great, but we took off on time." Adehm lowered her voice. "I tried bribing the captain to step on it and get me here faster, but apparently they like being right on time or something silly like that."

"What did you try to bribe him with?" They walked slowly toward the baggage carousel.

"That's for me and the captain to know," Adehm replied saucily. "I might be persuaded to tell you later."

"You can keep it to yourself," Anne said. "If it didn't work on him, it definitely won't work on me. I expect a far bigger bribe."

"Why would I try to bribe you? I was just trying to get some speed out of him."

"You mean you wouldn't want things to move a little faster between us? Hmm, my mistake, I guess." Anne turned to the baggage carousel as the mechanism started up, leaving Adehm with a grin of appreciative amusement on her face.

*   *   *

Adehm turned the rental car north onto Highway 99. They had decided to leave Anne's smaller vehicle in the airport parking lot, opting to take Adehm's car, which had been in the lot, waiting for her return. The powerful engine easily brought the vehicle up to the speed of the flow of traffic.

"You're eventually going to tell me where we're going, right?" Anne asked.

"Don't you trust me? I thought we established you had a spirit of adventure."

"I do. Some of my other fine qualities include a wonderful sense of humor, the ability to prioritize, and the good manners not to answer a question with a question."

Adehm laughed. "Touché. Okay, I thought a weekend up at Lake Tahoe would be just the thing for us. I hoped you weren't sick of the woods quite yet."

"Now you're talking. It may be more woods, but at least it will be different woods." Anne settled back into the plush leather seat. "Good call." She lazily reached over and lightly stroked the blue denim covering Adehm's right leg. She could feel a mild tremble under her fingertips.

"And they say talking on cell phones while driving is distracting. I don't think they took into account how distracting an engineer's hand on your leg is."

At Adehm's words, Anne started to bring her hand back, until it was held in place by Adehm's. "Hey, I didn't say I didn't like it." She kept Anne's hand folded in hers as they continued the drive in comfortable silence.

\* \* \*

The afternoon wore on, and three and a half hours later, Adehm brought the car out of the mountains and down into the Tahoe Valley. The late afternoon sun reflected off the bright blue lake, giving the whole area a golden glow.

"Anne, wake up. You don't want to miss this."

Slumped down in the passenger seat, Anne had been asleep for over two hours. She rubbed her eyes and yawned.

"Sorry, I guess I drifted off there for a bit. Yesterday was a little busy for me." She looked out at the scenery.

"It's spectacular," she said. "I've seen pictures in books, but they don't do it justice. I've been a lot of places, but this is breathtaking." She sat up higher and craned her neck to take in the beauty.

"Wait until tomorrow. We'll take a walk along the shoreline. The water is so clear you can see straight down to the bottom. I hope you don't mind if I keep my eyes on the road. Highway 50 into Tahoe has a lot of places where it isn't good to be caught gawking at the scenery."

"Just get us there in one piece, and I'll be happy." Anne lowered the window a short way. "You can really smell the pines, and the air is so crisp it reminds me of home a little," she said wistfully.

"Albuquerque is like this?" Adehm asked.

"No, I meant my first home, the one in Germany."

"I hope that's a good thing."

"Very. I was happy there as a child. I didn't understand the political situation at the time, and I understood it even less after the reunification. I knew how it affected us on a daily basis, but I thought how we lived was the same as everyone else lived, except for the language differences. East and West were quite opposite then, but not so much anymore. We've grown into quite the civilized country, with even a fast food place on every corner."

"If you think that's civilized, maybe you need to hit the woods more often. Sometimes I wish we were a whole heck of a lot less civilized than we are."

Anne smiled. "Does this mean I'll be seeing an uncivilized Adehm Trent this weekend?"

"You can see as much of Adehm Trent as you'd like to these few days."

Anne refrained from commenting on the double entendre as they drove into the outskirts of North Lake Tahoe. The motels didn't seem very busy. Maybe it was the wrong time of year for tourists. She assumed they would be packed soon with skiers, snowboarders, and others out to enjoy the winter playground.

"I guess reservations weren't a problem," Anne observed as they entered the city and she lost sight of the lake.

"No, reservations weren't difficult at all, but that's because we aren't staying in a hotel. I borrowed a friend's house for the weekend. We have to put a little food into the fridge and remember to turn the heat down when we leave, but for our first date, I didn't think I'd need anyone to put a mint on my pillow." Adehm turned off the main road and onto a side street, moving away from the lake. "The house is in a quiet neighborhood. You can hear a pine cone drop." They drove another quarter-mile before making a right turn and pulling up in front of a two story, A-frame house.

"This is it." Adehm got out of the car and stretched muscles cramped from sitting for the past few hours. "I love it up here. When I was young, my parents would rent the place and bring us up here in both the summer and winter. There isn't a season in Tahoe that doesn't attract me."

Anne watched as a squirrel crossed the scrubby front lawn and scampered up a nearby tree, carrying rodent foodstuffs in its mouth. "Some of us aren't taking the weekend off, I see."

"Poor guy. Let me go around back to get the key and turn the water on. Then maybe we can show that very industrious squirrel how to take some time off."

\* \* \*

"I can't believe it. It has to be beginner's luck," Anne said, as she slipped the white paper into a machine that would give her cash for the credits she had racked up on the quarter slots. "I started with just ten dollars, and now I'm cashing out sixteen dollars and seventy-five cents."

"You're a real high roller, that's for sure. I'm surprised the casino hosts haven't descended on us, trying to comp us food and a room, just to try to win a little of that largesse back from you," Adehm said.

"You can try to diminish my success, Miss I've-Got-Nothing-Left-In-My-Pockets-Except-Lint, but it won't work. Six seventy-five profit is six seventy-five profit. Okay, what's next?"

Anne had taken a liking to the bright, flashing lights and noise of the slots as the reels spun. After they promised to limit their gambling money, Adehm had shown Anne the ins and outs of casino action. They had put a dollar on the Wheel of Fortune, made a five dollar bet on a horse in the Sports Book, and played brightly colored chips on the roulette wheel. Anne had held her own, especially when they started on the slot machines, while Adehm's tiny bankroll had vanished in a short amount of time.

"I'm but a pauper now," Adehm said, "but I might have saved enough money to buy you a nice dinner. How about the steakhouse upstairs?"

"Sounds good to me. I saw their sign for steak and lobster, and if you're buying, I'm eating."

The women took an escalator up two floors to Jeremiah's Steakhouse. They were seated beside a large window, which looked out over the crystal blue waters of Lake Tahoe.

"The lake takes my breath away," Anne said as she gazed out the window, ignoring the menu provided to her by the hostess. "Too bad it's so damn cold right now. It looks good enough to jump right into."

"I've got news for you. The lake is damn cold in the middle of summer, too. It takes away the heat of a summer's day, but after a short dip, you're glad to get back into the warm sun again. Hey, don't get so mesmerized that you forget to order. Your glass of water isn't going to sustain you very long, and it's going to be hours yet until breakfast."

Adehm's comments seemed innocent enough, but Anne blushed anyway at the thought of what might preclude an early breakfast. She noticed that Adehm had put both their bags in the same bedroom of the borrowed house.

Anne quickly turned her attention to her menu. "I don't see anything more tempting than the steak and lobster I saw before," she said, scanning the offerings.

The waiter arrived with warm sourdough bread in a basket and took their orders. Adehm settled on a bowl of stew loaded with chunks of beef and brimming with vegetables.

They ate dinner in a comfortable companionship. The hostess lit the small candle on their table as they watched the sun set over the western edge of the mountains. Eventually, the Sierras claimed the bright orb, the sky changed to a deep purple, and the water took on an ebony appearance.

"Ready to go?" Adehm asked. "I think I want to get a good fire going in the fireplace tonight. It's going to be chilly."

They settled the bill, leaving a generous tip, and took the escalators back downstairs. Adehm directed them toward the parking garage, but as they passed the various gambling games, Anne's eye was caught by a round machine with numbered ping pong balls inside. The balls were being bounced around in a haphazard manner, like popcorn just heated to the right temperature so the hull burst.

"What's that?" Anne asked, watching as a few of the little balls slid randomly up two tubes.

"Keno," Adehm replied. "There are eighty numbered balls in that machine. They're mixed before each game. They pull out twenty of the balls for every game, at least the machine does. If you can guess which ones come out, you win."

"That's pretty simple. How much does it cost? I want to try it one time."

"You can play a lot of different kinds of combinations, but why don't you just pick a couple of numbers and give them a dollar? I wouldn't want you to invest too much in it."

"Why?" Anne glanced around the Keno parlor and saw several people making themselves comfortable at small desks, filling out their selections with the paper form and marker provided. "It looks like a popular game."

"To some extent, it is. If you play a lot of combinations, you can win enough to keep going for a while. The hard truth is that this is one of the most difficult games to win big. The odds for the player are actually less than those for roulette, and you saw how difficult that can be."

Anne hadn't even once hit the number indicated when the roulette ball finally fell into a slot. When she had picked odd, the number was even and when she picked black, it invariably came up red.

"Okay, I'll play this game only once, just to say I have. Besides, I'm using the casino's money, remember? It'll shave my profit margin down, but what the hell?"

Adehm showed Anne how to mark down the six numbers she had decided to play, smiling when Anne told her she was choosing birthdays and other numbers of days special to her. Her last choice was seventeen, the day of the month they had first met in Wood Mill. They took the ticket to the Keno writer, who exchanged the hand-marked paper with a computer-generated one showing Anne's numbers.

The balls began bouncing furiously in their round, plastic home. As the numbers escaped into the tubes, they were lit up on a large board behind the Keno counter. Simultaneously, the numbers were lit up on smaller boards located around the casino.

"My odds may be small, but it's kind of fun anyway," Anne observed. "Hey, I got one." She pointed out a winning number to Adehm, who nodded.

"You only need to get two more numbers to get your money back." Adehm couldn't help but smile at Anne's enthusiasm. It was the way Anne approached everything, with one hundred percent effort. Adehm leaned over and whispered in Anne's ear, "When we get back to the house, I'm going to show you just what a winner I think you are." She reached out the tip of her tongue and briefly touched the delicate earlobe with a quick move.

Anne's attention was completely claimed by the declaration and brief, but sensual, caress.

In front of them, the whirl of balls ceased and the last number was lit up on the Keno results board. Anne studied her ticket, checking her numbers against the twenty winning ones.

"Ich habe sechs!" Anne yelled. "Alle sechs."

"You can have that later, but there's no need to tell the crowd about it," Adehm said trying to encourage Anne to moderate her volume.

"No, sechs... not sex," Anne tried to explain. "I got all six numbers! What do I win?"

Adehm double-checked Anne's results, and all six numbers had, indeed, been drawn. They took the paper to the Keno window and watched as the Keno writer put the ticket in the machine. Then they stood as patiently as possible, waiting to be paid off.

\*　\*　\*

"Fourteen hundred dollars! Fourteen hundred dollars! Can you believe? Now we're talking beginner's luck." Anne fanned out the hundred dollar bills in her hand. This will keep Angela and Helmut in gourmet vegetables for a year. Hell, it might even keep me in gourmet vegetables."

Adehm smiled as she drove back to the house. Anne's excitement and sense of fun were infectious. Adehm had listened with silent amusement as Anne went over at least thirty different scenarios on how to spend the money.

"You don't have to decide about it tonight," Adehm said. "Why don't you just relax and bask in the knowledge that you're temporarily wealthy?"

"Good idea." Anne included Adehm into the smile that encompassed a major amount of the world at large. "This has been a lot of fun, and you're a remarkable tour guide."

Adehm kept her eyes on the road as she replied. "That's what this first date is about, remarkable things. Lake Tahoe, the mountains, the gambling, all of that."

"Those things are all for me," Anne said. "But technically this has been your first date, too. What's been new and exciting for you?"

"That would be you," Adehm replied simply.

Anne's gaming win suddenly seemed diminished when compared to the jackpot she had hit in being with Adehm.

# Chapter 12

Using a towel to dry the damp tendrils of her hair, Anne skipped down the final three steps of the staircase.

Adehm turned from her spot next to the fireplace to watch Anne's approach. Feeling her breath catch in her chest, she turned her back to the robe-clad woman and busied herself with arranging the fireplace screen to prevent stray embers from popping into the room.

"Find everything okay?" Adehm asked over her shoulder.

"Yep, I did. I almost finished drying my hair with the blow dryer when I remembered you saying you were going to start a fire. I decided I'd rather sit here with you than sit by myself upstairs." She glanced around the living room. An open bottle of wine sat next to two empty glasses. "You've been busy."

"I thought a toast to celebrate your big win would be in order," Adehm said, rising from the hearth. "The wine has been open long enough, I think." She poured two glasses and handed one to Anne. "To you, oh victorious conqueror of the casino." She clinked her glass against Anne's and took a sip. She could see Anne suppress a grin. "What?"

Anne's smile broke through. "I'm not naïve enough to think I had any skill in that win. It was luck, pure and simple. The image of anybody conquering the casino amused me." She raised her glass. "To you, who brought me to Lake Tahoe, entertained me lavishly, and made me feel more special than I've felt in a very long time." Never losing eye contact with Adehm, Anne sipped her Cabernet. An approving look appeared on her face as she tasted the wine. "Very good."

"It's one of my favorite wines. I slipped a bottle into the basket when we bought the groceries earlier."

"The wine is nice, but I was also referring to the weekend, the location, and the company." Anne leaned forward and placed a soft kiss on Adehm's lips. "This is very nice as well." She moved forward a fraction and kissed Adehm again. The heat in the second kiss rose perceptively.

When the women parted, Adehm's eyes were warm with emotion and anticipation. "We shouldn't waste this fire. Come sit with me?" She extended her hand toward Anne.

"Love to," Anne replied, taking Adehm's hand and allowing herself to be led to a large, fuzzy rug in front of the blazing fire. Crossing her feet at the ankles, she gracefully dropped to the floor.

Adehm settled behind her, wrapped her legs around Anne's body, and took the towel from her.

"Just sip your wine and let me do this," she whispered, her mouth very close to Anne's ear. She used the towel gently to remove the last of the moisture from the ends of Anne's hair. "Your hair is so beautiful. It feels like silk in my hands." Adehm tossed the towel onto a nearby chair and began almost reverently touching Anne's hair with her bare hands, letting the thick strands slip through her fingers. Anne responded to the attention by moving back more tightly against Adehm.

Adehm moved the hair from the nape of Anne's neck and deposited a gentle kiss there.

Anne twisted her shoulders to look at Adehm. She didn't speak as her right hand came up and touched Adehm's cheek. Using gentle pressure, she urged Adehm toward her, and the kiss she initiated left all thought of wine completely forgotten. The kiss lasted much longer than the previous two had, and both women were a little breathless when it finished.

Adehm moved the wine glasses to one side and returned her complete attention to Anne. She wrapped her arms around her in an unspoken request for more access.

Anne complied, turning around until she was seated across Adehm, almost in her lap. Anne brought her arms up and draped them around Adehm's neck. Pulling her forward, Anne kept her eyes open until the last second before the kiss.

Adehm thought the look in Anne's eyes was the most erotic thing she had ever seen. She returned the kiss enthusiastically, feeling her heart rate kick up.

"So long," Adehm murmured against Anne's lips. "This has been so long in coming."

"Too long," Anne whispered, seeking out Adehm's lips again. She felt Adehm's hands moving over her back, pulling her closer. The kiss ended, and Anne dropped her head to Adehm's chest, hearing the rapid thud of her heartbeat through the thin long-sleeved shirt. "This was inevitable, you know. From the very first."

"It was? Are you a fortune teller in addition to being a very talented engineer?"

"In some things. In the way I feel and in the people I'm attracted to. When I first met you and found out you weren't a man, I had a very difficult time keeping my eyes off you. You're a very lovely woman, you know." Anne could almost feel the smile appear on Adehm's face.

"Thank you, but you aren't exactly lacking in that department either," Adehm said with complete honesty. "I never noticed you trying not to look at me. Maybe that was because I was trying to keep you from noticing I was noticing you." Adehm was silent a moment, as if trying to figure out to herself what she had just told Anne. "I used to be much more articulate than this. The dazzling company must be muddling up my speech as well as my mind."

It was Anne's turn to smile. "Your speech is just perfect, as far as I'm concerned." She snuggled closer to Adehm, bringing her arms down over her shoulders in an enveloping hug.

They shifted so they could face the fire and watched the reds and oranges behind the screen in silence, enjoying their proximity to one another and the delicious anticipation.

"Anne?" Adehm said quietly.

"Hmm?" Anne replied from her place in Adehm's arms.

"When we were on the phone when I was in Detroit, you said something to me in German. Do you remember that?"

Anne thought about the conversation. "Yes, I said 'Du machst dir keine Vorstellung was dich erwartet' to you."

"You told me you would tell me what that meant when I got back."

"I did indeed." Anne lifted her head to look into Adehm's eyes. "It means 'you've got no idea what you're in for.'"

"Promises, promises," Adehm said as she moved in for another kiss. And another. And another. Adehm's hands roamed over the terrycloth expanse of Anne's robe before bringing her hands up to grasp both sides of the collar. She tugged gently but persistently, and the garment opened, revealing a fully nude Anne underneath.

Adehm broke the latest in a series of kisses to let her eyes feast on the exposed flesh. "Did I say you weren't lacking? I meant to say you're exquisite."

"You're recovering your ability to speak. What will we do about that?" Anne asked.

"I'm sure you'll think of something." Adehm leaned forward and chastely kissed Anne's cheek. That kiss was followed by one to the strong line of the jaw and another to the sensitive underside of Anne's neck.

Instinctively, Anne's head tipped back, allowing Adehm unfettered access.

Adehm took immediate advantage of Anne's inviting move. She placed a kiss on Anne's collarbone, while bringing her hand up to softly follow the path her lips had just traversed.

The touch of Adehm's hand produced a lashing of excitement in its wake. Anne strained for more of the touch, and Adehm didn't make her wait.

Adehm's right hand caressed Anne's breast lightly, trailing the fingers across the nipple, while her left hand and arm supported Anne, who was leaning even farther back. The budding under her fingers let Adehm know her efforts were being appreciated.

Anne closed her eyes and softly moaned her approval.

"Anne, look at me," Adehm directed, almost demanded.

When Anne's blue eyes opened, a fire was present there, every bit as blazing as the one in the hearth. "Anne, I want to make love to you. I want you right here, no more waiting. I want to touch you and taste you and love you."

Anne understood that Adehm needed this last bit of permission. She was struck by the generosity of the woman touching her. Even in the most passionate of circumstances, Adehm was letting her make the call. "Can't you tell I want that more than anything? Maybe more than anything in my whole life? Love me. Please love me." Anne realized Adehm had been holding her breath, waiting for her response.

Adehm moved her legs, allowing Anne to fully recline on the rug. Opening Anne's robe the rest of the way, Adehm gazed hotly at Anne's body.

A flush rose on Anne's skin under the intense scrutiny.

"You are beautiful," Adehm said simply. She pushed the robe off Anne's arms, then she rose to her feet. Their eyes met and held as Adehm undressed slowly, allowing Anne to enjoy watching her undress.

Adehm pulled her shirt over her head and tossed it over to join Anne's towel. Reaching behind her, she unclasped her bra, letting the straps drop off her shoulders. She removed the bra completely, giving Anne an open view of her generous breasts and hardened nipples. Adehm's chest rose and fell rapidly under Anne's torrid gaze.

Adehm's hand went to her jeans. She unsnapped and then unzipped the closures. Panties joined jeans in an inexorable descent down Adehm's long legs. She felt a rush of wetness as Anne's eyes followed the movement, lingering at the triangle at the juncture of Adehm's legs.

Adehm kicked the garments aside and knelt at Anne's side. Picking up Anne's hand, she directed it to her center. She pressed Anne's fingers into herself.

"Feel what you do to me. You've barely touched me, and I'm wet for you."

Anne slid her fingers through the abundant moisture she found there. "Ohhh," she moaned, feeling the silky wetness coat her fingers. Just as she moved to increase the contact, Adehm caught her wrist and gently removed Anne's hand.

"Not me yet. We have plenty of time for me. First, I want you. I've dreamed about this. Now it's time to make that dream real." She stretched out at Anne's side, dragging her hand up Anne's thigh, circumventing the area where Anne most wanted her attention, to once again touch Anne's breast. Adehm leaned over and put her mouth over Anne's, kissing her thoroughly. "I'll be back for more of that."

Adehm moved her head lower, now using her lips, tongue, and teeth in addition to her hands, to pleasure Anne. Slow strokes of Adehm's tongue, accompanied by sweeping touches of her fingers caused a moan to escape Anne's lips. Adehm looked up to see Anne's eyes close in pleasure. The sight caused her to redouble her efforts. After taking a taut nipple into her mouth, Adehm used her teeth to gently tease it into even further firmness. Releasing one nipple and moving to the other, Adehm took her time, creating a slow burn in herself.

Adehm's hand drifted lower, moving across Anne's soft belly, down to the softness of neatly trimmed curls the same color as the hair on Anne's head. The moisture Adehm found there assured her that Anne was ready for the most intimate of touches. Slipping her fingers through the dampness, she found the lips already open, inviting her touch. Adehm did not refuse the invitation.

Using her middle finger to glide up and down the opened furrow, Adehm found Anne's clit yearning for her touch. Circling and stroking the firm bundle, she felt Anne's hips take up an almost involuntary motion, matching the movement of Adehm's fingers.

Making her strokes longer and lower, Adehm found Anne's opening. Dipping a finger tentatively inside, she glanced up to see if Anne had any apprehension at the penetration. Finding none, Adehm continued her exploration, finding the heat and wet intoxicating.

A desperate whimper of pleasure from Anne stirred Adehm, and she lowered her head to Anne's wet mound. Reaching out with her tongue, she swirled it around the bundle of nerves as she kept up an even rhythm with her finger inside.

Anne jolted perceptibly when Adehm's mouth reached her. She leaned up off the rug until Adehm settled her back with her free hand.

"Please," Anne whispered. "I can't wait anymore. More inside me. Make me come."

Adehm added a second questing finger inside Anne, feeling an even greater rush of moisture as she did. The tempo she set up was faster, the stroking of her tongue outside matching the deep touches inside. Increasing both the rate and pressure, Adehm felt Anne's hips take on a frantic rhythm in response.

"Yes, yes..." Anne panted. And then she was there. Her back arched as a long groan escaped her lips.

Adehm held her tongue firmly against Anne's clit and stilled her fingers, holding them deep inside as Anne rode out her orgasm.

Long moments later, Anne relaxed back against the rug, unable to move except for the twitching in response to the small aftershocks of her climax.

Adehm gazed up from her place at the juncture of Anne's legs, over the flushed skin and damp flesh. Watching Anne as she reached her pinnacle turned a switch on inside Adehm, one she had thought couldn't be moved again. She slowly withdrew from Anne and moved up her body to cradle her lover in her arms.

"That was so beautiful, Anne. I loved watching you come for me. You're everything I could have imagined and so much more." The words flowed from Adehm, coming straight from her heart and entirely bypassing her brain. "I love you," she said, depositing small kisses along Anne's shoulder and neck.

Adehm felt Anne's body freeze. Realizing what words had last come out of her mouth, Adehm silently berated herself for pushing too far, too fast. She summoned her courage to lift her head to look at Anne. To her amazement, Anne was looking right back at her with a smile of satisfaction and happiness.

"You say the most phenomenal things at the most interesting times," Anne said.

Adehm blushed under Anne's scrutiny, more self-conscious than when she had stripped her clothes off earlier.

"I'm sorry. I didn't mean to say that out loud. Yet, I mean."

"I don't know why," Anne replied, her voice suddenly heavy with emotion. "I've wanted to say it to you for weeks. If you'll help me up, there's a perfectly good bed upstairs where I intend to show you just how much I mean it."

Adehm moved to her knees and then rose to her feet, pulling Anne up and into her arms.

"You're incredible, you know that?" Adehm said, kissing Anne with intensity that conveyed more than she could explain with words.

"I know," Anne said when the kiss finally ended. She nibbled Adehm's lower lip with her teeth. "But I'm going to want you to repeat that opinion when I have you on the receiving end of what you just gave to me." She moved out of Adehm's arms and led her to the staircase.

* * *

Entering the bedroom at the top of the stairs, Adehm was conscious of the chill in the house when it wasn't augmented by a fireplace or the heat from two very excited bodies. She went into the small bathroom off the bedroom and flipped on the heat lamp in there.

Anne pulled back the blanket and quilt from the bed.

"Don't jump in yet. There's a—" Adehm's words were cut off by a sudden shriek from the next room.

"My God, those sheets are cold!" Anne ran from the bedroom into the bathroom and into Adehm's arms. She tucked in close and murmured, "Now that's better."

"I was trying to tell you there's a heated mattress pad on the bed. Turn it on, and the chill will be off the sheets in no time. If you spend any time at all up here in the late fall or winter, you learn to appreciate that little detail." Adehm disengaged from Anne long enough to return to the bedroom and turn on the mattress pad.

"And what will we do for heat until that contraption works?" Anne asked when Adehm came back to the bathroom.

"We'll think of something to pass the minutes." She pulled Anne to her. "This, for instance." She kissed her, a loving interplay of lips and tongue.

"Good idea." Anne leaned back and looked Adehm directly in the eye. "You may have eluded me for a few minutes, but when the frost is off the sheets, I intend to generate enough energy to power several large cities."

Adehm's eyes didn't reflect her smile.

"Is something wrong?" Anne's hand went to Adehm's cheek in an encouraging touch.

"I wanted this to be everything you could ask for in a first date. While I'm not sure I could have held out from you physically for one additional second, I'm pretty sure I didn't have it in mind to tell you I love you."

"I'm not seeing what's wrong here," Anne said. "I adored hearing it. I feel that way myself. I do love you. Is the problem that you said it, but maybe you didn't mean it?" Concern clouded her eyes.

"No, absolutely not. I need for you to believe that, Annegret." Adehm held Anne's arms, willing her to see the truth of that statement in her eyes. "I've only told one other person that in my whole life, and maybe the problem is, I never thought I'd say it again." She brought Anne up against her, loving the feel of Anne's warm breath on her skin.

"You've surprised me," Adehm said, "with how quickly you've become the person I need near me all the time. When I was in Detroit, I'd be sitting in one of those boring meetings and be thinking about how much nicer it was when I was working in the office at Big Tree with you. I could see the little line on your forehead that comes out when you're deep in concentration. I could smell the scent of your perfume and the way it interacts with your skin. I couldn't get you out of my mind, and I realized it was because you're already firmly entrenched in my heart." Adehm turned her head and placed a light kiss on Anne's temple. "So here I am. I'm in love. In love and standing naked in a bathroom. Not the most romantic of places to clarify my declaration."

"I don't know. If you think about it, it's highly appropriate. Wastewater treatment is my specialty, and I like the image of being entrenched in your heart. I don't think you could have made it more perfect for the engineer in me."

Anne heard a small laugh emanate from Adehm. "I love you, too, Adehm. It doesn't matter where or when you tell me. I know you're not a woman to give your heart lightly, and if I'm only the second person you've said it to, then I'm in rare and marvelous company."

She hugged Adehm even tighter. "I hope those sheets are warm, because frozen or heated, I need you now." She pulled Adehm into the bedroom and down onto sheets that had lost their earlier chill.

"I loved it when you took your clothes off for me downstairs," Anne said as she settled onto Adehm's left side. "And I loved it when you teased me with that preview of how wet you were and what it was going to be like to touch you. The time for previews is over. I need to touch you. I need you to feel the love you inspire in me." Leaning over Adehm and bringing one leg up over Adehm's thigh, she dropped her mouth to Adehm's in a searing kiss that reignited all the passion they had experienced earlier.

Anne leaned up farther, training kisses across Adehm's jaw and neck. The movement forward brought Anne's wetness into contact with Adehm's thigh, and Adehm groaned with the sweet memory of Anne's taste on her tongue. She shifted a bit, bringing even more of Anne's mound into play.

"You made me so wet. Can you feel it? I'm still dripping with the pleasure you gave me." Anne used her fingertips to roll and tease Adehm's nipples into exquisite firmness before lowering her mouth to the rosy peaks. She lavished attention on the nipples.

"Now I'm going to touch you," Anne said, her voice filled with passion. "I'm going to touch you and make you know how much you're loved." Following through on her promise, Anne dropped one hand to Adehm's shaved mons and nudged her thighs apart. She placed her thumb directly on Adehm's clit, stroking across it with an easy rhythm, the way being eased by the copious moisture Anne found.

"You're so hot and wet for me. I want to taste you so much, but I'm greedy for myself, too," Anne whispered hotly. "I want us to be as close as we can get. Open your legs more for me."

Helpless to do anything but comply, Adehm spread her legs wider and watched as Anne lifted herself up and into the space that was created.

Lowering herself, Anne's tight curls came into contact with Adehm's shaved area.

Seeing Anne's intentions, Adehm felt a fresh flow of moisture between her legs.

"Oh yes, just like that," Adehm begged.

Anne ground her crotch against Adehm and then pushed her hand between their bodies. She first opened Adehm's lips, followed by her own. Removing her hand, she brought their mounds together. Anne angled herself up and initiated a sensual grinding. She tugged one of Adehm's legs up and out for even more contact.

They writhed together, the friction pushing them both toward their climax. Rhythmic movements soon gave way to erratic, frantic grinding.

"Come with me, love. Oh, God, I want you to come with me. So close... so close." Anne felt the beginnings of her orgasm stir within her and slid hotly against Adehm, determined to bring her with her when she went over the edge. Anne saw the torrid look in Adehm's eyes, and the huge rush was upon her, making her buck against Adehm in spasms of pleasure.

The additional contact released Adehm's climax, and she groaned in ecstasy. Eventually, the sexual St. Vitus's dance slowed, leaving the sound of heaving breaths and the scent of sex heavy in the room.

Anne dropped down to Adehm's chest. The body-length contact soothed her nerves, raw from the enormity of her orgasm. She placed her head on the sweat-slick breast under her.

"Too heavy?" Anne asked, not really caring about the answer.

"Don't you dare think of moving. Stay there. Just let your body touch mine."

"I'm not going anywhere. I'm right where I'm supposed to be."

# Chapter 13

"The rat bastard," Adehm said. "The dirty, scheming, rat bastard."

"I believe you called Mr. Neil Hammond that once before," Anne noted from her desk in the office at Big Tree. "I can only assume you're referring to him again, or you really need to add to your verbal repertoire."

"It's him all right," Adehm confirmed, fuming at Rodney's e-mail. "He's doing an audit of all West Coast projects. I just wonder who that's aimed at. I can feel the bull's-eye on my back."

"How is an audit going to affect you here? Nothing's wrong with the financials on this project. I should know. I submitted them all to you."

"There isn't anything wrong with our numbers," Adehm said, including Anne in ownership of the project. "This is a time waster and an annoyance for me. Neil knows the amount of time and work it takes to get ready for a project-wide audit. He's doing it to piss me off, and in that, he's succeeding famously. I've sent him every shred of paper on this project. I didn't need to be included in this witch hunt, and he knows it. That's what bugs the crap out of me."

"Can you do anything about it?"

"I highly doubt that. Bohannon is big on accountability, and he's sure to have cast a wide enough net that any protest I make will be viewed as suspicious." Adehm rose from her desk to pace the length of the office.

Anne moved to intercept Adehm as she passed by her desk. Reaching out, she pulled Adehm into a warm embrace. "Then if you can't do anything about it, let me work with you to make it as painless as possible. You know I'll do anything I can to help." She looked earnestly into Adehm's eyes.

"Can you kiss it and make it better?" Adehm asked, easing her tense posture and wrapping her arms around Anne.

"Gladly." Anne leaned forward and softly placed her lips against Adehm's.

Memories of their weekend together flooded through Adehm at the first touch. She moaned quietly as her body involuntarily responded to Anne's simple gesture of affection.

The kiss became more demanding than affectionate as moments passed and they continued to cling together. Adehm pulled back reluctantly, the realization of where they were strong in her mind.

"If we weren't at work, I'd show you the kind of audit I'd like to do."

That prompted two raised eyebrows from Anne. "Oh, really? You say that to me, and now you're going to leave me guessing what you'd be interested in?"

"I have a wide range of interests I could discuss with you. For instance, I'd be sure to note the softness of your hair, how it falls across your forehead when you move in to kiss me. It's so soft in my hands." Adehm brought one hand up from where it still rested on Anne's hip to touch the brunette tresses.

"It's beautiful. Like your eyes. The blue reminds me of the lake in Tahoe. When we were up there, I thought several times that you gave the lake a run for its money." She trailed a gentle fingertip along Anne's jaw line and over her full lips. "Then there are these two lovely assets. Your mouth intrigues me, awes me, and enchants me. You can drive me wild and drive me to distraction, sometimes both at the same time."

She leaned in and, forgetting her withdrawal moments earlier, placed a gentle kiss on the spot her fingertip had touched a second before. "There are so many obviously wonderful things about you. I could go on for hours and hours, and if you agree to meet me in my room after work tonight, I'd be glad to go over them in depth."

The playful, yet sensual, banter brought a smile forth from Anne. "I believe it would be my pleasure to—"

Anne's comment was interrupted by the ringing of her cell phone. A short piece from Wagner's *Die Walküre* indicated the call was coming from Anne's father. She shot Adehm a look of regret even as she moved out of her embrace. "I have to take this. It's my father."

"Of course," Adehm said. "I'll give you some privacy." She exited the office as Anne answered the phone.

"Hello, Vati."

"Annegret, you need to come home now." Her father's pronouncement startled Anne.

"What's wrong?" she asked anxiously. "Is it Mutti? Is something the matter with her?" Anne's decibel level rose with each question, and she could feel her heartbeat picking up as she waited for an answer.

"No. Well, yes. I mean, I don't know anymore." Marcel's voice broke, and his distress came across the line loud and clear.

"Calm down, Vati. Just tell me what's happened."

"It's Dieter. When he came into town to visit, I told him how Karina had begun to fail and her memory was nearly nothing now. I told him she could not be left alone at all, and I was looking for a place to give me some time off from being your mother's fulltime caregiver. The extra hours that we arranged for when she left the hospital after having her arm put in a cast have helped, but I don't sleep well. I worry that I will not hear her if she needs something, or I won't feel her get up in the night. She wanders."

Anne felt the pang of guilt slap at her conscience. If she had been back in Albuquerque, maybe she could have helped her father. Maybe she could have eased some of the burden on him.

"I have even taken to tying a shoelace to my wrist and hers at night so I will be aware if she gets up. It's becoming very difficult, Annegret. Karina needs feeding most of the time now, or she will just sit and stare at the food. She no longer has any control over her bathroom functions. I must crush her medicines and put them in jam so she will swallow them."

Then Anne heard something she had heard maybe one other time in her life. She heard her father start to cry.

"I only needed some time with your mother in a safe place. I just needed some good sleep so I can be strong enough to take care of her." He paused a moment and Anne heard him blow his nose. "Dieter came for his visit and saw Karina. You know it has been a long time since he last saw her. I think it must have been the shock of seeing her so much worse than before. She did not know him at all. This upset him very much."

Dieter. Anne's jaw tightened at the mention of her brother's name. Dieter had always left the care of their mother up to their father and her. He occasionally sent some money with instructions to do "something special for Mutti." Their mother was long past the time where she could appreciate much of anything out of the ordinary.

"What did he say, Vati?"

"He said we had not been doing a good job of taking care of Karina and that you should not have left for this job in California. He thinks I should sign over a Power of Attorney for your mother. He says it will be for the best, that I won't have to worry as much, but I think he feels I cannot make good decisions for Karina. Annegret, I am so tired. Maybe he is right. I thought that if I only had some extra rest, I could be strong enough again. Dieter thinks if I don't have all the paperwork and legal things to worry about, that I can still take care of your mother at home."

*And join her in her grave when she dies,* Anne thought. *Alzheimer's is robbing me of one parent. I won't let it take both of them.*

"We talked about this," she said. "We know that one day, Mutti will require care we can't give her at home anymore. This is all happening much faster than we thought it would. I don't think we're prepared for all this may entail. Listen, please don't sign anything right now. You have always been the best decision maker for Mutti. You still are."

"What will I tell Dieter? He wants my answer soon." The uncertainty in his voice was a testament to his distress. Marcel had never in his life been uncertain about anything.

"You don't have to tell him anything. I'll do it. I'll get the quickest flight home that I possibly can. On second thought, you can tell Dieter something for me. You can tell him I'm coming home, and I'm going to kick his ass when I get there."

"Annegret, I don't think that kind of—"

"I don't have time to debate my language at this moment. I need to book a flight back there. Don't sign anything or agree to any changes yet. I do want you to make an appointment for Mutti with her doctor. I don't understand what's going on with her. This isn't the way he said things would progress. It's all too fast." Anne chewed her bottom lip in thought for a moment.

"I'll call you about my arrangements, but don't worry. Patrick can pick me up at the airport, or I'll get a cab. Everything will work out. I'll be there soon." Anne hung up, not leaving her father room to question her plan. She opened a window on her Internet connection and typed in the Web address of her favorite travel planner. She was connecting to her destination when Adehm returned to the office.

"I'm glad you're done with your call, because I don't know what in the hell this means and I'm going to need your expertise to translate this stuff." Adehm held out a letter and the registered mail envelope it had apparently come in.

"Adehm, I know it's short notice, but I have an urgent..." Anne's sentence trailed off as the words on the paper started to make sense to her. "What the hell?"

Adehm shook the piece of paper in frustration. "What is it? I'm not sure what they mean by aeration vent fan. What is it, and why do we need one? And if we need one, why does this letter say we aren't getting one?"

"Hold on, let me read through this." Anne took the letter from Adehm and finished reading it. "I don't understand this. This was all ordered and taken care of a few weeks ago."

"Would you mind filling me in on what you mean? I realize I'm only the supervising executive on this project, but maybe I might have a clue how to fix this if I know what's broken in the first place."

"Okay, an aeration vent fan is a critical piece of the wastewater treatment plant," Anne explained. "When you process wastewater, you put it through a biological unit tank. There are several things that have to happen, but one of them is that microorganisms, plain old good bacteria, work on the carbonic matter. They render that matter into carbon dioxide and water, the kind of water we can release safely into the environment. There are a lot of factors that go into figuring out how this all comes about, but the whole process depends on the bacteria getting a couple of things... food and oxygen. The food we supply in the form of the waste we process. The oxygen is delivered by the aeration vent fan."

"I can understand that. Basically, if we don't supply the needed oxygen, we choke off the process."

"That's about the size of it. The aeration vent fan is essential. We never would have made an error in the order for that."

"That's what they're saying happened? I can check on that." She went to the filing cabinet that held all the invoices related to the Big Tree project. "Give me the company name again."

"Spanos Manufacturing. I've worked with them before, and I've never had a problem." She watched as Adehm fingered her way through the alphabetically-filed paperwork.

"Here it is." Adehm pulled a thin beige file folder from the cabinet. "We ordered that over four weeks ago. I don't get this."

"We knew when we ordered the fan that it would take some time," Anne said, "because they needed to specially fabricate it based on my calculations of the COD and other things."

At Adehm's shake of her head and lost look, Anne clarified her statement. "The chemical oxygen demand. Spanos did do the job to our specifications. That isn't the problem."

"Then what is?" Adehm asked, her exasperation showing.

"Apparently we cancelled the order."

"What the hell?" Adehm yelled as she crossed back to Anne's desk. She snatched the letter back. "There's got to be some mistake. Our records clearly show we placed the order and confirmed the invoice number with them." She took both the file and the letter to her own desk.

"Here's the problem," Adehm said, flourishing the letter. "The 'Send to' and 'Bill to' addresses are the same on their letter. Our order form shows that the part was to be sent to us here at Big Tree and that the bill for payment was to go to Bohannon Corporation in Detroit. They have the Detroit address in both places. I'm surprised they got this letter to us, but that at least shows they have the right address somewhere in their system."

She slumped back into her chair. "Good grief, it was only a clerical error on their part. My mind is boggled. Detroit should have figured out what was going on and fixed the address problem. I mean, how many aeration vent fans can Bohannon have ordered? The invoice number would have let them know the part was for the Big Tree project."

Adehm turned to her computer and began typing at a furious pace.

While she was occupied with that, Anne continued her search for airline connections to Albuquerque.

A final sharp rap on the Enter key and Adehm was back on her feet. "I've put Rodney onto finding out what happened back at Corporate. Meanwhile, let's get on the phone, clear this thing up, and get the part here pronto."

"It isn't going to be that easy," Anne said. "Did you see the last paragraph?"

Adehm lifted the letter again. "I came a little unglued when I read the first part. What's the rest of the bad news?"

"They want to charge us a restocking fee."

Adehm blew out a long breath. "Is that all? No problem. They should waive the fee when they realize that they made the mistake in the first place. Good business practice will take care of that."

"If you say so," Anne said. "But they didn't just put the part back on their shelves. That was a custom piece we requested."

Anne's news made Adehm stand very still. Every fiber in her body was taut as she carefully phrased her next question. "What did they do with it?" she asked.

"They've salvaged the raw materials for future use. The restocking fee they were requesting was only for the fabrication. Our aeration fan is destroyed."

"Mother fucker," Adehm said quietly. "Son of a bitch."

Anne found the low, intense words to be more intimidating than if Adehm had screamed them. She could see Adehm's mind working feverishly, using business acumen combined with sheer instinct to try to come up with a solution.

"If we can get Spanos to start on a new vent fan today, how long will it take to get here?"

"Probably the same four weeks, maybe less if we put some pressure on them."

"You can count on that. And once it's here, how long to install and get the treatment plant up and working?" The questions came rapidly.

"Another week, with perfect luck."

"We're going to make our own perfect luck. Okay, that's four weeks, maybe five at the outside." She walked to her desk and glanced at the project calendar. "That puts us in the same week that the State's inspectors are going to be here. That's going to be close, but maybe we can just make it."

"But Adehm, that means we won't have any time to run the plant and do our own testing. We'll only have the one shot to get everything right. That's a big chance to take. Is there any way to get the inspection put off another week or more so I can get some numbers for you and make adjustments if we need to?" Anne rose and went to Adehm's side. "Not testing first might mean the difference between passing and being shut down for good."

"The six months was a hammered-out deal. The fact we got that amount of time was only because we could prove economic hardship for this area. There won't be an extra minute, much less a week." Adehm reached out to take Anne's hand in hers. "Good thing we've got a talented and incredibly lucky team here. We're going to need that, but I swear, nobody's going to beat us if we work together."

Anne's reply to that statement was delayed by a sound from Adehm's computer alerting her to an incoming message. She left Anne to check the e-mail. Adehm tapped a few keys and read the news. A slight twitch in her jaw was the only indication of any reaction to what she was reading.

"It's my reply from Rodney. He didn't sugarcoat the news. He says, 'notification of pending shipment from Spanos Manufacturing to Bohannon Corporation was received by mail six days ago. I just confirmed. The invoice number for Big Tree project checks out. Spanos called, and order was cancelled by Corporate as made in error. The name on the order to cancel is—'"

"Let me guess," Anne interrupted. "Neil Hammond."

"Got it in one. I'm going to cut off his left ball."

"Why would he do that? Wouldn't it cost the company money? How did he think he could get away with it?"

"Want to place any of your recent gambling winnings on the coincidence of this sudden audit? His choices were going to be catching me red-handed at being incompetent, or waiting until time ran out and I screwed up this project anyway by not having the plant functional enough to pass inspection. Either way you look at it, I'm out. For good, very likely. In business, it's usually a case of what have you done for me lately? My history wouldn't be enough to save me from a disaster of this magnitude."

Adehm smacked her hand down sharply on the desk. "He has us in a corner, but we've got time to pull out a major comeback. Yeah, we have our backs to the wall, but I believe in us. We can do this. I've seen your work, and I know what I'm capable of. We make one hell of a team. I've got the woman I love, who's a brilliant engineer as well, on my side, so I'm pretty fortunate there. Maybe you aren't the only one with a little luck."

Anne fidgeted under Adehm's intense gaze.

"What?" Adehm asked, finally noticing. "What's bothering you? We can make the deadline, I know we can."

"The deadline will be extremely difficult, but it's not that..." Anne's voice trailed off. She found it hard to come up with the words which wouldn't make it seem like she was abandoning Adehm in her hour of need. Which she was. The feeling of being torn between her family responsibilities and her professional commitment was almost overwhelming. No, it wasn't just professional. She knew she was leaving the woman she cared about most in the world in the lurch. Tears welled up in her eyes at her divided emotions.

"Hey, there. You're starting to worry me now. Please tell me what the matter is before I start imagining the worst." Concern tinged Adehm's tone. She started toward Anne, to pull her into a hug, but hesitated. "Is it us? Have I done something wrong?" Concern now warred with fear in Adehm's voice.

"Oh, no. You haven't done anything wrong." Anne closed the space between them and wrapped her arms around Adehm tightly. "I love you. You could never do anything wrong when it comes to us. It's me who's about to do something wrong."

They were practically cheek to cheek in the embrace. "Tell me," Adehm said, her voice barely above a whisper.

Anne disengaged from Adehm, feeling as if she were already taking the first step away.

"I need to go home," she said in a voice devoid of all emotion. The flat tone belied the emotional turmoil under the surface. "The call from my father earlier wasn't good news. My mother seems to be failing at a much faster rate than we expected. My brother, Dieter, is putting enormous pressure and guilt on my father. I don't know how much more he can take. He needs me. Please understand."

Adehm's hands, which were still on Anne's arms, suddenly dropped to her side.

"I thought you had everything taken care of at home."

"I believed I had. I hoped I had. I don't know why the changes have happened, but something's wrong. I can't leave my father to fight everything on his own."

"But it's fine to leave me," Adehm spat out. Angered flared in her eyes. "You knew from the start that this project needed you every inch of the way. Now something happens at home, and you're ready to drop everything."

"I don't want to. I *have* to. My parents need me. I have an obligation to them."

"And you don't have one to me? You tell me you're in this job until the end. You tell me we can get this done together. You tell me you love me, and now you run out on it all? You run out on me?"

The harsh words stung like the crack of a whip. Anne hung her head, knowing she'd let everyone in her life down in one way or another.

Adehm stalked to her desk and picked up the phone. "Lucas? Arrange for someone to drive Ms. Schneider back to Wood Mill. Yes, she's leaving immediately." She dropped the phone back on its cradle and stared blankly at Anne.

"Adehm…" Anne took a step toward her.

"Don't." Adehm raised a hand in a command to stop. "Just don't. Get out of here. Go now. I'll have your things packed and sent back to you. We're done."

Anne received the message loud and clear. Being done didn't merely refer to their business dealings. Tears filled her eyes as the realization struck her. She went to her desk to retrieve her laptop computer and her shoulder bag.

"I'm so sorry, Adehm. More than you'll ever know," Anne said as she gathered her things and headed for the door.

"Not so sorry that you'll stay. Not so sorry that you'll finish the project. Not so sorry that you won't leave me in one of the toughest spots of my life." Adehm raised her chin, daring Anne to deny it.

Anne couldn't. "No, not that sorry." She opened the door. "Much more than that."

As Anne left, Adehm could only gawk at the open door, unable to muster enough of her business mask to hide her complete devastation.

# Chapter 14

*She left. I can't believe she's gone. Bullshit to the left and right of me, and she bails.*

It had been two hours since Adehm had watched Anne walk out the door of the manager's office. Nothing had happened in that time to abate her anger and hurt.

*I shouldn't have relied on her. I shouldn't have trusted her. Where were my brains? I know better than to trust anyone. You broke your own rules, Adehm, and this is what it got you.*

Adehm paced the office, wishing the décor included something unimportant and inexpensive that she could throw and break. The emotional turmoil took its toll, and Adehm's temples throbbed with the beginnings of a dull headache. She went to her desk and retrieved a bottle of ibuprofen from the top drawer.

*I wish I was one of those executives who keep a bottle of whiskey in the desk. I could use a belt about now.*

She took four pills from the bottle and popped them into her mouth. After washing the pills down with two large swallows of the cold coffee from the mug on her desk, she leaned back in her chair. Using her fingertips, she gently massaged her temples.

*I can't think about this now. Work is what's important. I need to get Rodney to deal with the Spanos order. The original invoice needs to be faxed and then followed up with a confirming letter reinstating the custom order. Then I need to get Lucas Barr up here and go over the strategy for the next few days. With the vent fan not here, progress might slow down, and I'll need to make a contingency plan for hiring a new engineer if Anne doesn't come back.*

She stopped massaging and dropped her hands to her lap.

*Who am I kidding? I need Anne.* As the words flashed across her mind, Adehm felt the simple truth of them.

*I do need her, but she's gone. Damn it, of all the times for family issues to come up. Doesn't she know that when it comes to business, family has to take a backseat?*

Adehm sat very still in her chair and then slumped forward, arms wrapped around her midsection. She knew the sudden queasiness she felt had nothing to do with the fact she'd taken twice the recommended amount of ibuprofen.

*What a joke. I've stomped around here for two hours like a sanctimonious bitch who's never known what it's like to deal with a seriously ill family member.*

She reached for her mug again, but pulled her hand back. Cold coffee wouldn't combat the bile rising to the back of her throat.

*God help me, I do know. I know exactly how it feels to worry about someone you love. I've experienced the grinding guilt of needing to work and at the same time, needing to be home.*

An emotional dam broke somewhere inside Adehm, and memories of Shannon's illness and death cascaded through her. She yanked her cell phone from her pocket. Finding the number for the Pine Palace, she hit the call button.

"Pine Palace Hotel," Len answered.

"Len, it's Adehm Trent. Anne Schneider was called away from Big Tree on an emergency, and she left something behind. I was wondering if she's still at the hotel."

"No, ma'am. She left with a small suitcase and her laptop computer about forty-five minutes ago. She gave me her room key, but she asked to hold the room, so if you need to put something in there, I can open it and then lock it back up."

"That won't be necessary. Thank you anyway."

She hung up without explaining that what Anne had left behind at Big Tree was Adehm. She opened her phone again and scrolled to Anne's number. Slowly, she closed the phone.

*This can't be over the phone. I need to look her right in the eye when I apologize and beg her forgiveness.*

Adehm booted her computer and searched for flights to Albuquerque. She realized Anne would barely make her first connection in Merced, and Adehm couldn't make it at all. She opened her phone for a third time and used the speed dial.

"Rodney, I need an enormous favor. Who do we know on the West Coast?"

\* \* \*

Anne used her lengthy layover times in San Francisco and Las Vegas to compose a long letter to Adehm. She knew there was no way she could explain about or apologize for her personal decision, but she had to try to salvage a bit of professional pride. She had broken her contract, and Clearly Perfect would pay dearly for that, but she was determined to do whatever she could to make the Big Tree project end in success for Adehm.

In as non-personal a way as possible, she delineated each step Adehm would need to take to keep the Big Tree plant on track and give Bohannon its best chance to pass the State inspection. Her handwritten notes were precise, detailed, and completely professional. Anne knew if she added even one line of personal regret, she risked making Adehm hate her even more than she probably already did. Maybe even more than Anne hated herself.

As she stepped off the ramp of the Jetway and onto the concourse in Albuquerque, she mentally ran over an agenda of things she needed to do immediately. She had phoned Patrick to ask for a ride from the airport, promising a complete explanation when she saw him. She needed to go straight home to assess the changes in her mother and to be sure her father had arranged a visit to Karina's doctor. Then she needed to meet with Dieter and find out exactly what his problem was. Another dozen notions occurred to her as she proceeded to pass beyond the security checkpoint.

"Need a lift somewhere?" a familiar voice asked at her side.

Anne's knees nearly buckled as Adehm stepped into her line of sight. Anne's carry-on bag fell to the floor, and her mouth opened with a million questions. She assumed it was shock that prevented one sound from issuing forth.

Adehm picked up Anne's bag and guided her to a grouping of chairs nearby. She set Anne's bag on the floor and indicated they both should sit. Then she took Anne's hands in her own.

"Before anything else, let me say this. I love you, Annegret Schneider. I was so wrong to be mad at you." She raised Anne's hands to her lips and kissed the back of them. "I love you. Please forgive me for not being there for you. Did I mention I love you?"

Anne smiled then, and Adehm's brief flash of humor helped her to find her voice.

"What are you doing here? How did you get here? I can't believe it's really you." Anne brought one hand up to cup Adehm's cheek. "But it is."

"You took commercial flights on a last-minute ticket. I drove like a bat out of hell straight up to San Francisco and called in a favor to hitch a ride on a friend's company jet. Okay, they weren't going to stop in Albuquerque, but a tiny side trip wasn't a big deal." Adehm gazed deeply into Anne's eyes. "We have a lot to talk about, but the airport isn't the place to do that. I haven't said this since college, but will you take me to your place?"

"Well, Patrick…" Anne glanced around.

"Is at home, waiting for your call to tell him you've landed safely. He was very accommodating about your transportation, especially when I dropped the Bohannon Corporation name."

"Then absolutely, but Adehm, aren't you going to lose everything back at Big Tree?"

"We'll solve one problem at a time together, and we'll start with the most important one first. Now let's get out of here and get moving."

Anne allowed herself to be guided to baggage claim to retrieve her suitcase and then out to Adehm's rental car. Before she knew it, she was giving directions to her apartment as Adehm drove them along Interstate 40.

*   *   *

Anne opened the door to her apartment, dropping her carry-on bag with her computer just inside the doorway. She dashed to the hamster cage located in one corner. She tapped gently on one of the plastic houses that formed the dwarf hamster city.

"Angela… Helmut…" she called softly as she scanned the cage.

Adehm closed the front door and deposited their suitcases next to Anne's carry-on. She came up behind Anne just in time to see a tiny, furry animal burrow its way out from the pile of bedding in the cage. Another quickly presented itself.

"Adehm, this is Helmut, and that one over there is Angela." Anne indicated the respective rodents. "The best dwarf hamsters on the planet."

"Or at least in Hamsteropolis," Adehm said, eyeing the elaborate cage.

"If you love something, treat it well. Wish I had remembered that when I was dealing with you."

"Hey, that goes both ways. I didn't exactly do my best to see what was going on with you either. You hadn't been gone very long when I realized you weren't the sort of person who would take off and leave an important project for less than the very best reasons. I decided I was going to help you work through those reasons, and if we did it together, as a team, we might just get back in time to finish up Big Tree. It's not like we can't run some of the project from here. We have our information computerized, and oddly enough, I heard somewhere that telephone lines go from Albuquerque to California. I also called Lucas Barr and told him if he wants to be more than an assistant to the interim plant manager when this process is complete, he better be ready to eat, sleep, and live wastewater treatment for the next little while."

"I bet that went over well."

"I don't care how it went over," Adehm said. "If he wants the top job, then now's the time to pull on his big boy jockeys."

"So, now that we have our intentions all cleared up, what's the battle plan?"

"First, I think we need to find out what's going on with your parents and your brother before we can formulate a battle plan on the Big Tree front. I have a conference call set up with Lucas for tomorrow, so that's on track. And as far as the 'us' front is concerned, it's my intention to kiss you very thoroughly before we think for one more second about our other problems." True to her word, Adehm pulled Anne into her arms and kissed her. The kiss was a mixture of longing and tenderness.

"I missed that so much," Anne said after the kiss. "It's not been that long, and I still missed it like crazy."

"Me, too," Adehm said, her lips now traveling over Anne's cheek to her jaw line. "I missed you."

The ringing of Anne's cell phone broke the intimate moment. Anne rolled her eyes at the interruption. She managed to open and answer her cell phone before it went to her voicemail.

"Hello, Vati," she said, having noted the caller by the individual ring tone.

Adehm stood by her, touching her arm and shoulder in an unconscious show of support as Anne listened to her father.

"We'll be right there," Anne said. She closed the phone and pushed it into her shoulder bag, looking for her car keys at the same time. "My mother has been taken to the hospital. My dad just gave me her room number. Apparently, they're getting a neurologist to consult on her case. I want to get there as soon as possible to see what the hell is going on."

Adehm turned away from Anne. Anne wrapped her arms around Adehm from behind.

"Don't worry, love. Later we'll pick up right where we left off." Moving around Adehm, Anne looked directly into her troubled eyes. "I promise."

\* \* \*

Adehm was glad they'd had a larger vehicle than this on their way from the airport. Anne's subcompact car would have accommodated them and their luggage, but not with more than an inch to spare.

"Like this model, do you?" she asked as Anne maneuvered the tiny automobile through the Interstate 40 traffic. Anne gestured noncommittally and made her latest lane change in what seemed to Adehm like a fraction of a second before flipping on her turn signal.

"It's okay. Gets me around, and it's sweet on gas mileage. I swap for one of Patrick's cars when I go out of town on a job. This thing won't hold all my equipment plus both computers."

"Or one passenger and their medium-sized legs," Adehm said. "Nice vanity plate though." The red and yellow New Mexico plate read "NGINEAR."

"I thought that one up myself," Anne said proudly. "Too bad you can't shorten high-powered and fabulously sexy corporate executive. Then you could have a vanity plate, too." Anne punctuated her words with a two-lane crossover, barely making her exit.

"Is the hospital your mom in a trauma center?" Adehm asked.

"Yep, it's the only one in New Mexico. Why?"

In reply, Adehm closed her eyes and made a swerving motion with her hand.

Anne laughed. "I learned to drive in the land of the Autobahn, remember? Albuquerque's easy compared to that."

"The difference is I'm fairly certain Albuquerque does have a speed limit," Adehm said.

"I like to think of it as a speed suggestion." The playful smile on Anne's face faded as the University Medical Center came into view. "There it is."

Adehm glanced up at the adobe-colored building. They were both silent as Anne pulled into the parking garage and found a spot on the third floor. They exited the car together; Anne grasped Adehm's hand. "Thank you for coming here with me."

Adehm nodded in reply.

They walked across to the main building and entered the lobby. After choosing the proper elevator, they rode up several floors. Anne consulted the paper she had written her mother's room number on and then looked at a sign on the wall. "This way," she said, leading off toward the left.

The door to Karina's room was open, and Anne could see her father sitting in a chair beside the bed. Karina was very pale and seemed to be asleep. Anne moved quickly to her father and threw her arms around him as he rose. She felt him return her hug with an awkward patting of her back.

"I'm so happy to see you, Annegret. I've needed you here. Karina has needed you."

Anne stayed in her father's embrace until he fidgeted in her arms. He had never been the demonstrative parent, and now Anne turned to the one who had been.

"How is she?" Anne asked, keeping her voice lowered and her eyes fixed on her mother.

"She's so quiet," Marcel said. "She doesn't even open her eyes when I call her name. I've never seen her like this."

Anne watched the blanket that covered her mother's chest rise and fall rhythmically. Intravenous fluid was regulated by a machine at the bedside. A catheter draining yellow fluid was connected to tubing that disappeared under the covers near her mother's thigh.

"Has the neurologist been in to see her yet?" Anne pulled her gaze away from her ailing parent.

"She was here earlier, poking and prodding and tapping your mother with a small rubber hammer. She said she was going to review the scans they took of Karina's brain and would be back to tell me... tell us... the results."

"And Dieter?"

"He stayed at the house this morning. He said he needed to take care of some paperwork for his business and answer messages on his computer. He told me he would try to come by the hospital later, but he asked that you call him as soon as possible."

"I'll bet he did. Unfortunately for him, I have other more pressing priorities right now. I only want to know what's happening with Mutti." Anne's voice rose a little with her words, and she looked toward her mother to see if she had been disturbed. If Karina knew anyone was there, she gave no indication of it.

It was then Anne remembered Adehm. She turned to introduce her.

"Vati, I'd like you to meet someone very special. This is Adehm Trent, and she's…" Anne's words trailed off as she realized that she and her parents were the only people in the room.

In confusion, she went to the door and glanced both ways down the hall. She was just in time to see Adehm step hurriedly into the elevator.

*   *   *

Anne walked off the elevator and into the lobby. She had given her father only a brief word of enlightenment before leaving. She had been at a loss to explain Adehm's sudden disappearance.

She surveyed the lobby area, but Adehm wasn't there. Through the glass doors, Anne saw her just outside the main entrance, pacing and punching numbers on her cell phone.

Adehm nearly ran into Anne as she emerged from the lobby.

Despite her curiosity, anger was Anne's first reaction. "Business now?" she accused, seeing Adehm on the cell phone. "Can't you leave your damn job behind for a few minutes?" Anne took a breath to continue, but stopped before the next sentence even started.

Adehm was pale, a sickly hue replacing her normally healthy color. There was a fine sheen of perspiration on her forehead, and her hand trembled as she held the phone. "I can't," she told Anne. "Please, I just can't."

"What is it, Adehm? What's the matter?" Anne steered them to the corner of the building, away from curious eyes.

"I didn't realize it would be so bad," Adehm said, her voice filled with anxiety. "I thought I could deal with it, master it like every other challenge, but this is one hell of a lot tougher than I expected."

A wave of uncertainty hit Anne like a blow to the solar plexus. She wondered if she had asked too much of Adehm and their recently-minted relationship. Apparently, her internal worry transferred to her facial features.

"No, no, Anne. It's not you, and not about us. It's just me and how I react to these places. When Shannon was sick, I went into more hospital rooms than you can imagine, including being in one every minute of the last twenty-three days of her life. I can describe every moment of that horrible time, but if I even think about it, my stomach hurts and my heart beats a mile a minute. I know it's all in my head, but it's in there in a powerful way. I figured maybe this time it would be different, but it's not. The smell of disinfectant, the linoleum on the floors, and every noise brings it all back."

Anne had never seen Adehm look as shaken as she did at that moment. "Was it that bad?"

Adehm let out a rueful laugh. "Bad? Not bad if you don't mind having your heart ripped out of your chest while you're wide awake. I saw someone I loved wither away, no matter what we tried. I was with her the day she woke up from surgery to find a bag on her abdomen. She was brave then, but when she was able to go home, she cried nearly every time it needed to be emptied or changed. She hated the colostomy and hated herself with it. We never made love again after the surgery. She shut the door when she showered, and when she got to the point where I needed to help her bathe, she wouldn't look me in the eye. Shannon would let me hold her and kiss her, but anything more physical than that was something she couldn't deal with." Adehm swallowed hard, her eyes filling with tears.

"There's not anything about hospitals I can't tell you. I can tell you what time in the morning the lights come on in the rooms so the lab person can draw blood. I can tell you which medications are going to make you so nauseated that you can't stand to have the lid taken off your supper tray. Worst of all, I can tell you how someone looks after they've died. One moment they're breathing, still the owner of that thing that makes us the humans we are, and the next moment, they're so still it seems like there was never any animation to the body at all." Adehm caught her breath, the tears slipping down her checks now.

Anne waited silently.

"It's the damnedest thing. Literally, one second is the difference between your lover being there, and then not. That body, that prison, is still there, but she's gone. And she's gone forever." Adehm's voice cracked with emotion.

Anne could stand it no longer. She pulled Adehm to her in a fierce hug.

"And this is the kind of place it all happened in. I can't be in there, Annegret. I love you, but I can't go back inside."

Anne nodded and tightened her hold. Moving back, she looked into Adehm's eyes. "I can't not be in there."

"I know, and I'm so very goddamned sorry... again."

Anne nodded as she fished her keys from her pocket. She removed one from the ring. "Here's the apartment key. You can get there?"

Adehm lifted her cell phone in reply. "This phone can do everything but drive me there itself. I can get a cab." She straightened her shoulders and wiped the tears from her cheeks.

"Well then, I suppose I should get back in there. My mother and father need me." Anne moved away, her hand running down Adehm's arm as they separated, until only their hands touched, then held.

"I love you," Adehm said again.

"I know," Anne replied as their fingertips parted. "But that might not be enough."

# Chapter 15

Anne lingered in the lobby long enough to see a cab pull up and Adehm slide inside the back door. The pain of that sight had to be pushed aside, so she could deal with the more pressing issue, which was her mother's health. As Anne neared the door, she heard her father's voice and a female one she didn't recognize.

"Annegret," her father said as she crossed the room and went to his side. "This is Dr. ..."

"Ebrahimi," the woman supplied. She extended her hand to Anne, who shook it. "I'm the neurologist consulting on your mother's case." Anne glanced at her mother, concerned their conversation might have news which would further confuse or agitate her. Karina seemed completely unaware of them. Perhaps sensing Anne's uneasiness, Dr. Ebrahimi suggested they continue their conversation in a small conference room located at the end of the hall.

"Of course," Marcel said, following the doctor out the door. Uncharacteristically, he took hold of Anne's arm for support, even though he outwardly appeared calm and prepared for whatever the doctor might say. From that one gesture alone, Anne knew he was anything but.

When they were seated at the small round table in the conference room, Dr. Ebrahimi brought out a writing pad with a large drawing of the exterior of a human brain next to a picture of a cross section of the same organ and a third picture showing the brain in cross section from the top. It was obvious the doctor had used the visual aid many times before.

"Mr. Schneider, I've taken a look at all the results of the tests we've performed on your wife since her admission. I've reviewed the scans with the radiologist, and we're in agreement with what we're seeing."

Dr. Ebrahimi took the pad and shaded in the frontal lobes of the brain on all three printed views. "These are the areas of the brain affected by Karina's Alzheimer's disease. Both the CT scan and the MRI films showed the same severe white matter changes associated with Alzheimer's. These changes in and of themselves could explain Karina's problems with swallowing and walking and also her cognitive issues. Her level of confusion and deterioration of higher functions, such as memory and the like, are something you are both aware of, correct?"

Anne and Marcel nodded.

"The Alzheimer's does not explain her loss of consciousness this morning," the doctor continued.

Anne jerked in shock. "When did she—"

"I tried to reach you, but you were on the way here," her father said. "Usually your mother wakes before me, but she didn't this morning. I called her name, but there was no response. I even shook her arm, but there was nothing."

"Your father called an ambulance and Karina's primary physician, who notified me," Dr. Ebrahimi said. "Your father and brother reported that your mother had been confused but responsive when they put her to bed at ten last night. Karina was already going to be scheduled for an outpatient MRI, so we went ahead and did it on an emergency basis."

An uneasy feeling began to gnaw at Anne's gut.

"The CT scan hadn't been helpful, but the MRI was. It showed that Karina suffered an infarct here." The doctor shaded in an area on the picture that showed the brain from the top. "This is an area that is supplied blood by the middle cerebral artery." She stopped her explanation and changed to layman's terms. "In other words, Karina has had a stroke."

The impact of the doctor's words sent a chill so severe through Anne's system that she almost missed the rest of the explanation.

"Not only has she had a large stroke, this was preceded by a series of smaller strokes. The MRI shows several areas that have been affected. It's quite possible the signs of these strokes may have been masked by her Alzheimer's disease. The symptoms were put down to a progression of her chronic disease. It does happen, and there really would have been no way to know, not until the symptoms were much more pronounced, much more rapidly."

Anne's voice became almost unnaturally calm. "And what does this mean for my mother?" She almost dreaded the answer.

"An ischemic stroke is very similar to a heart attack, but in the brain. The affected area in the brain loses its blood supply, usually from a blood clot or disease in the vessels of the brain itself. Once the blood flow is interrupted, that part of the brain does not receive adequate oxygen, and the tissue dies. The amount of injury to the brain tissue determines if the symptoms are mild, such as slurred speech and weakness or, as in your mother's case, an altered level of consciousness."

Anne glanced at her father. He seemed to understand what the doctor was saying, but he wasn't asking the one question she knew they were both wondering about.

"Will she wake up?" Anne asked.

The doctor took the pad off the table and slipped it back into the pocket of her lab coat. Karina's pathology disappeared from view.

"I don't know, Ms. Schneider. I've started Karina on an anticoagulant. You may have heard it called a blood thinner, and we are giving her fluid and electrolyte support, but I can't say right now if she ever will awaken."

"Is she going to die?" Marcel asked. His voice was quiet, only a little above a whisper in a church.

"I don't know that either. I wish I could be more definite, but I'd like to observe her another day or two and see what happens. To be very honest, I think I should ask you to consider the question of what we should do if her heart or breathing should stop."

Marcel nodded, saying nothing. His gaze dropped to the tabletop.

"Meanwhile, Karina's internist will follow her care overnight and call me if any new problems arise." Dr. Ebrahimi stood and hesitated, giving them the time to ask any other questions they might have. Marcel and Anne had none. "I'll see you both tomorrow." The doctor left the conference room and the despair of the two people who remained there.

\* \* \*

"I don't care which airline gets me back to California, just make some reservations, and I'll get to the plane."

"I'll get right on it, Adehm." Rodney said. "I'll text you the information."

Adehm snapped her cell phone shut. Leaning back into the seat of the cab, she took in her surroundings. The driver was guiding the cab through the traffic. His attention was on his driving, but a radio played softly in the background. Adehm realized she didn't understand the language on the selected station.

"What are we listening to?" Adehm asked. Since she'd left the hospital, she felt much more relaxed.

"It's the big Navajo station from Window Rock, Arizona."

Adehm listened to the unfamiliar language. "Do you understand what they're saying?"

"Most of it. My grandparents were full-blooded Navajo. They lived up near Tuba City in Arizona. Sometimes I like to listen in on TNN, just so I don't forget the language. You never know when the Army will need some wind talkers again."

"I suppose not," Adehm said. "I take it you don't speak Navajo at home?" She waited for a reply as the driver yielded to oncoming traffic before making a left-hand turn.

"Not likely. I'm married to a third generation Irish-American. We don't speak Gaelic either." The driver caught her eye in the rearview mirror and winked at her.

Adehm felt a smile cross her features for the first time since watching Anne at the dwarf hamster palace earlier in the day.

*Anne.*

"As a matter of fact, you're the last fare of the day, then my shift's done, and I'm driving home. It's my turn to cook. My wife's a high school teacher, and some days those kids walk right on every last one of her nerves. She called me earlier, and it sounds like they did that today, so on days like this, I like to do the cooking for her."

"That's really sweet of you."

"Nah, I'm just afraid she'll be so pissed off one night that she won't pay attention to her cooking, and she'll accidentally poison me. This is just self-preservation." He grinned as he pulled the cab up in front of Anne's apartment building. "The funny thing is, I hate to cook, but it's what you do when you love somebody, right?"

He clicked off the meter. "That's fourteen bucks."

Adehm handed him a twenty-dollar bill. "Keep it," she said.

The driver acknowledged the generous tip, and Adehm climbed out of the back seat. Her earlier agitation had left her completely.

A chilly breeze caused her to pull her jacket collar up, but other than being cool, the early evening was turning out to be beautiful, with a scattering of stars just becoming visible in the twilight. She pushed her hands into the jacket's pockets and felt the key Anne had given her. The metal was cool in her palm but began to warm up as she held it. Instead of heading into Anne's apartment, Adehm walked slowly down the street.

* * *

Anne sat silently in the chair at her mother's bedside. After sending her father home for the night, she was restless and unsettled. She had watched as the nursing staff cared for her mother. They turned her side-to-side, carefully using pillows to provide support behind her back and under her motionless extremities. They cleaned her mouth with dampened swabs and used an ointment to moisten her lips. They placed rolled up washcloths in Karina's hands to help prevent contractures, as her body naturally curled the hands closed. Each time the nurses attended to her, they talked to their unconscious patient, explaining what they were doing. When the nurses left, the silence began to bother Anne.

"Mutti, I don't know if you can hear me or even know me right now, but I want you to know I'm here." Anne reached over to straighten a tiny wrinkle in the bedspread. "I sent Vati home. He looked so tired tonight. I'll do my best to make sure he takes care of himself." Anne watched for any sign that her mother heard or understood. She saw none, but continued to speak anyway.

"I wish I hadn't gone to California, and I wish I hadn't left you." She paused. "That's a lie. If I'm going to talk to you, then at least I'm not going to lie. I loved California, and I loved the challenge I had there. And I met someone very special to me." Anne kept her hand on the covers, stroking her mother's arm through the fabric. "Don't ask me how any of it is going to turn out, because I don't have a clue. Things are unpredictable right now."

Anne stood and slowly walked to the sink at one end of the room. She looked at her reflection in the mirror before turning back to her mother. "Unpredictable is as good a word as any. I have no idea what I'm going to do about the relationship or the job. I have commitments there, but I have bigger ones here."

"And we should talk about that," a man said from the doorway. Anne turned at the sound of Dieter's voice.

"I was wondering when you'd finally show up." Anne didn't bother to hide her irritation. "Get a lot of work done?"

"Yes, I did." Dieter entered the room and set his coat and a brown paper bag on the bedside table. "And I got some sleep, as well. I was with Mutti all through last night. Vati wouldn't try to sleep unless I promised him I would stay up with her. He had been trying to stay awake beside her for hours when I got him to agree to lie down. When she wouldn't wake up at all this morning, I persuaded him to call an ambulance."

Anne knew his words were true, having gone through similar scenarios with her stubborn father.

"I made him something to eat when he got home. He hadn't had more than coffee since he left the house this morning."

Anne felt a pang of guilt shoot through her. Despite her recent promise to her mother, she had all but ignored her father's condition in her worry about her mother's.

"Has there been any change?" Dieter asked.

Anne shook her head. "Not that I can tell." She didn't have the strength or the inclination to fight with her brother. It seemed they had been at odds with each other most of their lives. She had to ask questions.

"Vati told me you wanted him to sign papers to take over dealing with her care. He said you wanted Mutti to be placed in a nursing home."

"Maybe I should have consulted you first, before I spoke to him, but yes, that's a fairly accurate description of what I said. And I'm right to have said it."

Dieter's calm manner irritated Anne even more. "What gives you the right—"

"Because I don't want to see Vati dead," Dieter interrupted. He went to the paper bag he had placed on the table. He took out two covered cups and one large sandwich. After handing the sandwich to her, he opened one cup. "Hot chocolate with whipped cream. Sorry, they didn't have marshmallows." He opened a second cup for himself. Pulling a small folding chair close to the table, he sat down and pointed to her chair. "Sit down and eat, please. We have a lot to discuss."

Since he was six years older than she was, Anne was used to his bossy and condescending tone. But his tone now was gentle and addressed from one adult to another. She sat.

"I'm sorry I didn't give you the opportunity to present a united front with me. My only excuse is that I was scared."

Anne's surprise didn't keep her from taking a large bite of the turkey and cheese sandwich. Her hunger had been suppressed by worry, but now it came back to the forefront. She ate as Dieter continued.

"You came to the United States for college, and that was a wonderful opportunity for you. I admit I was a little envious, but our parents were very proud. They were determined that nothing should get in the way of your education. Not even Vati's heart attack."

Anne coughed as her brother's revelation caused her to choke on a bite of sandwich. She took a sip of the hot chocolate.

"When?" she asked.

"About eight months after you left Germany. He didn't want you to know and feel obligated to come back because of him. That was his decision, and you know that made it the final word."

Anne knew her father had been master of the house up until her mother's illness revealed his vulnerability.

"It was a mild heart attack, and he's been watching his blood pressure, salt intake, and cholesterol since that time. Mutti's problems lately have put a huge burden on him. Some of it couldn't be helped, but much could. Did you know that almost two weeks ago, he dismissed the caregivers you'd arranged for?"

Anne was stunned.

"I thought not," Dieter said. "He told me they weren't doing their job, that Mutti seemed to be getting worse, and he put it down to their ineptitude. He decided he could do everything himself. He thought he could watch her constantly, deal with her physical problems, and still work on his own project. When I got here, I saw a worn out old man on the brink of becoming very, very ill. That was something I had to deal with immediately." Dieter glanced over at Karina.

"I know I haven't handled Mutti's illness well. Vati had always seemed so strong and in command of everything. I used that as my reason for not being involved in what happened with her after her diagnosis. When you had them move to the United States, I was too ashamed to admit I hadn't been paying enough attention to them. I had my world and my work, and it wasn't until I heard Vati's voice on the phone a few days ago that I realized how bad the situation was." He turned back to Anne. "So maybe the combination of guilt and fear made it seem like I was suddenly too concerned." He set his cup aside and leaned forward, clasping his hands together between his knees.

"You are my sister, and they are my parents. Let's work together on this, okay?"

Weariness and relief filled Anne. "Okay," she said.

*   *   *

The cell phone in Anne's bag rang. She glanced at the caller ID, then at Dieter in apology.

"I need to take this." She stood and walked into the hallway as she answered. "Hey there."

"You haven't gone home yet," Adehm said.

"I'll be on my way home in a little while. My brother's here, and he's going to spend a couple of hours with my mother, then I'll come back toward morning. Did you find everything you need in the apartment?"

"I found your apartment, but everything I need is still at the hospital."

Anne blushed, and the words warmed her far more than the hot chocolate had.

"Did you know the car I rented at the airport has a global positioning system in it?" Adehm asked. "I'm thinking of having one installed in my car at home. It worked pretty well when I needed driving directions."

"Where did you have it take you?" Anne asked.

"It helped me find the lobby of this hospital again."

"You're here?" Anne had to keep her voice lowered, but the happiness came through loud and clear.

"Yeah, is it okay if I come up?"

"Sure, but I really am about to leave. You don't have to come all the way up here. I love it that you did this for me."

"That's just it," Adehm said. "I didn't do it for you. Maybe you gave me a reason to look at the situation, but after a lot of thinking, I came to the conclusion I needed to do this for me."

"Whatever the beginning, I'm happy about the results. Let me get my jacket and say good night, and then I'll be down."

"I'll be waiting."

Anne returned to Karina's room and stood next to the bed. Leaning over, she kissed her mother's forehead.

"Goodnight, Mutti. I love you, and I'll be back in a few hours." She then repeated the words in German.

"Just in case," she said to Dieter. She went around the bed and pulled her brother into a fierce hug. "And I love you, too." She took Dieter by surprise by giving him a quick kiss on the cheek. "Just in case you needed a translation as well."

He grinned and helped her on with her jacket. "I'll see you in the morning, and I'll call if there are any changes before then."

Anne walked out the door and down the hall to the elevator. She tapped the call button a few times, even though the button was already illuminated. A phlebotomist with a cart of blood-drawing supplies joined her and observed the extra button pushing.

"I feel like that at the end of my shift," he said. "I want to get home as fast as possible."

"I'll settle for getting to the lobby," Anne replied as the elevator finally arrived.

Stopping only once to let the phlebotomist off two floors down, the elevator car soon reached the lobby. Anne stepped out to find Adehm waiting for her.

Adehm pulled Anne into a powerful hug. "I love you," she whispered.

"I'm so glad," Anne whispered back. "We've got a hell of a lot to talk about, so let's get out of here." She started toward the lobby door, but was pulled back when Adehm caught her jacket sleeve.

"Hold on, Speedy Gonzales. I barely got my nerve up to come back in here. Let's not race off." She continued to tug at Anne until she'd led them both to a small waiting area.

"Okay," Anne said when they were seated. "Do you want to tell me how you got your nerve back? I could swear it was you, or a reasonable facsimile, who only a few hours ago told me she couldn't deal with being in a hospital."

"That was me. And it was true, but I've done a lot of thinking and walking since then. Did anybody ever tell you it's damn cold in Albuquerque after dark this time of year?"

"I know. It's one of the things I like about it."

"I took that time and thought about the things we do for love. A pretty smart cab driver got me on the road to understanding a few things about myself. I know I loved Shannon very much." Adehm saw her words made Anne slightly uncomfortable. "I also know it's very possible to be in love with more than one person in your lifetime, and it wasn't a cabbie who got me to realize that." Adehm smiled softly and took one of Anne's hands in her own.

"I realized tonight my fear and hatred of these places came from my love for Shannon. I hated what I saw happening to her, I feared losing her, and then I did lose her, and it all came about in a hospital. I guess in some warped way, I figured if I didn't create almost a phobia about hospitals, it would be like I was disloyal to her or something." Adehm sighed in frustration. "I mean, it would be like I…" She searched for words to express her feelings.

"Didn't care for her enough to hate the place she died in?" Anne finished for her.

"I guess that's how I felt. I saw tonight that I had combined my hatred of the disease that took her, how much I missed her, and how guilty I felt that I was still here, and I translated that into a loathing of all things medical. Does that make sense?"

"Not the feelings themselves, but I wasn't in your shoes. I didn't go through what you did. I wish I could take some of that off you, but I know I can't. What I'm really curious about is why things changed tonight."

"It was love again, but this time it was for you." She frowned slightly. "I want you to understand what I mean by that. I'm not a starry-eyed kid or a big believer in fairy tales. It isn't my love for you that has magically transformed me into someone who could all of a sudden overcome all the obstacles and fears in my life." She squeezed Anne's hand. "It's my love for you that makes me want to try."

Adehm drew a breath and went on. "I never questioned my fears. I never wanted to know why I felt the things I did. Not until today, that is. I wanted to give you the support you needed, and I just couldn't. So, if I loved you, and I do, then it was time I figured things out."

"Now you're better, and that's all that matters," Anne said. "I'll tell you the truth. You left me here, and that hurt. It hurt like hell. I'm glad you managed to work things through, but I hope you'll understand if I wanted you to suffer a little."

The blunt honesty took Adehm by surprise, and she laughed uneasily.

"You don't have to worry on that count. The GPS directed me to three gas stations on the way here. My brain may understand why I felt the way I did, but it doesn't mean my lower intestine has kept up with the changes."

"How awful for you. What do you say we get out of here before anymore of you physically rebels?"

"You're sure? I'm willing to stay with you here if you need me."

"I know that, and knowing is enough."

Keeping hold of one another's hands, they stood and quietly left the medical center.

# Chapter 16

Anne sat on the sofa in her apartment, curled into Adehm's side. Adehm's arm was draped over her shoulder.

"Long day, huh?" Adehm asked.

"Definitely. I'm so glad to be home with you. I'm worn out from being concerned, angry, overwhelmed, and about a trillion other emotions. Add that to my father trying to do everything on his own. He could have killed himself proving he wouldn't kill my mother. Stubborn, mule-headed *dickköpf.* That's a fathead, for you tourists."

"I'm glad his daughter didn't inherit any of that."

Anne tapped Adehm lightly in the ribs. "I'll have you know that for Germans, being stubborn is practically a prerequisite."

"I'll try to remember that, but feel free to remind me if I forget. So, what's going to happen with your mother?"

"We don't know, and I don't think the neurologist does, either. We might have an idea by tomorrow. Pretty much, it's out of our hands." Anne felt Adehm tighten her hold, physically showing her love and support. "I feel more helpless now than I did when my mother was diagnosed with the Alzheimer's. At least then, she and I could still talk to one another, and I knew what she was thinking, if she needed anything, if she was scared…" Anne trailed off and gave a deep sigh.

"How about you?" Adehm asked. "What are you thinking? Do you need anything? Are you scared?"

Anne toyed with a loose thread on the cuff of her sweater. "I'm scared as hell. Scared and guilty."

"For Pete's sake, why? You dropped everything to come home when you were needed."

Anne sat up and looked Adehm directly in the eyes. "I feel guilty because I should have known everything about my parents' health. I feel guilty because I wasn't the one to bridge the gap with Dieter for our parents' sake, and I feel most guilty because there's a small part of me that wishes this stroke would end my mother's life. That she might go quickly and not have to endure an even slower and less dignified death." Anne shook her head. "Or is it so I don't have to endure it?"

Adehm knew the last question was the toughest. She tried to formulate some words of comfort. "Annegret, I think as a society, we're conditioned to take reverence for human life very seriously. There's a lot less guidance when the life we revere becomes a life we can't live with. If it's your own life, the choice is clear—you live with the situation, or you end your life. If it's the life of someone you love, then the whole situation becomes much murkier. There are so many more people to take into consideration, so many decisions to be made, and not a single one with a guarantee of being correct. You can only try to have the decisions you make come from a place of love. That's what I realized when Shannon was dying."

"I'm so tired now, I wouldn't trust any decision that came out of my head."

"Then how about we go lie down for a few hours and we look at things again in the morning? Some rest might make things clearer."

Anne nodded and allowed herself to be led to the bedroom, where they stripped off their outer clothes and slipped between icy sheets.

"Adehm, please kiss me."

It was a simple request, and Adehm was glad to reply. The kiss reconnected them and, in momentary peace, they fell asleep together.

* * *

Anne woke after only a few hours of rest. She slipped out of bed, smiling when a still-sleeping Adehm whimpered once. She showered, left a note for Adehm, and drove to the hospital.

The eastern sky hadn't begun to lighten when Anne pulled into a space in the University Medical Center parking garage. She called Dieter's number on her cell phone, not worried about disturbing her mother.

*Maybe I'm even hoping it will wake her a little.*

"Ja," Dieter answered. His voice sounded weary to Anne's ears.

"It's me," Anne said. "I'm here at the hospital. Can I bring you anything?"

"No, but why don't I meet you outside? I could use a cigarette."

"I thought you gave those up."

"I did, on a temporary basis, apparently. I'll meet you at the front door."

Anne locked her car and walked slowly to the hospital entrance. She pulled the hood of her jacket up and zipped the front as high as it would go. Dieter emerged from the sliding glass doors, pulling a cigarette and lighter from his overcoat pocket. He kissed her cheek before shielding the flame to light his cigarette.

"Any change?" Anne tipped her head in the direction of the hospital entrance.

"No." Dieter took a deep drag on the cigarette. "Nothing."

Anne nodded. She looked down, and scuffed the toe of her shoe on the sidewalk.

"But we continue to hope, correct?" Dieter asked.

Anne glanced up at him. "Correct." She shook her head. "You realize you've taken me a bit by surprise here, don't you? I came back to Albuquerque expecting to find Mutti ill, Vati uncertain, and you indifferent. Where was this concerned brother all these years?" Anne's tone was curious, not accusatory.

"I was eighteen when the wall fell. You were twelve. Those six years meant our worlds were going to be very different. You were always meant for Vati's world. Your aptitude for academics was apparent at a young age. My destiny was in building things."

Anne remembered when Dieter entered an apprentice program in construction.

He continued. "In the East, my choice of profession was equally as honored as the one you've chosen. Comrade Builder was as valued as Comrade Engineer, even making as high a salary and earning civilian medals. That changed with reunification. There was plenty of work, but equally as much suspicion of me by colleagues who were raised in the West. I was a citizen of the same country, but made to feel like a lesser one. It's strange. When I worked outside Germany, I was German, and therefore, disliked. When I worked inside Germany, I was a former communist, and the feelings were the same. So I worked, and worked hard. I had to prove myself loyal as well as capable."

Anne could understand a bit of her brother's feelings. She had encountered some prejudice of her own, but never to the degree Dieter described.

"I'm sorry. I didn't know it was like that."

"I was lucky in one sense. Most of the construction in Germany was on the former East side. So much modernization to be done. I was able to visit the family, but not often. That distance... insulated me, I think."

Dieter took a last pull on the cigarette before stubbing it out in an ashcan adjacent to the entrance. "I started my own business as you were leaving for the university. Although I could visit Dresden more, it felt like less of a home to me." He put his arm around Anne's shoulders and guided them inside the hospital entrance. "I don't blame the circumstances. I blame myself. I should have worked harder at things that weren't work."

Anne put her arm around Dieter's waist. "You aren't a bad guy."

"You mean like you thought I was for several years?"

Anne blushed. "Yeah, like I thought you were."

"It's okay. I'm not all that happy with myself lately. Two weeks ago, I asked Vati for a Medical Power of Attorney for Mutti. I think that was what made him dismiss the caregivers. He wanted to show me he could take care of her. I had the intention of taking stress off him, and instead, I must have increased it terribly."

"We'll both talk to him this morning. There's no sense in putting off what we both know we need to say to him. We'll remind him three Schneiders are better than one."

"I only hope it won't need to be two against one."

"Agreed," Anne said.

*　*　*

Marcel walked into his wife's room at the hospital. Anne and Dieter looked up at him from chairs at Karina's bedside.

"Good morning," Anne said. She rose and walked to her father, placing a quick peck on his cheek.

Marcel went to the bed and stared down at Karina.

"Guten Morgen, Karina," he said. He leaned over the bedrail and kissed her forehead. "Hast du gut geschlafen?"

"There's been no response from her overnight," Dieter said.

"Warum?" Marcel asked. The question was not directed to either Anne or Dieter.

"I don't know why," Anne said, "but I know we are Mutti's family, and we'll wait together for her to wake up."

Marcel glanced at Anne, but said nothing.

"Dieter and I need to speak with you today. There are several things we need to think about with Mutti so ill."

"Such as?"

"We need to speak about plans for what will happen with Mutti when she is ready to leave the hospital," Dieter said. "Also, I think we need to talk about her wishes for the end of her life."

"There's nothing to decide. She will wake up and come back to her home with me."

"And if she doesn't wake up?" Anne asked. "Or if she does wake up and can't do anything for herself anymore? Not walk? Not feed herself? Not speak? Let's be honest. You know Mutti was becoming more and more difficult to care for at home. Even when you did have the caregivers..." Anne saw Marcel flash a quick, angry look at Dieter.

"Yes, Dieter told me everything, and I'm glad he did. Vati, it isn't as if this is all coming as complete news to me. You and I talked many times when I was in California. I knew things were getting harder for you." She sighed as Marcel set his jaw, a look of stubbornness Anne knew well.

"I don't give a good goddamn if you want to play at being obstinate," she told her father. "There are bigger issues here than you needing to be the one in charge."

Anne heard Dieter rise from his chair and come up behind her.

"I agree with Annegret. We have far bigger issues. We don't want to do anything but make the situation as easy as it can be, for you and Mutti both." Dieter reached forward and took his sister's hand.

Anne saw her father notice the gesture.

"I see," Marcel said. "So now I am to be the child and you two the parents."

"Never," Anne said. "We're going to be partners."

* * *

"Hi there," Anne said over the phone.

"Hey, you left early this morning. It was lonely waking up without you, especially when I'd gone to sleep with you," Adehm said. She pushed the lever down on the toaster, dropping two slices of wheat bread from sight.

"I wanted to get over to the hospital early. I needed to talk to Dieter again before we spoke with my father."

"Ooh, how'd that go? It doesn't sound like something easy to tackle with so little sleep."

"And without coffee. I'm in the cafeteria now, trying to get a caffeine infusion."

"I can bring you some, if you'd like. There's a Starbucks on every corner, and I'd be happy to provide you with some fresh-brewed java."

"Not necessary. This stuff is okay for now."

"Then how about if I come over to the hospital a bit later and buy you some lunch?"

"Honestly, I was so impressed you came back last night, especially after what you shared with me. Give yourself the day off today. Besides, I really want you to be there when I come home. I'll need you then."

"You'll have me, I promise. Do you have any peanut butter?"

"Look in the cabinet over the stove. I don't have any peanut butter, but try the Nutella."

Adehm found the jar. "This looks like a chocolate spread. I thought you were health conscious."

"It's a hazelnut spread. The chocolate is a mere bonus."

"I'll try it. Seriously, I will come over there. I had allergy shots as a kid. Eventually, I was able to eat strawberries without getting hives. I can do a little hospital time."

"And I love you for the offer. It's actually gone better than I expected. See? I did eventually answer your first question. Getting some rest brought back the father I know."

"Is that good or bad?" Adehm dipped a finger in the jar and tried the Nutella. She closed her eyes at the luscious taste.

"Both. He's strong and stubborn again, but it also brought back the man of reason. He's someone who can be swayed by a good argument and a well-thought-out approach. I think Dieter and I gave him both of those things when we talked to him at Mutti's bedside."

"Bravo, Anne. I'm very proud of you." Adehm found a knife and spread a generous dollop of Nutella on her toast. "If I can't bring you coffee, is there anything you can think of I can do to help you?"

"Just be there and be ready to take a long and well-deserved nap with me when I get back. Oh, maybe you can give Angela and Helmut some fresh vegetable pieces. There should be plenty in the fridge."

"I'll do it. I suppose nobody's ever died of a dwarf hamster bite, have they?"

Anne laughed. "Never mind, I'll be there shortly, so I'll do it. I want to see the doctor, and then I'll be on my way home. Vati will stay here with Mutti during the day, and I'll come back in the late afternoon. Dieter has the night shift."

"I'll be waiting for you."

"I'm happy to hear it. And thank you for the only laugh I've had in a few days. Watch out for those fatal dwarf hamster bites."

"Make fun of me if you want to, but at least I've helped by making you laugh. See you soon."

"Bye."

\* \* \*

"I'm very pleased to meet you, Mr. Schneider. I wish it could be under happier circumstances," Adehm said. She extended her hand to Marcel. After a brief pause, he took it.

Anne and Adehm had returned together to the hospital in the late afternoon to relieve Marcel at Karina's bedside. After Anne greeted her father, she had pulled Adehm forward. Adehm knew her disquietude at being in the hospital had made her palms cool and clammy. She had taken care to surreptitiously wipe her hand on her slacks before reaching out to Marcel.

"It's good to meet you, Ms. Trent. Yes, the circumstances could be better, but there are things over which we have no control." He glanced at Karina before making eye contact with Adehm again. "Annegret hasn't told me much about you, but everything she said was complimentary."

"It's been a great pleasure and honor getting to know Annegret," Adehm said.

"I am proud of her," Marcel said.

Adehm noticed the startled look on Anne's face. *Didn't hear much of that growing up, Annegret? Your surprise gives you away.*

Marcel turned his attention to Anne. He gave her an update on Karina's condition.

Adehm focused on their conversation. Anytime her gaze drifted to the woman in the bed, her stomach lurched in unease.

"Maybe Ms. Trent would walk me to my car," Marcel said.

"Certainly. The bracing Albuquerque air will be good for me."

"I'll be here when you get back," Anne said. "Take your time." She helped her father put on his coat.

"Dieter will be here after midnight. It's a good time for him," Marcel said. "He can use his portable computer to contact his office, which opens at that time in Germany."

Adehm understood about working away from the office. While Anne napped earlier in the afternoon, Adehm had been in contact with Detroit and Big Tree. Though Rodney was covering for her at the corporate office, pressure was building in her to return to supervising the project in California.

Marcel led the way from the room. They didn't speak until they emerged from the front entrance of the hospital.

"Annegret told me you and she are more involved than merely as business associates."

Adehm jerked slightly at the unexpectedly frank statement. She decided that honesty in return was her best course. "We are, and that has also been a great pleasure and honor. She's a remarkable person."

"That's from her mother. Karina was... is... a most singular person. Forgive me, the current situation makes me unsure of how to think of Karina. She is here, and yet..."

"I understand. I lost someone very close to me a few years ago."

"One of your parents?"

"No, they're still both alive and well. This was someone I thought I would be with for the rest of my life. It's very difficult to lose someone so early in their life. It seems wrong somehow."

Adehm and Marcel walked slowly toward the parking garage.

"We spoke earlier of Dieter working while he's here. Is that what you are doing?" Marcel asked. "I know Annegret told me many times that your project in California was extremely important and had a rigid deadline. Won't this trip to New Mexico interfere with the completion of that undertaking?"

Adehm laughed softly. "To be truthful, yes, it well might interfere with it. I'd like to be able to work, but I also very much want to be here to support Annegret. If I must make the choice, then she will always come first."

"It's unfortunate you have to make that choice at all. It seems as if there isn't an easy answer."

Marcel stopped by a Volkswagen Jetta. "This is mine."

"Mr. Schneider, I'm not asking for an easy choice. I'm only asking for Anne."

"I told you, she is like her mother. She is the only one who can give you what you ask. For other things, there may be some assistance."

"I'm not sure what you mean," Adehm said.

"It's enough that I do," Marcel said. He climbed into the Jetta.

Adehm watched Marcel back out of the space and drive off into the early evening. She walked back into the hospital, still mulling his words.

\* \* \*

The conference room down the hall from Karina's room was full of the people who cared about and were caring for the still-unconscious woman. Marcel, Dieter, and Anne had asked to meet with Dr. Ebrahimi again. At the doctor's suggestion, the charge nurse of the Neurology Unit, the unit's discharge planner, and the social service worker were also included.

Forty-eight hours had passed with little change in Karina's condition. During the night, Dieter observed some voluntary movements in her, but none with purpose or in response to a request. The doctor found that Karina withdrew her arm when an uncomfortable pressure was applied to her fingernail. Though small, these signs were deemed positive.

"We know my mother can't go back to the same living situation she had prior to coming to the hospital. It's clear that her requirements have changed drastically," Dieter said.

"I agree," Dr. Ebrahimi said. "Karina will need around-the-clock care, and that's too much for one person to manage."

"I wish I was able to take her home again," Marcel said quietly.

Ellie Simpson, the social worker, said, "You did everything for her you could, Mr. Schneider. You gave her as much time and care as possible. I really believe it would be best now to hand over the job of being your wife's caregiver to those who do that professionally. Allow yourself to just be her husband and support. That's what will help her the most. She needs you to love her and make decisions for her. Let others make her bed."

Anne was impressed by how Ms. Simpson spoke to Marcel. The short, African-American woman was kind yet direct, and she exuded an aura of competence and compassion.

"I know what you say is true, and I need to accept that Karina's needs go beyond what I can provide, but it is difficult to give over my responsibilities," Marcel said.

"We understand, Mr. Schneider," Dr. Ebrahimi said. "That's why we try to approach these situations as a team. We can assist you with those responsibilities. Your daughter asked the nurses this morning about skilled nursing facilities. Pat Wood, our discharge planner, has a list of several possibilities, and she can provide the necessary financial information as well. She will also assist in arranging transportation when we're ready for that."

The group spoke for several minutes regarding the level of care Karina would need, including medications and therapies. It was decided Marcel and Dieter would tour the appropriate facilities and make a decision by the next day.

"My father and I have agreed we will both hold my mother's Medical Power of Attorney, and we'll have those papers drawn up today," Dieter said.

Adehm sat quietly off to one side of the room. She tried to keep her mind off her own discomfort at being in the hospital by concentrating on supporting Anne. She noted with approval how Anne was working out things with her brother and father. She was glad, when faced with both of his very determined children, Marcel had listened to reason.

"Mr. Schneider, have you made a decision regarding nutrition for Karina? She obviously can't take in anything orally to support herself now, and we need to know what you and your family have decided regarding that," Dr. Ebrahimi said.

Dieter explained the family was opting for a nasogastric tube feeding for the present time as opposed to the more permanent gastrostomy tube that could be surgically inserted into Karina's stomach. If there was no improvement in Karina's condition, they would decide whether or not to withdraw the enteral nutrition. He also informed the staff that Karina had previously expressed a wish that she not be kept alive on machines, therefore no heroics were to be attempted if Karina's heart or lung function should cease.

"I'll write the order for Do Not Resuscitate," Dr. Ebrahimi informed the charge nurse. "I think that wraps up everything for now. Thank you all for working together for Mrs. Schneider," she told the group. "I'll see Karina again on my afternoon rounds," she told Anne, Marcel, and Dieter.

"You have a few things to do today, so I'll stay with Mutti until you get back," Anne told her father and brother, as the non-family members of the group left.

"That won't be possible," Dieter told Anne. "You're going to be very busy yourself this afternoon."

"Whatever you need me to do, I will," Anne promised her family.

"Good," Marcel said. "Then I know you won't mind getting on a plane and going back to California today."

"What?" Anne asked loudly. She lowered her voice immediately. "What are you talking about, Vati?"

"Annegret, whatever happens with Karina will happen if you are sitting with her or you are in California. You have done so much for her. Now Dieter and I can take care of things. I believe you made a commitment to work on a very important project with Ms. Trent. You should honor that obligation."

"But—" Anne began to say.

"Vati talked to me last night," Dieter said. "This is his idea. If it makes any difference, then I should tell you, I agree with him."

"But you wanted me to come back," Anne argued. "You said you needed me."

"I did ask you, and I did need you. I needed you to help me see the facts of Karina's situation and accept that I will have little hand in her destiny. I will merely have a say in how she arrives at that destiny. That was not easy for me to understand. I could have only done it with some rest and the help of my children."

"So you don't want me to stay? You don't need me?"

"We will always need you," Dieter said. "Vati believes at this moment you are needed more elsewhere."

Anne was clearly perplexed at the attempted change in her plans. She placed her hands on her hips.

"I can see where you get your determined streak, Annegret," Adehm interjected. "Your father thinks you take after your mother, but I see a great deal of him in you, as well. I wouldn't want to get into a disagreement with either of you, but right now, he's making a very persuasive case."

"Do I get a say in any of this?" Anne asked.

"Of course you do," Marcel said. He put his hand on her shoulder. "I can only hope you say the right thing."

Anne watched as Adehm held up her cell phone.

"The transportation back to Big Tree that Rodney was going to arrange for one is just as easy to arrange for two. As unappealing as it sounds, I think there's a wastewater treatment plant in California with your name on it."

# Chapter 17

"We'll be back in the manager's office at Big Tree at 9 a.m., West Coast time. I want you to be ready for a conference call then. Anne and I need to get updated on the progress made during our absence." Adehm moved her phone to her other hand and hefted her bag from the back of the car, then followed Anne into the lobby of the Pine Palace. "I'm beat from the flights, the layovers, and the drive. I want some sleep, and I want to wake up in the morning ready to work like hell. We've got less than two weeks now. Oh, and call Lucas Barr and have him meet us in the office, too."

"No problem," Rodney said. "I'll e-mail you the information as well, so you'll have hard copies. I'll cc Ms. Schneider, too."

"I'm sure Ms. Schneider will be happy to hear that, and I'll tell her momentarily. She's getting our room key."

Adehm stopped speaking as she saw Len hand Anne one room key and one room card.

"Keys," Adehm corrected. "She's getting our room keys."

"I'll speak to you at nine then," Rodney said and hung up.

Adehm closed her cell phone and dropped it into her coat pocket. She waited as Anne approached her and reluctantly reached out to accept the card key to her room.

"I was kind of hoping we were past separate rooms for good," she said in a quiet voice.

"There hasn't been a single night since Tahoe that I haven't wanted to be with you. What I don't want is to tarnish your professional reputation in any way. You're the very visible representative of the mighty Bohannon Corporation, the biggest employer in these parts. That comes with a huge responsibility." Anne hooked Adehm's arm as she steered them across the lobby, stopping at the foot of the stairs with her suitcase.

Adehm appeared crestfallen.

"Did I ever tell you that I polished up my English by watching old American movies on television? The subtitled ones really gave me an understanding of American pacing and inflection," Anne said.

"That's an interesting story. Any point to it, or are you just making conversation?"

"Only that I've always wanted to say this line like they did in those old films." Anne leaned forward and lowered her voice. "Your place or mine?"

As realization of what Anne was saying struck, a wide smile lit up Adehm's face.

"Mine, for tonight. Tomorrow, your place. As long as I'm with you, it could be the moon, for all I care."

"Then I'll put my suitcase in my room, grab a few things and be at your door in fifteen minutes. Shall we set up a password or something so you know it's me?"

"No password," Adehm replied, shaking her head. "You don't have to say anything, and you don't have to do anything. Not a thing. Oh, maybe just whistle. You know how to whistle, don't you, Anne? You just put your lips together and... blow."

Anne grinned as Adehm played along with her game. "For that, I'll be there in fourteen minutes." Anne turned and quickly climbed the stairs as Adehm watched appreciatively from the lobby.

"God bless Hollywood," she said softly. She turned, picked up her bag, and walked rapidly to her room.

*   *   *

"It's the home stretch, Annegret. We've got everything done, and we've got two days to spare. We even got that aeration vent fan installed." Adehm tipped her chair back and propped her feet on the corner of the desk. Her pronouncement didn't seem to have the effect she wanted on Anne, whose frown of concentration never left her face.

"I'm glad you're happy," Anne said, eyes flicking from one of her computer screens to the other. "It's gone too smoothly. There's always something else to be done. I already know the files need fixing."

"And Rodney has checked into his room at the Pine Palace and is on his way here as we speak. It won't take him more than a day to have the paperwork in apple pie order and ready for the State team to dive into them."

Anne glanced up from her screens. "That was a great idea of yours, if I've failed to mention that before," she said. "Without adding the tidying of the plans, purchase orders, permits, and the rest of the ton of paperwork to our schedule, it's made the difference in our timing. It's made up for my running out on you."

"And my running after you. Don't forget that." Adehm took a deep breath and let it release slowly. "We made the decisions we did, and I believe we both made the right ones. There's no need to second guess a correct decision."

"Even if it meant sixteen-hour days, needing to double up on our double checks, and having far too little time for…"

"International relations?"

Anne was amused by Adehm's euphemism.

"Don't you know," Adehm said, "that every moment I spend with you counts toward that?"

Anne made a dismissive sound at the statement.

"No, it's true," Adehm continued. "I haven't been the easiest person to work with. You can get Rodney to testify to that when he gets here. I chafe at sharing my space, much less my power. I get impatient with delays and have no tolerance for incompetence."

"All of which makes you an excellent executive and problem solver. Like your decision to bring Rodney here. You know how to make the puzzle pieces fit."

"I admit it, Rodney coming here was inspired, but I can never reveal that particular move of genius at Bohannon. All they know is that Rodney is down with a nasty virus. Neil Hammond shot down my request to get someone here from the accounting department, so I bribed Rodney into calling in sick and hopping on a plane."

"Out of curiosity, how much is Rodney's bribe? Maybe I can save you some money."

"And how exactly would you accomplish that?"

For a moment, Anne allowed her German accent to come through freely. "As a former resident of the German Democratic Republic, I will appeal to his sense of loyalty to his fellow man and ask him not to take more than a fair share of our economic wealth. All for the good of the people, of course."

Adehm moved her feet from the desktop to the floor and crossed to Anne's desk. She grasped Anne's upper arms and pulled her to her feet. "Ms. Schneider, I do so love your German accent. Do you know you let it slip out even more when you're in, shall we say, the throes of passion? I feel a little like Gomez Adams wanting to kiss my way up your arm right now, but I just adore that accent."

"Ich liebe dich," Anne said softly. She watched as the momentary flare of heat banked a bit in Adehm's eyes and was replaced by a loving warmth.

"I don't need a Rosetta stone to translate that for me. I love you, too."

"We have ways to make you be quiet," Anne said, stressing her accent. She ran her index finger across Adehm's lower lip.

"Show me," Adehm said, leaning in to kiss Anne with passion and intensity.

There had been scarce minutes in the last four-and-a-half weeks for the women to tease, play, or indulge in anything more intimate than wrapping exhausted arms around each other as they fell asleep at night. Adehm shifted a little in Anne's arms, turned her head, and reclaimed Anne's lips. At that moment the office phone rang. Adehm reached behind Anne to pick up the handset.

"Adehm Trent," she said, her voice soft. She listened a moment and then said, "Give him directions and send him up to the manager's office." As she reached to replace the phone on its cradle, she kept moving Anne backward until she was lying on the desk, Adehm above her.

"There's a barbarian at the gate. A barbarian named Rodney Burnett who has very rotten timing." She kissed Anne again and pushed off the desk, bringing them both back to their feet.

"I suppose we need to get to work so you can start amassing Rodney's bribe," Anne said.

They parted reluctantly.

"It's not money, it's you," Adehm said. "I promised him he could meet you, and you'd tell him just how you managed to snag a catch like me." Adehm returned to her desk.

"At the current exchange rate, that's not much of a bribe." Anne resumed her perusal of her computer screen.

"With his crappy timing, he's lucky his reward doesn't consist of a swift kick from the toe of my shoe to his backside."

"That's it! That's what I'm missing!" Anne cried. "Toe boards!"

\* \* \*

"You did meet her," Adehm said.

Rodney lifted his eyes from the stack of papers on the desk in front of him. He had commandeered Adehm's desk, which meant his boss had moved to Anne's. He snorted in mild derision.

"I don't count a hurried hello in the hallway as much of an introduction. You promised I could meet her, and I'm determined to do that. I've got to see just what makes her so special." He took a paper from the top of the stack and placed it facedown on a scanner now attached to Adehm's computer. "I mean, she's really well put together and sort of hot, in a bookish way, but there's got to be more to the story than that. There's been plenty of eye candy going in and out of your office, and if you didn't notice it, I did. Thank you for that, by the way. There are the occasional perks to being an executive assistant, as well as the numerous drawbacks."

"You mean like everybody assuming you're gay?"

"That's actually my secret weapon." Rodney looked at the pile of paperwork on the desk. "Nobody thought of backing these things up on the computer before this week?" He removed the scanned item and used the touch pad to electronically file the image.

"Thought of it, but didn't have the time to do it." Adehm labeled a hanging file folder. "Besides, I knew from week one I'd be bringing you out here eventually to arrange things. Don't tell that to Anne. She thinks my brilliant idea of bringing the Master Organizer to Big Tree spontaneously occurred."

"Master Organizer," Rodney said, trying out the title on his tongue. "That ability, along with my flair for fashion and love of gossip is what makes the other employees think I'm gay."

"Possibly."

"As if a heterosexual can't be fabulous."

"It makes the female assistants trust you." Adehm stated it as the fact it was.

"Implicitly."

"Thank goodness you're devoted to only your very demanding boss."

"About whom I must complain periodically to keep up your slave-driver reputation."

"I thank you for your very loyal... disloyalty."

"Anytime," Rodney said. "I'm learning a lot from you. You're a fantastic boss, but please don't think my presence is guaranteed forever by loyalty and a great paycheck. One of these days, you're going to have to fly without me."

"You're too good to stay an executive assistant forever, and I accept that. Just as long as you stay one this week."

"Granted."

They worked in silence for a while, Rodney tied to the computer and Adehm readying the office file cabinet for rearranging.

"So what's Anne doing anyway?" Rodney asked.

Adehm grinned at the question, appreciating that Rodney possessed the essential trait of keeping goals in focus, despite distractions and disturbances.

"She's gone to have toe boards installed."

"And a toe board would be?"

"The way she described it, it sounds like something to keep errant crescent wrenches and the like from falling off a work platform and onto an unsuspecting employee's head. It's a safety feature for the plant."

"Sounds like it. She was pretty cute in that hard hat."

Adehm dropped the hanging files onto the rails in the file cabinet drawer and then closed it.

"It's what's under the hard hat that caught me. She's got brains, heart, perseverance, compassion, and a ton of other wonderful qualities. Mix that together with her own style, personality, and attitude, and you've got a winner. There's no other way to explain it."

"No way to explain what?" Anne said as she entered the office. Her hair was sticking out at odd angles from under the hard hat, her old coveralls were grimy, and she was trailing a few flakes of sawdust as she walked.

"No way to explain why I want to put off the rest of this work until tomorrow and take you and Rodney out for an early dinner."

"Even if I show up just like this?" Anne asked. She waved a hand down herself, indicating her grubby work clothes.

"Even if you do." Adehm put her hand up to her mouth and spoke to Rodney in a stage whisper. "There's always takeout."

\* \* \*

Anne, Rodney, and Adehm sat in the dining room of The Rose, enjoying tea and coffee after their meal.

"You want to start the plant up in the morning?" Adehm asked. "I thought we'd need to wait for the inspectors."

"No, I checked with the State inspector's office. The person they're sending will want to see the treatment plant in operation, go through the files, check for compliance, and more importantly, take samples from the outflow pipe and possibly the river. Each part of the inspection is important, but the results of those samples will be critical."

"The paperwork's covered," Rodney said. "I'll be done by noon, at the latest."

"Six months of damn hard work all comes down to a few bottles going to the lab. It may be a town's survival riding on those samples," Adehm said.

"We're going to pass." Anne's tone wasn't boastful or wishful, it was merely confident.

For Adehm, that was enough.

*　*　*

Anne snuggled close to Adehm under the quilt. Room 12 at the Pine Palace was quiet except for the sound of that movement between the sheets.

"I had a call from Dieter while I was out in the plant control room this afternoon," Anne said.

Adehm lifted her head from the pillow.

"Why didn't you tell me? What's happening? What did he say?"

"I didn't tell you because we were busy, and it wasn't anything that couldn't wait until we were alone to discuss it." She took a deep breath. "They moved my mother to a nursing home today. She's more responsive than she'd been. I was so glad when they were able to take out the feeding tube. Dieter told me the physical therapists still haven't been able to walk her. They don't know if she'll ever be able to walk again. Dieter thinks this might be the best she'll ever be."

Adehm dropped her head back to the pillow and held Anne a little tighter.

"How do you feel about that?"

"I don't know, really. I go from being grateful for not losing her, to not grateful for knowing how she is, and then I go back again."

"I know your dad will be happy to have you back home. Win, lose, or whatever, we're done here in two days. You don't need to wait around for the reports to come back. I'll let you know, of course."

Silence returned. Anne contemplated the conclusion to the project that had dominated their working lives for the past several months and what that would mean to their personal lives.

"Annegret, when this is over—"

Anne interrupted Adehm by placing a finger over her lips. "Not tonight, Adehm. I promise we'll talk about whatever happens next when the business part is ended, okay? For tonight, could you just please love me?"

Adehm nodded her head slowly, her lips moving under Anne's fingertip. She kissed the fingertip lightly as she gently rolled Anne onto her back.

# Chapter 18

"You can't tell anything by just looking at it," Edward Shively said. Anne was sure the grinding of her teeth was audible as her jaw clenched yet again. The inspector from the State of California had uttered the same words at least a dozen times.

"Excuse me while I exchange my Master's degree for a dumb shit sign," Anne whispered under her breath to Adehm. They were several steps from the man who continued collecting samples produced by Big Tree's wastewater treatment plant. He was loftily perched on a plywood stand, his right arm extended with sample bottles he filled and then placed into a leather valise.

"Right here," he said, "is where the concentration of undesirable elements will be highest. If you can pass the analysis here, the Prussian River should be safe. Because you were shut down for violations, I'll take three times the usual number of samples. I'll have one tested at the State labs and send the other two samples out for independent verification."

"Because you can't tell anything by just looking at it?" Adehm asked. An amused grin crossed her face as she heard an annoyed squeak from Anne.

"Exactly." Mr. Shively turned around to face them. "I'll seal and initial the bottles to prevent tampering, and that should be that. I've already checked your files, and may I say, they were impressive. You've done a top-notch job with the building inspections as you went along. And on a purely personal note, I'd like to add that I'm grateful for this sampling platform." He indicated the plywood stand under his feet. "You've no idea how aggravating and sometimes dangerous it is to get to some of these outflow pipes."

Anne seemed soothed by the praise from the State inspector. The sampling platform had been her idea.

"A little public relations never hurt," she'd told Adehm while drawing up the plans for the simple structure. "It will be easier and safer to get samples for your own internal monitoring, as well."

Adehm saw that Anne's close attention to detail was paying off, and she was once again impressed by Anne's expertise in her chosen field. Clearly Perfect was currently a small company, but it looked to her like they would be a success.

"That wraps it up for me." Mr. Shively closed the valise. "The results will be back in about five days, and we'll move quickly after that. Either you'll be cleared to run at full capacity, or you're closed for good."

As much as that information caused concern in her, Adehm appreciated the honesty.

"Mr. Shively, I want to thank you for coming up here, and I'm confident of the outcome of the tests. Big Tree is a responsible company, and you'll find we meant what we promised about making sure we're not adversely impacting the environment." Adehm looked around her. "We'll take much better care of this."

The trio made their way to the nearby access road and drove the short distance back to the main part of the mill. Mr. Shively shook hands with Anne and Adehm before he got in his car and drove off through the entrance. The security guard closed the large gates behind him.

"With any luck, we'll soon have those gates back open for business," Adehm said. She noticed the large number of mill workers who had shown up to demonstrate their concern and support on the day of the crucial tests.

"Ladies and gentlemen," she said, raising her voice to be heard by the workers. "I want to thank you all for your hard work and great patience while Bohannon Corporation upgraded this facility. I've appreciated getting to know many of you on a deeper level." Her eyes turned briefly to Anne before scanning the crowd again.

"I'm proud of the huge job we accomplished in such a short time. The tests have been taken, and we'll know the results soon. Call me an optimist, but I think we'll pass easily. To that end, I'd like to call Lucas Barr up here."

Lucas had been standing near the door of the Operations building. He made his way to where Adehm stood. She clapped her hand on his shoulder.

"We might as well make it official. Lucas, you did an outstanding job as assistant to the interim manager, so rather than go outside of the plant to find the right person, you're the new manager at Big Tree."

Applause broke out, accompanied by several calls of congratulations.

"Lucas's first job as manager will be to bring me his recommendations for assistant managers and shift supervisors and to work with those people to get this plant up and running."

More jubilant cheers broke out from the workers.

Adehm nodded at Lucas and walked toward the manager's office. Anne caught up with her in a few strides. Adehm glanced over at her as they walked.

"As my father would say, I hope my mouth didn't just write a check my ass can't cash."

"It hasn't," Anne said. "We did it. I can feel it."

"Even if you can't tell anything just by looking at it?" Adehm was surprised when Anne didn't rise to the bait. Instead, she stepped ahead of Adehm to open and hold the door for her.

"Sometimes you can tell a good thing with just one glance," Anne said warmly.

"How right you are, Annegret," Adehm said as she passed through the doorway.

*     *     *

"So, what's next for you?" Rodney asked Anne. They were working in the manager's office, packing up in preparation for leaving Big Tree. Anne secured one of her computers into a shipping container.

"My business partner, Patrick, has already put in bids on two more projects. They're both near Albuquerque, so I'm looking forward to spending a lot more time with my family."

"That sounds good. I'm hoping Adehm will take some time off, too. She's worked really hard on this project. You both have, but you had her, and she didn't have much backup or support from the company."

Any reply Anne might have made was cut off when the person under discussion walked into the office. She waved a paper at them.

"This is Lucas's list of assistant managers and shift supervisors. Will you make copies of this for the Payroll department, Rodney? And have Bohannon send out copies of the standard managerial contract when you get back to Detroit. We'll want to get everything nailed down for the restart of full production."

The phone in the office rang. Adehm glanced expectantly at Rodney.

"Don't look at me," he said. "I'm not even supposed to be here, what with my terrible virus and all." He used the first two fingers on each hand to make quotation marks around the words "terrible virus."

"I'll get it," Anne said, picking up the line. "Manager's office." She listened a moment and then said, "Just a minute, please. I'll put you on hold and see if she's available."

Punching the red hold button, she extended the handset in Adehm's direction. "It's Neil Hammond."

"My best friend," Adehm said sarcastically as she took the phone from Anne. "How many calls does this make in the last three days?"

"Six," Anne and Rodney said in unison.

Adehm pushed the button to talk. "Neil! This is a pleasant surprise. What can I do for you... now?" Adehm was gracious in victory, but not overly so. She pantomimed gagging as she listened to Neil Hammond.

Anne clapped her hand over her mouth to keep from laughing.

"I'm planning to be in the office on Monday. Everything's done here except for the final chemical analysis. It should be back in five days. It's the BOD five that takes the longest to run, of course."

Anne gave Adehm a thumbs-up sign to indicate she had correctly regurgitated the information Anne had given her earlier in the day.

"Oh, sorry. That's the biological oxygen demand for the five days. Anyway, with those results in hand, we'll be ready to push back up to full production and start making Bohannon Corporation some good return on its investment. We're already profiting by some great local press coverage. We're on the road to having the reputation of a good corporate citizen again."

Anne's cell phone rang and she checked the number.

"Dieter," she whispered, silencing the ring. "He's probably checking my travel plans. I'll take it outside."

Adehm nodded as Anne slipped out the door to the hall.

"What?" Adehm asked, realizing she'd been intent on watching Anne and had missed Neil Hammond's last comment. "What board meeting?" She listened again and, as she did, she felt a touch of heat rise in her cheeks.

Rodney stepped back from her a little.

"The team? As in you and I?" Adehm closed her eyes for a moment. When she opened them again, she had regained the cool manner of the corporate executive. "I'll tell you what, Neil. If I'm not back in time for the meeting, you can start the presentation without me. Be sure to fill them in on all the fine details of how *we* saved Big Tree." She hung up the phone without saying good-bye.

"Now it's all crystal clear," she said to Rodney. She smacked a hand to her forehead. "I guess working these last few months with straightforward and honest people put me off my game. I should have seen this coming." She began to pace.

"Seen what?" Rodney asked. "What's going on back at the Temple of Doom?"

"As self-appointed team leader, Neil Hammond has arranged for us to brief the board of directors on *our* achievement."

"You're not serious. Neil Hammond, who tried his best to be a stumbling block to everything you did out here, is now trying to take credit for it?"

Adehm perched on the corner of her desk as Anne came back into the room.

"Not trying, has done. We're both getting letters of commendation and a nice little extra something added to our Christmas bonuses."

"Oh sweet mother of God, that is just too much," Rodney said.

Adehm turned to get Anne's reaction to the news, but stopped short when she saw the look on Anne's face. She was pale and drawn.

"Annegret? Honey, are you all right?" Oblivious to everything but her concern for Anne, she left her seat on the desk and went to where Anne had dropped into her chair. Adehm put an arm around her shoulders. "What's the matter, love?"

Anne turned tear-filled eyes to Adehm.

"About half an hour ago, my mother passed away." Anne launched herself completely into Adehm's embrace as the terrible wracking sobs broke through.

\* \* \*

Anne dropped her keys on the small table just inside the door of her apartment. She wandered slowly through the living room to the kitchen and filled an electric kettle with water. She flipped the switch on at the base of the appliance before returning to the living room where she removed her long black coat and hung it on a peg near the door.

She walked to the cage containing her dwarf hamsters. Angela was in one of the plastic tunnels nibbling on a piece of vegetable, but Helmut was nowhere to be seen. Anne suspected he was sleeping peacefully, burrowed under the pile of shavings in the house in the corner of the cage.

"I wonder if they make human-sized bags of shavings?" Anne asked the visible hamster. Angela stopped chewing for a moment and tilted her head thoughtfully to the side, but made no helpful reply.

"Good grief, it's freezing out there." Adehm let herself into the apartment. She slid her lined trench coat off and placed it on a peg adjacent to Anne's. Rubbing her hands together, she quickly walked toward the hamster cage. She stepped behind Anne and wrapped her arms around her waist.

"Seems like plenty of food in the cage," she said. "How about something for you? You haven't had anything since breakfast, not even after the service."

"I'm not really hungry. I put water on for some tea. That's enough for now."

"Then go sit down on the couch and let me make the tea, okay? It's been a really long day for you."

"That sounds good," Anne said. "Let me go change out of this dress and into something less... funereal." She left Adehm's embrace and went into the bedroom. She slipped out of the black dress and quickly changed into comfortably-worn sweats. Running her fingers through her hair, she straightened it where the sweatshirt had knocked it askew.

"I got a call from Neil Hammond a few minutes ago," Adehm said to Anne when she reappeared in the living room. "That's what took me so long with parking the car." She handed Anne a steaming mug of tea and took her free hand to lead her to the couch. They sat down together, Anne leaning slightly against Adehm's shoulder.

"What did he want?"

"The usual. He made the formal presentation to the board and crowed about our glowing report from the State. He told them all about the plant start-up. He also wanted to know when I was coming back. He figures I was only here in Albuquerque in a corporate goodwill capacity."

Anne took a sip from her mug and made an appreciative sound, as the tea had been prepared exactly as she liked it.

"And when are you going back to Detroit for your showdown with him?" she asked. "With all the arrangements, the service, and cremation, we haven't really had time to talk about that. I've just been very, very grateful you came back with me. You've helped me hold everything together."

"I haven't lost a patient yet. I'm not sure I can even imagine what you, Dieter, and your father are going through. If I've helped you in some tiny way, then I'm happy. That's the whole reason I'm here. I do like Marcel and Dieter, but I believe I thought only of you."

Anne gave a small smile. "Nice sentiment, but I know when I hear Jane Austen being paraphrased."

"I love a smart woman," Adehm said. "Especially a smart woman named Annegret."

"A smart but tired Annegret. Tomorrow won't be as bad. I just have to get Dieter and Vati to the airport."

"The funeral home arranged to have your mom's ashes sent to Dresden, right?" Adehm took another sip from her mug, then set it on the coffee table in front of them.

Anne nodded. "Dieter and Vati will pick the ashes up the day after tomorrow at a mortuary there."

"Are you sure you don't want to go with them? We can still get you a ticket."

"No. Dieter won't actually go along with Vati when he scatters her ashes. Vati promised Mutti it would be only the two of them that last time along the Elbe River. They used to love walking there together. Dieter's only going along to keep him company on the plane." Anne set her mug on the table next to Adehm's.

"Your dad loved your mother very much," Adehm said. "The way he spoke about her at the memorial today really touched me. He looked a little lost. Do you think he'll be okay?"

"I think so, yes." The weariness in her voice allowed her natural German accent to come through. "In some respects, he's been preparing for this day since Mutti's diagnosis, but I'm certain that another part of him will be counting the days until he joins her on that river bank again."

"Annegret? You know I adore your accent. Would you do me a favor and not Americanize it when it's just us?"

Anne leaned her cheek into Adehm's shoulder.

"Not a problem. Just don't ask me for a Marlene Dietrich impersonation."

"Agreed." Adehm pulled Anne to her. They sat quietly for several minutes.

"So when will I need to be taking you to the airport?" Anne asked, returning to her earlier question.

"I've been giving that some thought," Adehm said. "I'm not sure Neil Hammond is worth my anger, even my cool, detached professional anger. Over the past several days, I've figured out there are a few things a whole lot more important than playing corporate mind games with a back-stabbing toad like Neil Hammond."

"You have, huh?"

"Yeah, and I think there are many, many more things I can figure out, as long as I'm figuring them out with you."

Anne's eyebrows scrunched together and she sat up, looking intently at Adehm.

"So you're saying..."

"That I think we'll need a much bigger place than this one. We'll each need a home office, and of course, we'll want a nice area for the kids." She gestured to the hamster cage.

"You want to stay here?"

"Here, yes. With you, yes. Hopefully together forever, yes. How do you feel about that?"

"I probably should think more about it, but it appears the popular answer today is yes. Who am I to buck a trend?" Anne leaned forward and softly kissed Adehm's warm, full lips. The kiss broke, and she moved back into Adehm's arms.

"Hopefully forever," Anne said. "I like that."

"All the way to our own riverbank," Adehm vowed. "I love you that much."

"Hoffentlich für immer... hopefully forever," Anne said. "We might as well start your German lessons now."

# Epilogue

"You said you didn't need to go to the airport. You said you wanted to stay together forever." Anne watched Adehm place her clothes carefully into the open suitcase on the bed. Anne stood with her feet slightly apart, hands on her hips.

"You have a very good recall of the things I said six months ago." Adehm put her toiletry items in a separate bag and then set it into the larger suitcase. "Maybe the reason you remember what I said back then is because you say it every time I leave town."

Anne laughed, unable to maintain her wounded façade.

"I do, don't I? Maybe there is a little Marlene Dietrich in me, after all." Anne brought Adehm's garment bag over so she could put her business clothes in it. "You'll be back on Friday, right? I better be sure I have your flight information in my Blackberry so I don't miss picking you up at the airport."

"I e-mailed it to you this morning. I don't worry. You're the most punctual person I know."

"Part of my Saxon DNA, dear."

Adehm's phone rang.

Anne noted the caller ID as she passed Adehm's phone to her. "Rodney."

Adehm nodded as she answered. "Hi, Rodney." She continued packing as she listened. "Right. Eleven in the morning." She walked around the bed to choose another pair of shoes to add to the suitcase.

As she passed Anne, she placed a light peck on her cheek. Then she laughed.

"No, that wasn't for you, Rodney Burnett. Trent Enterprises pays you an excellent salary as Vice President. You don't need phone kisses from me as a bonus. I'll call you from Phoenix tomorrow." She closed the phone and tossed it on the bed.

"Rodney says to remind you that you're a lucky woman and that my consulting business may drag me away for short periods, but I'll always come back to you and our home, because there's absolutely no place on this earth that I would rather be."

"He said all that?" Anne asked, feigning awe.

"You bet. You can call him tomorrow at the office and verify it." Adehm sat on the edge of the bed and drew Anne to her.

"I might do that." Anne reached up to adjust the collar on Adehm's silk blouse. "Better yet, I'm dropping off some plans downtown for the new municipal facility, so maybe I'll go by and see if he wants to have lunch."

"He'd like that," Adehm said. It was true. In the six months since Adehm had resigned from Bohannon to open her own consulting firm in Albuquerque, Anne and Rodney had become great friends. Anne had assisted in Rodney's relocation from Detroit, even recommending the same realtor who had helped her and Adehm find their house and the location for Trent Enterprises.

Anne leaned over to drop a light kiss on Adehm's lips. "I'll miss you."

"I'll miss you, too. And this." Adehm returned Anne's kiss with several of her own. "I'll call you every night I'm away, just like always. Maybe that will make the separation better. I know it does for me."

"Don't call me until later in the evening on Thursday. That's the night I'm going over to Patrick and Robyn's house for dinner. Patrick wants to go over those résumés again. I think we have our choice for our new engineer narrowed down to three people."

"Good. You guys are getting too busy to just be a two-person outfit anymore, but I'm surprised Patrick asked you over for that. He knows you don't think of business when you're around your goddaughter." Adehm stood up and worked on the finishing touches of her packing.

"Guilty on that count," Anne said. "Oh, did I tell you Rodney mentioned some office space is opening up in your building? Patrick and I are going to look into getting Clearly Perfect a permanent home. We can finally put that generous Bohannon money to good use." Anne zipped up the garment bag as Adehm closed and locked the suitcase.

"I've loved having you work out of our home, but I suppose I'll just have to trade that for having a very beautiful woman in my carpool."

They carried the bags out to the living room, where Adehm retrieved the jacket that completed her traveling outfit.

"You've got your briefcase?" Anne asked.

"Already in the car."

"Then I guess you're all ready to go."

Adehm closed the gap between them and took Anne in her arms. "I'm prepared to go, but when it comes to leaving you for five days, I'm never really ready." Adehm leaned in and gave Anne a slow, deep kiss which was returned enthusiastically.

"I love you, Annegret," Adehm said after the kiss broke.

"You'd better, Adehm Trent, because you're going to be stuck with me for many, certainly dozens, and possibly hundreds, of ecstatically happy years."

Adehm laughed at Anne's playfulness as they gathered her bags.

"Wow, not only can you build a plant to treat it, you're pretty good at shoveling it, too."

Anne and Adehm left their home and headed out to their future, together.

Author Val Brown                    Photo Credit: Picture Perfect

# About the Author

Val wishes she could tell you all about her adventurous life as an international jewel thief and the intriguing people who are enthralled by her every utterance, but that would be a second work of fiction in this book.

The truth is that Val was raised in a military family: one mom, one dad, one sister, one brother. The family moved around a lot, as one expects of families in such situations. Val became a hit-and-run student, leaving the scene of the school after a year or so at each one. However, her unique upbringing allowed her to experience things most people only dream of getting to see in their lives. Perhaps that beginning is why Val finds people so fascinating.

Val worked her way through a community college. It was just like a real college, but cheaper! She became a nurse many years ago and hasn't quit that day job yet. Writing is something that isn't nursing, and Val loves it, and all the great people she's met through her writing.

Currently, Val is working on home ownership, where she'll be able to lead a terribly serene middle-class life with her dog. A modest goal, admittedly, but one with great potential.

If you insist on knowing more about Val and have nothing better to do some rainy day, you can visit her recently hatched website, www.valbrownwrites.com. She'd be happy to hear from you anytime.

# Coming soon from Blue Feather Books:

## Playing for First, by Chris Paynter

Lisa Collins is an Indianapolis sportswriter who covers the city's minor league baseball team and freelances for the newspaper. She leads an uncomplicated life of covering sporting events and chilling out at The Watering Hole, a bar owned by her best friend, Frankie Dunkin. But uncomplicated goes to complex when Amy Perry enters her world.

Amy, the all-star first baseman for a professional women's baseball team, dreams of playing in the major leagues. The Cincinnati Reds are about to give her that chance.

While covering Amy's ascent through the minor league system, the out and proud Lisa finds herself falling for the closeted ball player. As they begin a relationship, Lisa realizes she's already given her heart away to someone else-Frankie Dunkin. The problem is, though, Lisa's not sure the feeling is mutual.

In her quest to break through the gender barrier, Amy faces harassment from her male teammates. She's confronted with difficult choices about her sexual identity. Lisa is torn between supporting Amy in her struggle and acknowledging her true feelings for Frankie. Meanwhile, Frankie has her own demons to face as painful physical and emotional scars from her past haunt her.

Will Amy succeed in achieving her dream? Can Lisa sort out her feelings and pursue the right woman to love? Will Frankie's haunted past keep her from loving again? Amy may be the only woman on the major league ball field, but in the very serious game of life, all three of these women are *Playing for First*.

## Detours, by Jane Vollbrecht

It should have been a typical day of trimming shrubbery and edging lawns, but Gretchen VanStantvoordt—known to everyone as "Ellis"—first gets caught in a traffic jam and then lands in the emergency room with a badly sprained ankle. Mary Moss, a newfound friend who was caught in the same traffic jam, convinces Ellis that trying to tend to her dog and negotiate the stairs at her walk-up apartment while she's on crutches isn't such a good idea. Without friends or family in the vicinity, Ellis accepts Mary's offer for assistance.

When Ellis meets Natalie, Mary's nine-year-old daughter, she's ready to make tracks away from Mary as quickly as possible, but her bum ankle makes that impossible. Ellis stays with Mary and Natalie while she recovers. Little by little, Ellis develops a fondness for young Natalie... and develops something much deeper for Mary.

Ellis and Mary work out a plan for building a future—and a family—together. Destiny, it seems, has other plans and throws major roadblocks in their path. Ellis is forced to reconsider everything she thought she knew about where she wanted to go in life, and Mary learns that even with the perfect traveling companion, not all journeys are joyous.

No GPS can help them navigate the new road they're on. Come make the trip with Ellis and Mary as they discover that when life sends you on a detour, the wise traveler finds a way to enjoy the scenery.

## Coming soon, only from

Make sure to check out these other exciting
Blue Feather Books titles:

| | | |
|---|---|---|
| Tempus Fugit | Mavis Applewater | 978-0-9794120-0-4 |
| Yesterday Once More | Karen Badger | 978-0-9794120-3-5 |
| Addison Black and the Eye of Bastet | M.J. Walker | 978-0-9794120-2-8 |
| The Thirty-Ninth Victim | Arleen Williams | 978-0-9794120-4-2 |
| Merker's Outpost | I. Christie | 978-0-9794120-1-1 |
| Whispering Pines | Mavis Applewater | 978-0-9794120-6-6 |
| Greek Shadows | Welsh and West | 978-0-9794120-8-0 |
| From Hell to Breakfast | Joan Opyr | 978-0-9794120-7-3 |
| Journeys | Anne Azel | 978-0-9794120-9-7 |
| Accidental Rebels | Kelly Sinclair | 978-0-9794120-5-9 |

**www.bluefeatherbooks.com**